WHAT READERS LOVE ABOUT *THE TIME SURGEONS*

"Best science fiction book I've read in years! Super engaging story, very interesting, great charters, plot and story, well integrated, evokes emotions, makes you think. I recommend for everyone, not only science fiction lovers."

"I only found this author a few months ago and have since read all his fiction. With fascinating, imaginative plots I look forward to his future fiction!"

"Brilliant read! Highly recommended."

TITLES BY ROBIN CRAIG

The Hunter Series

Frankensteel

The Geneh War

Time Enough for Killing

Leonardo's Child

Time Travel and Alternative History

The Time Surgeons

Hannibal's Witch

The Passion of Judas

Short Stories

Past, Present Future

Non-Fiction Philosophy

Dialogue on the Two Chief World Systems

Good Without God

Cloning Around: The Ethics of Human Cloning and Stem Cell
Research

For the latest news visit robin-craig.com or follow on
fb.me/authorcraig

The Time Surgeons

ROBIN CRAIG

ROBIN CRAIG

DEDICATION

To my daughter Kira, as she travels through time. And to two men whose decisions may have saved the world.

CONTENTS

My thanks go to my wife Sonja Bernhardt OAM for reading and loving the drafts: her suggestions made this a better book.

CAST OF CHARACTERS

First Timeline	
Vasili	A Russian heading into hot water.
The US President	Unlucky in any timeline.
General Smythe	A man with a plan.
General Rushman	A man with another plan.
Ravan Harlington	A brilliant scientist with a dangerous thought.
Vickie Gray	An eminent historian who should have stopped looking.
Second and Third Timelines	
Another Russian	Calm, collected and about to destroy the world.
Praximar the Mighty	A barbarian general out for conquest. Not a nice man.
Pachmeny	A student with a far too bright future.
Shemsak the Exact	Pachmeny's Sage, not a happy man.
Timmony	A student on holiday about to become famous.
Arragath	A stellar student, in love with Pachmeny.
Sage Kuchalki	A geneticist with some good advice.
Baronak	The brilliant son of Pachmeny and Arragath, who lends himself a helping hand.
Geldamur	A cook who makes a fine sandwich.

Jennara	Food delivery with benefits.
Emmerline	A very quiet girl with a very clever idea.
Salidor	A man on a mission, with the gift of the gab.

Fourth Timeline

Ron	An author with a cunning plan, afraid he's been conned.
Jensen	An unobtrusive servant wondering what is going on.
Tamorabi	A hunter with a tragic past, looking for a better future.
Frenislan the Wise	An obscure Sage about to become famous.
Cherigaline	A famous Sage about to become more famous.
Praximar the Mighty	Like a bad smell, you can't get rid of him.
Vermaxakon	Wanted to be a Sage, doomed to disappointment, but carrying a golden legacy.
Accimbali	Another brilliant mind, faced with a terrible decision.
Sharalay	A woman who always does what she has to do.

Fifth Timeline

Stanislav	A lucky Russian, given a second chance.
Hireld Banekaro	A survivor watching the show.

PROLOGUE

Glittering eyes in the night. Hot breath panting, steaming, melding in the rolling mist of a still winter's night. A chill howl rises lonely to the sky, soft with menace. Times have been hard, and killers of the night course through a dark forest, driven by hunger and bloodlust, as wolves are.

Pale embers glow dimly in the grass by an icy stream, trailing thin tendrils of smoke into the night sky, a small ward of warmth against the chill of evening. Nearby lies a man, huddled in rough furs by his woman and child. Times have been hard, and they travel to find new lands where their lives may prosper, as men are wont to do.

It is not to be, this time.

The pack strikes, too quick, too silent, too many. Pitiable tools of stone and steel are no match for such as these. But the man fights, as men will, for what he values. And somehow, at the end of it all, he lives.

But those he loves are lost. Now nothing remains to him but memories, and their blood on the grass. Memories, of the warmth of their touch. The smell of her hair as they lay together in the dawn of a sunlit spring morning. The laughter of his child in the delight of discovery. Smiles lighting their faces, for no reason, no reason needed, but the joy of the living in life. And in his pain and in his anguish he screams to the stars and the sky, but there is no answer. And all he can do is ask his gods the question: Why?

To the east lies a Holy Place, a place of fear and reverence in the embrace of the ancient forest. There he journeys, heedless of the biting

1

snow riming his hair and frosting his furs, thoughtless of all but his goal, step after step after bitter step, his world empty of all but the dark forms of sleeping trees and the howling icy winds of winter. He enters the Holy Place, as a man who needs to know but knows not what or how. And there in his grief and in the pain of his soul, he kneels and prays, and cries his frozen tears, as men may. Then in the weariness of his body, he sleeps.

And with sleep come dreams.

And in his dreams come visions.

Fields of grain ripple white in the gentle breeze of a warm summer day. Here the wolf and the lamb lie at peace together, both tamed by the mind of man for his use and pleasure. Children, growing strong and fed and fearless in their mastery of the world, splash in the cool of the river. And in the midst of the grief in the dreamer's heart, faint hope stirs. But where some men create, and wrest value from the world by the power of their mind and the strength of their will, others take by force: for no excuse but their need, no reason but their want and their envy. Then the man dreams of fields aflame, of glittering eyes in the night. And he dreams of blood on the grass.

Then in his vision a prophet rises, a man who speaks for God:

> Men must not cheat and kill each other.
> Live not for yourself, but for your brother!
> Value not this world, it is merely shadow:
> Have faith in God, who rewards you in another.

The vision shifts, as visions do, and so it comes to pass: by chance and time the prophet's men now hold the seats of power. They live by faith and care not for reason: for they are so sure though they cannot show, so right though they cannot prove; too stern to let others be. And so the heretic and unbeliever die, for no better reason than a different faith or a mind that questions. And the eyes of the faithful glitter in the shadows, as they reflect the pain of ten thousand witches burning; and their ears are deaf to the pleas of the innocent, for faith is right and needs no reasons; and their feet tramp without a care through a river of blood on the grass.

Yet men live on, as men do, and a new ideal arises. That a man's life and freedom to seek happiness are his by right: by no lord's permission, by no virtue other than he is a man, a thinking being. So men begin to grasp a truth, a truth to live and die for. That each can live of and for himself, sacrificing himself to no one and no one to himself, but trading value for value. Humanity blossoms in the light of this, that men can deal with one another not by force, but by choice; not by arms, but by reason.

And hope rises as a sun in the dreamer's soul.

"But stop," they say, "this is not good, for some gain more than others. He who creates, he has not earned: he who needs must needs be given. To rise from the mud into a hut is not a gain when another has a palace: you have no right to the fruits of your work, if another man has less! Keep you some, for we need you so, yes sore we need your power: but our right it is to take what we will, for the sake of lesser men. Their want, their need, their noble need, is our lien on your soul."

Yet men work on, as men must. Now shining towers pierce the sky and fill the night with light, while golden arches glow afire, and ships of flame rise to the stars: and earth to sky and sky to sea, man's glory fills the world. Riches beyond imagining pour forth from just one fount: the minds of men who think and by thinking, create. And in his dream the man smiles at last, at the wonder that was man.

But some still live by force, and more still live by envy. Now mighty powers bestride the Earth: some standing for freedom, others seeking to rule; some to defend, others to take. And so they glare, their glittering eyes, burning in lust and fear; gathered and glittering in the night behind shields of iron and fire.

And so they risk it all, and risking all they fall. And the glittering eyes they whirl and burn and hate and howl, in night and fear and blood, until the towers rise now broken and dark from an ocean of blood on the grass. And in his dream, the man screams; and screaming, dreaming shatters into shards on the newborn snow.

The man wakes to a cold white sun on a cold white dawn. Snowflakes drift swirling around him in the chill still breeze of morning. Then he lifts his eyes to the Holy Place, to the dead dark towers piercing the sky, to the crumbling rusting hulks of a long forgotten past. And the wind sighs through the skeleton of the city, moaning, mourning, a million ghosts of a million dead, who almost reached the sky then faltered, then fell, then died.

There are no answers here. Nothing but the ghosts of the past, wailing as they have done for untold centuries past, and perhaps will continue for as long as the Earth itself bears witness to their loss. Nor are there answers in the forest beyond, only his own loss and pain. Perhaps he should find his own peace. So easy to lie down and let the snow draw him into its cold embrace, until finally his soul and his voice join in the chorus of the past.

Then slowly the man stands, as men will. In the light and cold and shadow, in the wind and the sun and the snow, he stands a man alone, a man bowed, but a man, proud. And he lifts his face to the sun.

And he cries, for the gods who are gone.

And for their blood on the grass.

And for glittering eyes in the night.

Part A:
Peace In Their Time

How far your eyes may pierce I cannot tell.
Striving to better, oft we mar what's well.

Shakespeare, King Lear

---

1. The Silent Deep

Vasili woke suddenly, a faint sheen of sweat on his brow testimony less to the heat than to the dream that had awakened him. But when he tried to grasp the dream it danced away from him like the shimmer of a mirage, and was gone.

He sat up on the narrow bunk in his cramped cabin, stretching the kinks out of his muscles as best he could. *Dreams do not matter when you may be waking into a nightmare,* he thought. *Let us hope we hear word, and that the word is for life not death.*

He knew they stood on the brink of war. It seemed so long ago now, but in truth had been mere decades, when men had fought a war so horrific they had thought it would be the last war of all. They had been wrong. The seeds of that conflict had spawned another, which had managed to plumb even greater depths of what men were capable of doing to their fellows. And in its turn, the seeds of that war had scattered to sprout yet more, like weeds in the vacant lot of humanity's soul. And now the inexorable drumbeat had brought the world to the edge of another, this one so terrible that perhaps it would truly be the war to end all wars. Not that men would look upon it and become too appalled, too afraid, or even too wise to wage war: but that this time there would be nobody left to fight.

The enemy were hunting him, that he knew. The enemy had placed a blockade, and he was running it. Thus they were running as silently and as deeply as they could. This they had been doing for days, and both temperatures and tempers had been rising steadily. The one thing that had not been rising was information. This deep they had no word, and little hope of receiving any. While safety lay in the dark, the deadly dangers of fear and ignorance stalked there too. And when the stakes were this high any decision could be deadly, and not just for them.

He hoped the enemy knew what they were doing. Not hoped that they knew enough to capture or kill him, but that they knew the dangers of continuing or escalating their hunt. That they had the sense to know when it would be wiser to give up their chase rather than pursue it to its end. For the longer Vasili's men were forced to evade and hide, the less they knew about the world outside the hunt; and so the more their own fears about the motives of the hunters would rise; and then the more likely they were to decide that their duty compelled them to stop hiding.

He did not think the enemy seeking him would like what they then found.

If the enemy knew what they were hunting, perhaps they would have already realized that wisdom lay in graceful withdrawal. Or perhaps they did know, and that was why they continued. Vasili remembered the sheen of sweat on his forehead, and knew that is what his dream had warned him. Or perhaps it had warned him that they did not know, and their finding out would be the end of the world.

Or maybe the sweat was just from the heat of his cabin.

He sat there for a moment, contemplating the vision of a choice made in ignorance, on the cusp of which his own fate and perhaps that of the world might hinge.

It was only a moment. He had risen to a position where such a choice might be thrust upon him through decisiveness, courage and an inability to give up no matter what the odds. He rose from his bed, straightened his uniform and left his room, his footsteps padding quietly down the passageway.

But as he walked the first boom and rattle sounded, and he knew the enemy had found him, or thought it had. Or with luck it was a random shot in the dark, a confession not of knowledge but of ignorance.

But then there was another boom and rattle, this time from the other side. *They are bracketing us. Showing us they know.*

He increased his pace, and as he hurried along the corridors the cadence of the enemy's rain sounded like the halting but ever approaching footsteps of a doom no longer to be denied or escaped.

~~~

When Vasili entered the room, the captain and political officer stood in greeting and respect but said nothing. He looked slowly from face to face and knew their thoughts. Beneath his own trademark calm, icy currents swirled to the darkest reaches of his soul. He knew what they would say. He knew what he would say if they did.

But they had to say it.

"Report status," commanded Vasili.

"Still nothing from Command," replied the Captain, "and we are now under attack."

"No word from command after all these days," added the Political Officer, unnecessarily voicing their thoughts.

"We have been hiding. We did not expect to hear word while we are this deep."

"We may be at war already, and we would not know," noted the Political Officer.

"But nor can we assume we are. We must be careful. As much as we do not want to lose a war by not striking when we should, our country will not thank us if we start one ourselves before she is ready."

"Surely you know that Mother Russia would win such a war?"

Vasili gave the Political Officer a searching glance. Such questions were dangerous, and meant to be recognized as such.

"Nevertheless, she will be hurt. It would be disloyal to bring that hurt upon her through hasty decisions."

"Hasty!" cried the Captain. "We are under attack! What more proof do you need?"

"We may not be under attack. They are bracketing us, not causing us significant damage. They are telling us they know we are here, and warning us to admit it or risk the obvious consequences."

"If they know we are here, perhaps they also know what we are. If they know what we are, perhaps they wish to trick us into surfacing, so they can destroy us with accurate and deadly force. Rather than risk an indisputable attack when they are not completely sure where we are, which could still leave us able to retaliate. A wounded bear is the most dangerous."

Vasili considered, looking from face to face, searching for doubt or perhaps salvation. Normally on a ship like this the decision would already be set. Attack required the agreement of the Captain and the Political Officer, no less, no more. It was only the accident of his presence on this particular vessel that made their decision more complicated. While he was junior to the Captain in authority on this ship, he was also the Commander of the entire flotilla.

That meant he had to agree too. It had to be unanimous.

Which made the decision his, if the other two voted for war.

He thought, another rattling boom underlining the urgency. If they were at war then the Captain was right: the enemy was playing it safe, attempting to flush them out for a clean kill. But if they weren't at war, the enemy was merely trying to enforce its blockade, and warn them that they had failed to run it. Slap their face, and turn them home in shame.

But if they know we are here, they know we are out of communication with command. If they know we are out of communication, what utter fool would drop depth charges on us, knowing we would fear it was an act of war, knowing how we might react? Knowing we would react exactly as we are doing? Surely they would not be so incalculably stupid as to gamble the fate of the world on our guess?

He looked again at his comrades. *Look at them. They are warriors, trained for war. They vote for what they know, fearing failure to act more than the consequences of acting wrongly. I knew what they would decide even before I saw their faces, and if I were not here it would already be done. And if I know it, surely those above know it too.*

He felt the ice grip his chest, knowing the decision was made.

"You know this is the death of us all?"

"We are dead anyway. Better to die heroes than cowards, and strike at the heart of our murderers with our final thrust."

He gave a curt nod.

"Captain, give the order."

2. OUT OF THE ASHES

"Torpedo in the water!" cried an operator in the aircraft carrier at the center of the flotilla blockading the island nation of Cuba. It was bad enough having a fanatical Communist regime so close to the homeland. It was unacceptable when their Russian masters chose to install nuclear missiles there, a forest of deadly fingers raised obscenely in their direction.

"How many?" asked the Commanding Officer.

"One! Sir!"

"Bearing?"

"Directly at us, Captain!"

"Time to impact?"

"Thirty seconds, Sir!"

For a ship this size evasion was not an option. "Countermeasures, now!"

"Trying! Sir!"

"Only one torpedo? Are you sure?"

"Still one torpedo, Sir!"

The Captain looked at his XO. "Oh, sweet Jesus. Oh. Holy. *Christ!*"

"Send top priority message to command, soonest! Advise under attack from the submarine we have been tracking. Only one torpedo, which suggests a nuclear warhead. Repeat. Nuclear torpedo. Attempting countermeasures."

He fought for inspiration and found none. He sent a quick prayer into the ether, hoping God was listening.

"Status!"

"Still coming, sir."

The Captain and his XO exchanged another glance. It was the last thing they would ever do.

The aircraft carrier disappeared in a nuclear fireball that left nothing of the carrier or the men in it, other than radioactive dust swirling in the mushroom cloud rising above its former location. The ships nearest the carrier were also obliterated, while others further out suffered varying degrees of damage from fatal to survivable. Those still able to fight unleashed their own fury on the submarine that had struck the deadly blow, and any others whose locations they knew or suspected.

Whether it was the shock from their own torpedo or the violence of the counterattack did not matter to Vasili or the other men on the submarine. Nobody would ever find the wreckage that was now their tomb and memorial, sinking into the black depths beneath a once balmy sea.

~~~

The American President rubbed his eyes. *Why, oh why, did I want this job? No number of willing actresses is worth this crap. More to the point why, oh why, did that idiot Khrushchev put nukes in our backyard?*

Much as he wanted to blame Khrushchev, he knew the problem went deeper than that. *The whole mess has this terrible feeling of inevitability about it. That bastard Castro wants something, that bigger bastard Khrushchev is happy to use him to get what he wants, we want something else, and none of us want it blowing up in our faces. Yet here we are, marching arm in arm toward Armageddon. And now my own goddamn navy is dropping depth charges on their triple-damned submarines.*

What could possibly go wrong? he thought bitterly.

He looked up. *I guess I'm about to find out,* he thought at the grim, ashen face of the man who had entered. He looked at the man, inviting him to speak.

"Sir. Mr President. I… that is… the… the Russians have hit one of our aircraft carriers with a nuclear warhead."

The President leapt to his feet.

The rest was as inevitable as the President had feared. The Americans had to react to this aggression, or the emboldened Soviets would sweep through the world; who knew how long the Russians had been planning this, and what they were about to do. *A nation renowned for their chess grandmasters. Who knows how many moves ahead they have planned and how many traps they have laid? Already they dangled their missiles in front of our noses as they thrust at us unseen from beneath the sea.*

The Russians knew how the Americans would react, and prepared as many missiles as they could, while wave after wave of nuclear armed bombers took to the air.

The revenge of the USA was swift and terrible, but the President was cautious: he would not unleash their entire arsenal, nor did he want to unduly risk his European allies by striking from there. But the Russians struck back, with whatever tactical, strategic and submarine weapons they had at their disposal. The Americans did not realize how overwhelmingly superior their own nuclear capability was: certainly the Russians had done their best to make them believe they were closer to parity. They did not hold back now.

Somewhere in Russia, a young man named Stanislav Petrov looked up to the sky at what looked like a falling star. His brain did not have time to let him see the flash that vaporized him. Thousands of others lost their lives in the same instant. Similar tragedies were repeated in too many other cities, on both sides of the war. Others were less lucky but no less dead, their inevitable deaths stretched out over minutes or weeks of pain.

By the time it was over, Russia had been obliterated as a power and indeed a country; much of Europe was in ruins, and the remainder was merely drawing breath before rushing after it; the USA was teetering on the edge of anarchy; even some distant allies had suffered attacks. Tens of millions had died in the USA; a hundred million in Europe.

The fires of combustion lit by the nuclear fires hurled great quantities of soot and other fine debris into the atmosphere and stratosphere, cooling the planet: not fatally, but enough to damage crop yields. Radioactive fallout caused deaths and illness on a worldwide scale. Worse, modern civilization is a delicate instrument: vast tracts of agricultural land barely populated, feeding giant cities; the giant cities making that productivity possible; an intricate web of transport, fuel, energy, water, food and trade tying the whole system together. And above all that, and supported by it like a delicate flower needing deep roots to survive, a thin web of security: medical facilities, police, the rule of law, fire services.

Europe had no chance. The USA descended into widespread anarchy. The rest of the world, damaged less at the start but also not as resilient to the shock, battered by the cold, the fallout, and the panic, followed it. Starving people care little about planning for a future they fear is unlikely to come unless they act vigorously in the present. The victims of their vigorous action were unimpressed by their motives, but the sheer numbers pouring out of starving cities could not be contained. But nor could those numbers, having ravaged the countryside, be sustained or survive much longer than the people who had grown their food, only to be consumed under their tide.

Within only a few years a billion people, one third of the world's population, had perished. Over the following decades more died: from famine, from residual radiation, from genetic damage. The world had long since lost count. And there was more. An optimist might have thought that being victims of such a war would have put an end to more wars. An optimist would have been wrong, as they sadly always have been on that particular question. Into the power vacuum left by fallen governments came replacements who were worse: using their guns to take whatever scraps others could still produce, until there were none left to produce them. The enormous productiveness of the food-growing regions on which the world had come to depend could not be maintained without the networks of goods and law that enabled and created the machines, chemicals and security on which it depended. When those networks were gone, food production and availability dropped to what it had been centuries before: and inevitably, the population followed.

The former United States of America was well on its way to dissolving back into warring tribes. Or perhaps it could have saved itself from that fate by turning to another: by bending its remaining strength into a dictatorship of iron.

Instead, something remarkable happened.

~~~

The uniform was perfect, and all medals were present and properly aligned. Examining himself in the mirror, General Smythe smiled, as much as he ever smiled, in satisfaction at the effect. He patted the sidearm in its glossy leather holster. *The die is not yet cast. But today it shall be, and one day the world will look back on this morning as the start of a new era.*

With one final examination of his attire, he crisply turned and marched out of his bedroom, heading toward the meeting and, if all went as he anticipated, destiny.

The United States had suffered terribly in the War. The only silver lining on the radioactive cloud, in Smythe's mind, was that the enemy who had started it had suffered even more, indeed fatally. *But still enemies remain, both within and without. Now it is time for the bold.*

The US armed forces had managed to hold on to most of their structure and enough of their chain of command, so could still project authority over most of the country, albeit somewhat loosely and in many places tentatively. The lower chains of command, however, were restless, their mood and loyalties worsening as their remoteness from high Command increased.

There was no civilian Federal government any more. Many had died in the early days of the war, including the President. Those that remained, including the new President, had been betrayed by a rogue military unit whose leadership had decided that the times called for a more vigorous, military government. The clique had in turn been crushed by forces still loyal to their oaths, even though those oaths now served an idea no longer embodied.

Now the top leadership of the armed forces were gathered in their mountain redoubt to discuss their strategies for the future, and General Smythe was determined that their decision would be the right one.

He walked into the room and looked around, judging each face in turn.

There was a group of five over to his left: hard-faced men who knew how to grasp the nettle; men with whom he had had many conversations, nothing specific, just about principles; men he knew he could count on. They lacked the true strength required of a bold leader, but they would follow a strong leader if one became apparent.

Scattered around the room were other groups, but his eyes skipped over them. They had varying opinions, but none had strong enough opinions or wills to cause trouble: like his core group, they would follow whatever man had the courage to seize the rudder and steer the ship through the dangerous waters ahead.

There were only two men on whom his eyes rested with cautious appraisal. General Schaffer was dangerous. A brilliant strategist and tactician, he could be a valuable ally and extremely useful asset for the future. However his loyalties lay with the man next to him, and worse, those loyalties were not merely ideological but personal. Schaffer's loss would be a blow, there was no denying it; but losses always happened in war, and there was nothing for it but to go on with what you had left. After all, that is what everyone in this room had been doing since the war started, and why they were gathered here today. But Smythe hoped there would be no loss. Yes, there was a danger that Schaffer's loyalty would make him do something precipitate, demanding an unfortunate response. But as long as he had time for a few seconds of reflection, he had the wit to see where the wise course lay: so with luck he would bow to historical necessity, whatever his personal feelings.

That left General Rushman, the top officer and man in charge, whom Smythe now studied carefully while trying to appear not to. Smythe had trouble understanding Rushman. His opinions were those of a weak man, yet he commanded the loyalties of his men as if he were strong. *He seems like a sheep, yet one who imagines he has teeth and claws. And somehow draws others into seeing them too.*

A memory from long ago floated sharply into Smythe's attention: some agricultural show he had attended as a boy on a holiday in far Australia. He remembered sitting next to his father on the rough wooden planks that provided seating above an open arena, the hot southern sun shining down through inadequate shade; he could almost still feel the trickle of sweat down the side of his face. His father was pointing to the arena, explaining the finer points of the trials, where a farmer was signaling his shaggy black and white dog to herd sheep into a pen. Smythe could recall the sound of his father's voice but not the words. What had struck him about the scene was not the ewes, milling about confused and docile, nor even the dog, circling around to cut off their escape and approaching, crouching, to nudge them in the right direction, but the sole ram of the flock. The ram had surprised the young Smythe, for it displayed what to him seemed the quite un-sheeplike behavior of facing down the dog, stepping forward and stamping his foot aggressively at it. To Smythe, the contest had seemed surprisingly even: the ram, threatening the dog, who had to be content with its own feints and threats. But eventually, inevitably, the dog had won and the sheep were penned.

Smythe smiled inwardly, the smile not reaching his lips. *Yes, my friend, that is what you are. One of the sheep, yes, but the brave ram, standing up for your flock. I could almost admire your courage. But no matter how brave the ram, still the dog outmatches him. And he stands no chance against the wolf.*

At the other end of the room, General Schaffer was conducting a similar assay of the men present. He held his head erect in his usual crisp posture, but he was worried. He glanced briefly in General Rushman's direction. He did not see worry there, only resolve. This morning he had warned Rushman of the overall mood of the group, noting that the only real danger was from Smythe. Rushman had nodded, but put his hand on Schaffer's shoulder.

"I know, Bob," he had said. "But don't do anything. Stand by my side, but it is vital that you make no move. Do you understand? Do nothing except follow my lead."

Schaffer could tell that there was a general mood but no general plan in the room. The men present had their opinions and their cliques, but no unified design. They were like balls in a roulette wheel: agitated and jumpy, wanting to end up somewhere but not knowing what slot they would finally fall into. But something in Smythe's posture and the way he scanned the room told Schaffer that if he was going to do anything, today was the day. Like Schaffer, Smythe knew that enough of the others would follow the lead of any man willing to take that lead.

He looked again at his friend, remembering their time in the Korean War. They had been ambushed and were under fire, with Schaffer cut off, pinned down and facing death: when Rushman had saved him in an act of daring and bravery, risking his own life and almost losing it. Rushman had dragged him out of the fire zone but Schaffer couldn't walk. Rushman should have escaped, but the two hid in the tropical foliage, trying not to breathe as enemy soldiers stalked past their noses. The two had been firm friends ever since. *And now we are coming under fire again, and you order me to stand aside. Do you see the danger? I hope you know what you are doing.*

Rushman called the meeting to order.

"The country is in ruins," he said. "But it can get worse. We're all that's left to stop its slide. The question is, how are we going to go about it? The main question is one of authority. You know my feelings on the matter. That even though the civilian government is gone, it is still the Constitution of the United States that we are sworn to protect and serve. That it is our duty, not only legally but *morally*, to return our great country to the civilian government that made it great as soon as possible. If any of you aren't on board with this, now is the time to say so. Our task is difficult, maybe impossible. We certainly can't succeed if we are divided among ourselves. So again: come on board or state your case now: or forever hold your peace."

For a few moments nobody moved or spoke. Then Smythe stepped forward.

"I agree we must be united. But your course is folly. The people are scattered and afraid. Those who aren't afraid are looting. Civilian government? Of whom, for whom? I agree, the task ahead of us is fraught with difficulty. We need strength, not squabbling. Action, not speeches. Authority, not votes. We have the power. We must use it."

The room took its collective breath, knowing that the future of the country and perhaps the world hung in the balance of this debate. Smythe stood rigidly, glancing around the room. He saw little hostility: what there was of it mostly the kind that hoped somebody else would stop him, rather than the kind that manifests itself in action. Most were just watchful. His own clique were not ready to come out in his support, not openly, but their watchfulness had a different tone: an edge of anticipation. Even Rushman and Schaffer did not look at him with hostility but with deep attention, as one might look at a bear, wondering if after its bluster it would run or attack. Then Rushman responded softly.

"You are speaking of a military dictatorship."

"A military government, yes. For the period of the emergency. We can worry about a return to civilian government when the time is right."

"And when in history, John, has a military dictatorship ever decided the time is right, unless forced to do so? And who is there left to force us?"

"If there are none left to force us, why should we bend the knee to their weakness and cowardice? Let us build something out of these terrible ashes: something glorious. We are the only real army left on Earth. Our country cries out for a new path to glory. The world lies open before us."

He raked his eyes across the faces in the room, baring his teeth in a way that could be confidence or the slap of a challenge. "There is a time for the wolves to serve the sheep. See where it has brought us! I say... it is time to do better! Time for glory!"

Rushman looked around the room, looking each man in the eye: those who did not refuse the contact. "Glory? We are the product of what may have been the greatest nation on Earth, the greatest of all time. A country founded not by accident but on ideals: for life, liberty and the pursuit of happiness. A country whose birth, yes, was aided by force of arms: but whose purpose was not continuing the rule of arms but bequeathing a life of freedom. Can we betray that legacy?"

He could see that some were moved; but that none would rise to his defense. "One of our greatest generals was George Washington.

Learn from him. He could have been king, but like the great Roman general Cincinnatus, he stuck by his ideals and, having won the war, left power to the Republic he helped create. Do not betray his legacy. Perhaps you can forget our legal duty. As General Smythe will remind you, there is nobody to enforce it except ourselves and our own integrity. But our moral duty is still to serve the Republic. Even if the Republic is no more, the idea of this Republic can never die, and it is the idea that is worth fighting for and dying for: but better than all, living for."

As he spoke, Schaffer's eyes darted around the room. *You are trying to win them with words, my friend. But you can only win with words when men are open to listen. Too many here have their own agenda. Too many feel the siren call of power. You must know this. What are you counting on?*

As if reading his mind, Smythe stepped forward. "Fine words, Arthur. But now is the time for boldness. We have the power. We must use it, and build something better upon the ruins." He rested his hand on his sidearm in silent but unambiguous signal, and the room tensed.

Rushman sighed. "Yes, I fear you are right, General."

He stood and bowed his head, leaning for support on the edge of his desk. "Some battles go only to the bold."

If the surprise in General Smythe's mind had had time to crystallize into words they would have been *I did not know he could move so fast,* as Rushman whipped the gun he had hidden under his desk and fired three shots. As Smythe's body crumpled to the floor, Rushman watched him fall. *You are not the only man to have read Machiavelli, John. For all his questionable ethics, the man had plenty of wisdom. Like never leave a dangerous enemy alive to plot his revenge.*

Then he lifted his head to address the room.

"Let there be no more talk of military dictatorships. Haven't we seen, around the world and throughout history, that the rule of guns does not work?"

He raked the audience with his eyes.

"It is the barbarian who sees a mighty pyramid rising above the desert and, not understanding how it grew, seeks only to take it. To build his palace on its crown, never knowing why it crumbles beneath him.

"Do you understand? That if we try to live as despots on top of a pyramid of slaves, then within our own lifetimes, let alone our children's, our lives will be more miserable and brutish than if we had been content to be equals in a free society?"

He looked at Schaffer, who had not moved from his side but whose own guns were now drawn, pointing in deadly emphasis at the men in the room. *Thank you for trusting me. It had to be me. Some of these men will hear reason. The rest will hear only strength. And it had to be me who had the strength.*

To the rest, he simply said, "So let us learn from history, not be seduced by dreams of plunder. We are not servants of sheep, but guardians of freedom: our own as much as that of our people. There is no room here for despots. If that is what you want, if you want to use the tragedy of an entire world as a stepping stone to your own power, then I suggest you slink away in the night—as the curs you are, not the wolves you imagine. We will not stop you. Try to set up your fiefdom far from here. But be warned. We will hunt you down. One day, we will destroy you."

Again he looked at each man in turn. This time, they all met his eyes. "There is no conflict between glory and right. What could be more glorious, and more right, than rebuilding greatness? So for all of you who retain the integrity of your oaths and the nobility of your souls: we have a lot of work to do. Let us work together as men, not brutes, and see what brighter future we might build."

~~~

Over the subsequent years, a government was formed with the strength of the military behind it but dedicated to the defense of the people, not their rule. They knew that things could never be the same, and they thought about the history of their country: whatever its flaws it had been a land of freedom, forged by men unafraid to both fight and think. From the city at the center of their power, Rushman and his generals called for a new Constitutional Convention, bringing the best thinkers from all the distant corners from whence they could acquire them. As in the first such convention centuries ago, perhaps these were flawed men; perhaps they made errors; but they worked to correct the errors of the past, and perhaps save the future.

This might have been impossible before the war: too many people, too many interests, too many conflicting ideals. But this was a smaller country, with fewer delegates and those selected according to the ideas that had founded the country, not those that had fought with and nearly destroyed it. And so a new Constitution was hammered out of the ashes of one country, to become the spine of the new.

The new government was named the Protectorate, as its role was not to rule but to protect; not to tell people how to live, but to allow them to live as they saw fit, provided that their way was to the benefit of others.

The Protectorate started as impregnable in its center of power, with thin tentacles stretching in many directions to its earliest allies. They had been the cities and regions still strong enough to maintain their own existence and still loyal to the ideals of the republic. As the decades passed the Protectorate spread its power and authority across the country. Where it could, it absorbed regions without violence via promises of protection, law and peace. Where it encountered warlords it crushed them. It had learned from the war and the wars before it, and had neither patience with appeasement of its enemies nor desire to make war with its friends. If a region did not want to join it, but had its own version of a peaceful government, then treaties were made. The Protectorate knew that winning the future required unification, but it had patience. It knew that war was not necessary; that eventually the advantages of trade and friendship would absorb the independent regions anyway. Only if a region would not accept peace was it considered a threat. Threats were eliminated with neither delay nor mercy.

In many ways it was a leaner and meaner version of the country it replaced. It was less free but not terribly so. The government knew how much had been lost and how desperately it needed to restore it. Its constitution banned nuclear weapons, but not nuclear power; it encouraged science, but not science that could destroy the world again. It sought to become a mighty industrial and technological power once more, but one lacking the fangs that could ravage itself. It was as if a viper had learned it could die from its own bite and, knowing it could not trust itself to never bite again, relinquished its venom.

Thus science, cautiously overseen, was treasured. In the early years that was difficult. Many of the finest minds had been lost. And no matter how great the mind, there is only so far science can go if all it has to work with is a blackboard or a magnifying glass. Much of the delicate equipment required for advanced science had been lost, the knowledge and machines needed to build more now dust as well. The Protectorate held on tightly to what remained; ensured that, whatever other priorities called on its wealth and manpower, education and science were never left to wither and die.

There was much to rebuild and little wealth with which to do it. When struggling even to survive, there was no room for fantasies that wealth could be created out of a vacuum simply by printing pieces of paper alleging it. So at first little could be done to preserve the knowledge which remained, other than hold on to it with grim determination. But as the rebuilding proceeded and production increased, slowly the scientists of the Protectorate approached, then equaled, and finally began to exceed the science the world had once known.

But if its scientists were imbued with the mandate to learn, they were also instilled with a desire for caution: new knowledge was carefully examined for its potential to help or to harm the human race. If the harm was too severe further work was avoided. Usually this was voluntary: they all knew the reasons, and believed in them with the fervor of survivors. If any mavericks thought they knew better and decided otherwise, they soon found their ability to continue in their chosen profession curtailed or lost forever.

The Protectorate valued freedom, as long as it stayed within prudent bounds.

Meanwhile, as the decades turned into centuries, the same process that had absorbed a country was applied to absorbing the world. The Protectorate spread rapidly across the devastated lands of Europe. In less shattered areas, there were often strong governments to resist its advance. But once again these were handled by treaty or force, whichever was appropriate.

In more ancient times, villages facing the outward sweep of the empire of Rome had learned that to surrender to Rome could bring peace and wealth, albeit under the yoke of governors and tribute; whereas to resist Rome was likely to bring fire and death. The countries of the new world learned something similar. Except instead of the yoke of tribute, the Protectorate offered only the benefit of knowledge and trade. Rome had wanted the world in order that its wealth could pour into its own coffers. The Protectorate merely wanted the world.

Life was still hard and neither the people nor the government of the Protectorate were squeamish, but nor did they wish to waste men and money on conquest. Yet their one driving force was unity: the world could not be left at the mercy of disputing powers. It had tried that and almost died.

They had one crucial advantage: by choice or circumstance,

nowhere else on Earth had retained as much advanced knowledge as they had, nor kept as much unified territory with which to sustain industries based on that knowledge. So they resolved the contradiction between peace and expansion. They invested in science and technology in order to maintain and enhance their superiority. They invested heavily in spies, in order to know their enemy. And if they learned that an enemy was becoming dangerous, they invested heavily in assassins.

And so the Protectorate spread its power across the globe, first as thin filaments of influence; then as thicker cables of treaty; finally by absorption.

Governments might not have liked this process. But governments by their nature are infested with people who enjoy power. The best of them seek it in order to improve the world; the worst of them, in order to trample over others. In either case the Protectorate was not interested in anyone else's desire for power, for it knew where that could lead, whatever the motives.

The people those governments ruled were more open to change. They might have been less so under the influence of their own governments' propaganda, but the Protectorate became expert in its own methods. And as more people came under the Protectorate's power, they learned that it was a good power. Not perfect, certainly: but generally better than what they had had before.

And so two things spread outward from the growing edges of the Protectorate's empire: their spies, and the knowledge that the Protectorate was a realm of its word. If it promised peace with honor and protection of rights, that is what it delivered. If it promised destruction, that came even more swiftly and certainly.

Not all countries were absorbed. Some were peaceful republics or democracies themselves, and happy to deal with the Protectorate as allies and partners. Some were more despotic, perhaps monarchies, even dictatorships, yet ruled by wise leaders: who were also happy to be friends rather than enemies of the Protectorate, especially when they knew what became of the latter. For its part, the Protectorate was happy with these arrangements. It had its spies in place to monitor for danger and betrayal and its assassins on call to handle such crises. And it was patient. It knew, from its own history, that eventually all would come into its arms, and the world would finally be safe forever.

3. Dangerous Thoughts

Dr Ravan Harlington was a product of his times.

He was brilliant, yes. But brilliance was not celebrated, except as it served those less brilliant.

He was handsome, yes, with a face chiseled by fortunate genetics and muscles chiseled by hours of effort. The loose curl of hair with a habit of dangling down his forehead, the bright blue eyes and the cheerful smile merely added to the ensemble. But nor was beauty celebrated, at least not in public utterances, except as it served some common good.

But in private his beauty served his own good quite well. He had no need to visit the Houses maintained by the Protectorate to provide for the physical happiness and psychological health of those, whether male or female, who were unable or unwilling to satisfy their most personal needs by their own efforts. Enough women sought out his charms that his schedule was full, and would still have been full were his appetites fiercer. No doubt it was an accident that most of those he chose would also be considered beautiful, if one had the bad taste to notice or worse, to comment.

That was some time ago. Ravan was now in his middle age, and though he retained his beauty it was not as remarkable as it had once been. There was a little more paunch and somewhat less chisel, for one thing. This relaxation of his body sometimes brought him a twinge of regret, but it passed quickly. For a man his age he was still attractive. His power, position and fame were even more useful for attracting female companionship. In the evolution of his race, a handsome face and muscular body were a mere promise of things to come, while actual success was the proof of good genes and even more alluring.

In another age a man like Dr Ravan Harrington might be proud, placing himself on a pedestal in his own mind for possessing the unearned traits of brilliance and beauty. He may even have been conceited, an even lower and more ignoble form of pride.

But in this age he was humble. He knew his genius but did not dwell upon it. He knew he had not achieved it, merely been born with it, and it was his happy duty to do good with it. He knew his beauty but did not flaunt it. Some of it he had achieved by hard work, but he told himself that was mere prudent exercise: for a healthy body made one a more useful member of society and better servant of the Protectorate. To the extent that his beauty helped him personally, why, that was just an indirect way to help others. A healthy, happy man was better able to serve the Protectorate and do so cheerfully, content with his lot. And he was a healthy man, and the kinds of benefits he gained were the mutual kind.

All these things Dr Ravan Harrington told himself. And all these things were true.

His brilliant mind had given him a brilliant career. Though not unique, still he was an oddity in the history of science: as exceptional an experimental physicist as he was a theoretical one. His earlier work in relativistic physics had led to breakthroughs in wormhole physics, and he was still the world authority in the field, deferred to by his colleagues and advisor to the highest reaches of government.

An exceptional mind is often a difficult one for those in authority, as the ancient thinkers Socrates, Galileo and others had learned to their cost, too often fatal. But Ravan had an even temperament which was a match for even his intellect. There had been few ripples in the course of his life to disturb his contentment in his present or endanger the projected path of his future.

He could recall only one of any substance, an event from his university days. He rarely chose to recall it except as a lesson in the virtue of not repeating it.

It was in his first year at university, which he had achieved at the age of fifteen. He could have gone earlier with great success but his parents, heeding the advice of the psychologists, had decided that a slower progression would meet his social needs as well as his intellectual ones, and he would be better for it.

Older students, sometimes professors, would often give impromptu talks to the lunchtime crowds. These were popular events, as they were generally prompted by either exciting new discoveries or an urge to amuse on the part of intellectuals who may once have dreamed of being entertainers.

On one such day, a student in archaeology gave a remarkable speech. Apparently the student, who specialized in pre-War USA studies, had found a cache of books and translated them from their original pre-war English into modern language. His speech was filled with strange ideas and claims, delivered in a manner as if making his audience understand were the most important thing in the world.

Ravan had settled himself on the lawn too late to hear the start of the speech, having been happily ensconced in the library until hunger drew him forth. The out of context snatches he heard meant little to him and he remembered as little of the speech, except one phrase the student had translated, which had struck a chord in his mind:

> There are no dangerous thoughts except one: the
> refusal to think.

He remembered much more of the aftermath. The audience were entertained if confused by this highly unusual speech, until men with the insignia of the security services on their shoulders and cudgels on their waists swooped down and carried the student away. They also barred the exits, allowing nobody to go on their way until they had been closely questioned about what they had heard. There was nothing brutal about either the abduction or the interrogations: this was merely an intervention for the psychological health of all involved in a possibly disturbing incident.

For there were many dangerous thoughts, especially the refusal to conform.

Ravan had little trouble with his own interrogation. It may have been his quick mind that saved him on this occasion: the wit and skill to blithely state that he hadn't really been listening, and the little he heard made no sense. Something about an atlas, he said, and Atlantis; though he confessed confusion on why an atlas including a mythical continent could inspire such unseemly passion. He suspected the student was drunk, or playing a prank. Neither the university nor the authorities thought it would be good for public order and tranquility to have too many people disappear, so only the worst affected students were in any danger of that. And the university had already marked Ravan's great mind, while the authorities did not want to waste such a useful future citizen on such uncertain grounds.

Others were not so lucky. He never saw the archaeology student again, nor a number of other people he had known somewhat and seen in the audience staring at the speaker with rapt attention, as if he were breaking new paths of thought open for them.

The rumor spread that the books the boy had found had driven him mad, though clearly no book had such power and the flaw must lie in the man. Yet still it was more evidence that all must heed the wisdom of the authorities and focus on their service to their fellows, and not indulge in dangerous ideas of no value to society. It was dangerous ideas that had nearly destroyed the world, and they could equally destroy one man. Obviously the Protectorate had not harmed the student or any of the others who had vanished from university life. The Protectorate was beneficent, and held the true interests of all to its heart. They were merely being cared for, perhaps under therapy, perhaps transferred to a new location far from the place that might stir up disturbing memories. Such memories might disturb their personal tranquility and thereby the harmony of society at large.

Most who remained were content to learn the official lesson. Ravan was more perceptive, or less compliant, and the lesson he learned was that there were many dangerous thoughts, and refusing to think about them was the path to a long and contented life. But it is the curse of any person of talent to think that their particular talent is king of them all; and the peculiar curse of superlative intellect to feel itself immune from the intellectual risks and errors that lesser mortals should rightly fear.

Ravan knew to express no unauthorized thoughts. But he retained the privilege of thinking them in the safe silence of his own mind. For the good of society, somebody had to bear the risk of such thoughts.

There were few lessons Ravan had which he then forgot, and this one was no exception. That served him well later in his university days, when he was doing his postgraduate studies in the physics of wormholes.

At the time wormholes were an exotic study, of little practical importance but some theoretical interest. There was little to be said about them except that they were a theoretically possible implication of relativistic physics. Since to create one required negative energy, an exotic imagining that nobody had seen or even knew where to look, theory is where they remained.

This is where Ravan made his breakthrough and his name.

Others had made progress in this area before him. It is one of the advantages of being a student that there is more time, as well as inclination, for wide-ranging and indeed eclectic reading into every nook and cranny of one's chosen field of interest. During this process, an obscure paper from many years ago had caught his interest. It speculated on the nature of time and proposed some novel transformations of spacetime equations, which hinted at the possibility of time travel via wormholes.

The paper had been widely ignored. Even its author had put it forward more as a theoretical exercise than with any intent to pursue it seriously. It dealt, after all, with an analogy not a reality.

But when Ravan read it, it reminded him of other speculations he had come across. He took a closer look and noticed something odd. With the equations transformed into a more timelike perspective, the negative energy aspects were transformed into something even more exotic. But now they looked strangely like a mirror image of another part of the equations, if the latter were passed through a different but still appropriate transformation.

Even Einstein would have been impressed by the mental gymnastics involved in his insight.

Once on its trail, Ravan pursued this line of enquiry like a ferret after a rabbit. As is often the case, the rabbit stood no chance. By applying his transformations, under some circumstances the negative energy equations resolved to zero! But, he thought, that would not help if those 'circumstances' were even more bizarre than negative energy itself. So he took a closer look at what they meant.

Some days later, he sat back, exhausted but stunned. *Oh my God. If this is right, the effect of forcing a wormhole back through time somehow creates something that mathematically looks the same as negative energy! We can't build a wormhole to the moon, but we can build one into the past! Without needing actual negative energy!*

He thought about it. The idea of moving into the past was exciting, and had been the theme of many a novel. But how could it evade the paradoxes of time travel? The famous 'Grandfather Paradox', in which you go back in time and kill your own grandfather: in which case you were never born, so who killed him?

He looked more closely. His intellect was enough that he had not only mastered the abstruse discipline of relativistic physics, but also could have been considered worthy of the upper, though not the highest, tiers in the equally difficult world of quantum mechanics. *You can do a lot with quantum mechanics,* he thought. *But can we do this?*

Another week passed, and became a month, then two. Finally he was ready, and took his work to his supervisor.

"What is it, Harlington?" Professor Theraney asked with some asperity, Ravan having rushed into his office while forgetting to knock.

"Sorry Professor!" he cried. "But you have to see this!"

He thrust his work under the professor's nose, and Theraney glanced at the dense set of equations. He gave Ravan a sour glance. "It is a dense set of equations."

"But don't you see what it means!?"

"Why don't we save some time and you tell me? Then I can decide whether to check your work and see if it really means what you think."

"Oh! Oh, sure! I should have thought of that!"

"First stop standing there hopping, Harlington. You look like a kid wanting to go to the bathroom. Sit down."

Ravan sat, then launched into his explanation. "If I'm right, you can't build a useful wormhole through space unless you can create negative energy, whatever the hell that is! But you can build one backwards through time, because that has an effect equivalent to applying negative energy!"

Theraney stared at him. "That would make you as famous as Einstein, if it's true. But several objections occur to me right up."

"The answers are all in the equations."

"Perhaps. But first let's dispose of the obvious. How do you avoid changing your own past, thus creating time paradoxes? That's always been the trouble with time travel."

"The simplest answer lies in quantum mechanics," Ravan replied, unconsciously slipping into Lecture Mode: to the irritation of the professor, who regarded that as his bailiwick. "At a small enough scale, the quantum wave functions are self-repairing: any distortions you introduce are obliterated before they can have any effect on the future."

"Then what use is it, beyond theoretical interest? We already know that wormholes are possible, it's just that they are too unstable. This sounds like just another kind of instability; maybe even, given your 'equivalent to' statement, exactly the same instability, only viewed from a different perspective."

"No, Professor. The scale that can be repaired is relatively large. Large enough that you can open a portal into the past and actually view what is going on. Obviously, doing that has to remove information-carrying energy from the past—light, sound, that kind of thing—but causality kind of flows around it at that scale due to the reactive, compensating forces on the wave functions."

"What about if you try at an even larger scale? At some scale, presumably your wave functions can no longer repair and must break into a new direction. Paradox. Say, for instance, you can open it enough to allow the passage of a bullet, and you shoot your grandfather."

Ravan hesitated, having seen hints of ideas but unwilling to commit himself to words yet. "I haven't taken it that far. I... guess... maybe it becomes impossible. But I thought now was the time to bring this to you."

"Yes, this should be enough for now," he deadpanned. "Leave it with me."

Ravan stood, bowed in farewell, and left, almost skipping out like a boy in a playground. The professor looked at the equations speculatively, then went to work.

A couple of hours later, he rubbed his eyes, put his hand on the sheaf and stared into space.

"Well smythe me!"

4. Causality

Ravan's work created quite a stir. Not among the public, who would have been as amazed as they were mystified: they certainly would not hear about it until it had been properly vetted. The Protectorate was keen on scientific progress, but even keener on ensuring that no dangerous technologies could be born; and preferably not even become a gleam in someone's eye.

Professor Theraney asked Ravan to prepare a paper on his findings and this he circulated among those luminaries with the expertise and clearance to see it. So in relatively short order, Ravan found himself standing before those luminaries and interested Protectorate agents, giving an account of his discovery.

This account went much as he had told his professor except with some simplifications and many colored images. These succeeded in conveying the impression to his audience that they understood what he was saying, especially if they did not.

"So," asked an elderly man with piercingly intelligent eyes but unrecognized face, "You are saying that we can look into the past, spy on it if you will, but not send things there to change it?"

"I am saying that we can look into the past without changing it, yes."

"That isn't quite what I asked."

"Well…" he started, and stopped.

"Well?" asked the man, somewhat more sharply.

"Well, I have not developed the equations that far. I've only looked at the small scales. In those, the past is not changed, no."

"Would you care to speculate about... other possibilities?"

For a student to be put up as the star in front of such an audience was of course thrilling for the student. In such circumstances it is easy to get carried away into imprudence. But Ravan had noted the silent men and women on the margins of the audience, and remembered the archaeology student.

Well, to be honest, sir, I think the wave equations do allow changing the past, through strange loops in causality, just as they allow physical effects to manifest from non-existent virtual particles, he thought.

"Well, I am sure that physics does not allow causality violations," he said. *And so I am.* "Just as the 'elasticity' of the wave functions allows us to view the past without changing it, I believe that very elasticity would push back against the creation of any wormhole capable of changing the past. Consider a rubber band or a spring: the more you try to stretch it, the more it pushes back against your attempt. Thus we would be back to unstable wormholes, and causality is preserved." *And that may even be true.*

"And how sure are you of that?"

Ravan spread his hands. "I am quite sure that causality cannot be violated. As to the exact mechanism whereby it may be preserved under all circumstances... I am afraid that is beyond me at this point. But causality is fundamental to reality, so I don't have to fully understand my equations in order to be sure of it."

The man nodded, and the questions turned to other matters. But Ravan noted that the glances of the silent men remained sharp.

Besides that one moment of danger, the seminar was a great success. At the end, Ravan received many congratulations. His doctorate in physics was a foregone conclusion, and so he embarked on his exceptional career.

When he wrote up the papers that formalized his work, he was careful to restate his assertion that using the technology to change time was impossible. He was even more careful to add statements to the effect of 'and of course, any such attempt would be extraordinarily dangerous, more dangerous even than atomic weapons.' *The last thing I want,* he told himself, *is for someone too clever for his or her own good to look too closely into that possibility. It's the last thing the world needs, too.*

If sometimes in the years following he thought he saw an occasional silent watcher in the shadows, perhaps he imagined it.

5. THE DAY

"What a lovely day," Vickie Gray said to her husband, as she looked out over the ocean, the early sun making the waves sparkle.

Their house was a modern one built at the top of a cliff, separated from the nearest public road by a winding access way through otherwise untouched coastal scrub, currently adding to the beauty of the day with its sprinkling of wildflowers.

If it were surprising that a historian could afford such a home in such a location, the fact was she couldn't. But her husband was high in some shadowy arm of the Protectorate, and between them they most certainly could.

Vickie was an ambitious woman. She had enough brains to do well in whatever career she chose, and also enough brains to know that in the world she was born into, mere intelligence was often not enough or even necessary.

Left to their own devices, her genes would not have made her notably attractive. But they had made a good start, with a fine bone structure and a tendency toward athleticism. Judicious application of the surgeon's arts had improved her, but not too much. People did not call her lovely; but they called her striking. She was attractive, but not too attractive: some teeth somewhat crooked, breasts well shaped but not excessive, a few minor flaws. These detracted little from her overall appearance, yet would suffice if someone wanted to avoid the reputation of being improperly concerned with physical beauty.

As well as investing in her body, she had paid chefs to teach her the art of cooking for maximum effect with minimum effort and expense. She had also paid prostitutes, not for the usual purpose but in order to learn how best to please a man. Having thus prepared herself for the two most traditional routes to a man's heart, at university she devoted her time to study for her career on the one hand, while seeking out a suitable mate to ease her career path on the other.

She was ambitious but not as an end in itself. She knew there was no point having position and money if she wasn't also happy. She supposed she would be happiest if she found love; but love was unlikely to bring with it the position and money. In any case her observations had left her jaundiced as to love's permanence, which rarely matched the glorious intensity of its birth. She was not the kind of woman to leave her destiny to chance.

But she did want to be happy. So if she did not hope for love, she hoped for someone she could live with and be neither abused nor bored. And someone destined for a high position. So that is what she set herself to find, joining the student societies generally regarded as breeding grounds for the political elite.

She made herself popular enough to be invited to the best parties and be asked out by an array of ambitious young men. But she did not make herself so popular as to become a commodity. She generally dated a man only once, to take his measure according to her criteria. She had the normal needs of a girl her age, and slept with some: but only those who were discrete, good, but not good enough to nudge the physical pleasure into the folly of falling in love.

She had one false start. The man was dark haired and dark eyed, with a stunning smile and a way of looking at people as if he cared. She suspected he had invested in his own future in a similar way she had in hers. *But hey, sauce for the goose...* Their first date was excellent. As was their second, and on that night she allowed him to seduce her. For a while they became an item. But to him, she was just a convenience. She foresaw that he would dump her for someone more advantageous, or if not, it would not be long before her life with him became a bore. He would be too wrapped up in his own career to share it with her. Or probably both. *Ambition in a mate is useful but dangerous,* she realized. So she engineered an event where she found him in bed with another woman, and ended it amicably but firmly.

When she met Trevor Gray, she was drawn to him. He had a quick intellect and ambition, and a concern for other people that seemed genuine, not part of his game. They dated once, and she found him charming but sincere: two independent qualities in her experience. And when she looked into his eyes, the concern she saw there for others seemed to draw her into its orbit, placing her on a special pedestal reserved only for her. They dated a second time, and this time she chose to cook for him. He loved it, and made it clear that this gratification of his physical needs left him hungry for another kind. But she demurred, citing a desire to know a man better before she went that far with him.

They had a few more dates, while she played her double game: playing him like a fish, while assessing whether this fish should be landed or released. Finally, on their fifth date, she relaxed into his hands when he placed them on her shoulders after dinner; allowed those hands to wander downwards; then followed him to his bedroom. This time, she applied all the arts she had learned for just this purpose, and the fish was well and truly hooked.

The fish stayed cheerfully caught and she was happy to have it wriggling on her line. Their romance turned into marriage and her studies turned into a career as a historian, while his turned into a career in the government. They were happy, successful and popular.

Had some of the seedier gossip reporters chosen to look into their personal life, perhaps their reputations would have been tarnished— or enhanced, depending on the reader's own predilections. Neither had entered their marriage imagining it was a match of passion and exclusive love until death did they part. Both knew it was more a mutual hand up the ladders of social and professional life than a union of souls staring into each other's eyes for eternity.

So they were relaxed about certain issues upon which other marriages have foundered when strict expectations collided with looser realities. She knew that he travelled, sometimes for weeks. She knew that a man had needs even when his wife wasn't waiting for him in his lonely hotel room. Had she been in love, she might not have thought that justified indulging such needs; but as it was, she did not care as long as he was keen for her own favors upon his return. More to the point for the purpose of their marriage, she knew that sex was a tool. After all, it was a tool she had used to acquire her beneficial marriage in the first place.

In times past, a prince would marry off his children in order to achieve political advantage. In the modern era things were more casual.

Powerful women would enjoy the attentions of an attractive man, and enjoy his company in her bed. Perhaps only one night, consummating agreements made during the day. Perhaps a week, during an extended negotiation, cementing an alliance. Perhaps illicit meetings in anonymous hotel rooms when they happened to be in the same city, adding both drama and welcome physical release to otherwise routine but stressful travels.

Or it might be a meeting in which some potentate showed his wealth and generosity by providing prostitutes, explicit or implicit, to his guests. A man who refused might be considered weak, even effeminate. It was expected that a virile, powerful man would take such gifts as his due, and his wife would just accept it.

Vickie knew these things went on. She did not enquire about them, being uninterested in the salacious details, though sometimes he would tell her about the most remarkable or amusing of his experiences. Sometimes he learned something from them, and she gained a more direct delight from his education.

She wondered whether any of his unions had been with men. He was not bisexual, but she was first of all a historian: she knew that in cultures like ancient Rome or Greece, sexual relations between men had happened for political reasons. Their own world was somewhat prudish on the matter. Officially, any sexual preference between adults was acceptable. But theirs was still a world recovering from disaster, where children too often were hard to conceive or flawed if they were, and hence were highly valued. The population had long since recovered but the trauma still ran deep. In such a society the heterosexual norm was tacitly regarded as the ideal, and deviations unconsciously frowned upon whatever the public face. Perhaps that same attitude is why Vickie preferred not to know what lengths Trevor might have gone to for the sake of his career.

For her part, Trevor well knew her skills in bed, and appreciated how valuable they could be. Just as in her time as a student she would not make herself a commodity to be passed around, now she held herself back for special purposes, so as to increase the value of her favors. Given the value of some of the deals she helped to close, she could have been considered as one of the highest paid prostitutes in history.

He too sometimes wondered whether any of her unions had been with women, but preferred not to know: not because it was distasteful to him, but because not knowing gave freer rein to his fantasies.

Vickie had a complex mind, and one could have taken a lifetime of study yet still not fully disentangled the delicate balances of its nuances. Her husband was a much simpler creature, as they often were.

Her marriage to a man with such position and influence eased the way to security clearances where such were needed. Her intelligence and dedication made her good at her job, and her social position made her known to those who, having seen it, would see her rewarded. Thus she rose in her profession.

In some ways the history of the world is immune to individuals. Its path goes on, perhaps slightly altered, but overall scouring its course over the small bumps and distractions introduced by the millions of people who briefly toil in some small portion of its immensity. There are some who by particular skill or sometimes chance will change its course, whose names reverberate down the centuries: warriors like Caesar or Genghis Khan; thinkers like Aristotle; scientists like Newton.

Some are unexpected. Few people in the world had heard of Vickie Gray, and if they did her name meant little to them. Those who knew her thought of her as a successful and popular woman, but not especially remarkable.

Nobody suspected she would destroy the world.

~~~

"What did you say?" asked Trevor, walking out of the en-suite while toweling his hair.

"I said, it's a lovely day."

He joined her by the window, put his arm around her waist, and admired the view.

"You seem particularly cheerful today."

"Today's the day they turn on the Machine."

"You'll always turn on this machine," he growled, nibbling her neck. She laughed, and the start of their working day became somewhat delayed.

6. The Machine

If the Protectorate liked to encourage the study of science, provided it was approved science, it also liked to encourage the study of history.

The war had given mankind a savage blow, and mankind had duly retreated to a safer place to lick its wounds before poking its head outside with much greater timidity than it had before.

Many who lived in past ages would have looked at the Protectorate with great disapproval. In most ages maybe not, as it was better than many; but those who enjoyed freer times would have called it repressive and intrusive, if not outright fascist.

Perhaps such charges would have been true. But the people whose experience, actions and ideas had led to the Protectorate in its present form had lived through different times. The result was repressive and it was intrusive. But above all, its founders had sought to prevent a repeat of the War.

There had been wars before, even a world war, then another. But the final war was just known as The War, as all others paled beside its fury. Its survivors had looked at the ruination around them and never wished to see its like again. They thought about what had led to it, sketchy and contradictory as the remaining evidence might have been.

And so the Protectorate was born, with its reason for being and core directive the prevention of literally earth-shattering technologies, the encouragement of a sense of community service, and through that the shepherding of society into a future where such a War could never happen again. The founders wanted a future where it would be literally inconceivable.

Freedom is always hard won, and the disciples of freedom might have been unimpressed regardless of these lofty motives. Had they been able to stand astride history and comment on its fate, they might have opined that it carried the seeds of its own failure in its own contradictions.

Perhaps they would have had a point. Its end came not from its failures but its successes. Nobody would have named those who destroyed it as other than model citizens, deeply imbued with the values of their society. Those individuals themselves would have said the same, and said so honestly.

~~~

The residual fatigue of the hours of her long flight fell from Vickie like water from an otter when finally she stood gazing at the Machine. The gleaming metal spoke of staggering powers under the control of arcane knowledge, and the thick cables leading to it bore further witness to their magnitude.

Nuclear weapons had long been banned on planet Earth but nuclear power, at least in its safer forms, had not. If the founders of the Protectorate had feared the nuclear genie that had spat its rage onto the world, they also had the wisdom to know that survival consisted not merely of escaping death but achieving life. They had no illusions that the future lay in some idyllic, pre-technological past. An industrial society was part of their solution and industrial society needed abundant, reliable power.

The world had struggled and many had died, but it had recovered, and by this age had exceeded many accomplishments of its ancestors. The thorny problems of controlled nuclear fusion had been solved, and its hellish powers were bent to the needs of men. With that landmark achievement all fission plants were removed as a now unacceptable and unnecessary risk.

The Machine Vickie stared at had its own small but dedicated fusion reactor.

She shook herself, and looked around the room. It was a select company. She recognized many faces, all eminent personages in the sciences and government. But one eclipsed them all. She saw the stately, still handsome form of a middle-aged man across the room, and recognized Dr Ravan Harlington. *The man who made it all possible.* He wasn't looking at anyone, seeming to barely acknowledge those who came up to congratulate him or shake his hand. He had eyes only for the Machine.

A large screen was set up, visible to all the company but currently dark.

There were no speeches. Dr Harlington had requested it. "If the Machine doesn't work, then speeches are foolish," he had opined. "If the Machine works, then speeches are superfluous."

The screen came to life, but nothing was visible on it but its background glow. Dr Harlington stepped forward to a console, checked the settings, placed his finger on a button, then looked around the room.

He broke his own rule to the extent of quoting, "O, call back yesterday, bid time return." Then he pressed the button.

The tiny leakage from the power going to the Machine set up a faint hum in the air, and they looked toward the large cavity inside the Machine. Faint sparkling lights danced in the cavity, like a miniature of the Northern Lights. Then they faded, and all that was visible was a tiny dot of black inside a ring of pale fire.

Vickie looked up at the screen, as Dr Harlington studied his console and made adjustments. There was a brief burst of static, and then the image cleared into something grainy but easily seen. It showed a bearded man dressed in strange garb looking at an instrument. He bent to its eyepiece, adjusted the instrument, then leapt away with a gasp, looking up towards the heavens.

Then the image winked out, and Dr Harlington stepped forward to address the room.

"That was Galileo Galilei, the first scientist, when he first looked through his telescope at another world. I could not think of a more appropriate test or tribute."

Vickie looked at him, stunned, as did the rest of the room. Then somebody began to clap, and the room erupted in applause.

~~~

The Machine was housed in a secure facility half an hour from a city, and they all went for formal dinner in a restaurant at the top of a tall hotel tower.

There was no way even Dr Harlington could prevent speeches now, and there were speeches aplenty. But his original words still stuck in her mind. *What is there to say, after seeing that? How can words express it, or hope to match it? Or stand in its memory?*

Harlington had been surrounded by dignitaries far more important than her and she had not yet spoken to him. But when coffee was served she had taken her cup outside, tired of the speeches and speculations, just to stand in the cool and gaze out upon the lights of the city and the darkness of the river winding through it.

She felt a presence at her side but before she could turn, it spoke.

"Dr Gray, our historian, I believe?"

"Dr Harlington."

She shook his hand, and when she said no more he looked at her with amusement.

"You are a woman of few words. Most people here don't know how to shut up. Or when."

"I confess I am quite tongue-tied."

"You must be a hard woman to impress."

"Quite the contrary," she laughed. "It's just that words seem inadequate. I can't find any to suit. That was... incredible. Beyond incredible. Beyond words."

"I understand completely. Thank you. For what the missing words say."

He paused. "Well, it has been nice meeting you, but I must go. So many people want to shake my hand for the tenth time. You'd think I've saved the world or something, not just opened a small window into its past. Good night, Dr Gray."

"Please wait."

He stopped and looked at her, but again she found she couldn't speak.

Despite her lifestyle she was not by nature promiscuous. To her, sex was too valuable for that: a union or a tool, not often a casual event like picking up strangers in a nightclub; not a fleeting pleasure lacking any other meaning. But looking at this man, her body was screaming at her that she must have him. She was shocked at her own reaction, but she knew the reason. *It would be like doing it with Einstein. And Newton. Together.*

"I'm flying out tomorrow," she managed lamely, then discovered to her horror that she was blushing like a schoolgirl. Exactly like a schoolgirl, she thought, remembering the day she had first invited a boy into her bed. The memory and the comparison just made her blush the more.

He saw and smiled. This of course just made her blush even more.

If that is even possible.

"You must think I'm an idiot," she stammered. *Stammering? Jesus!* "I'm sorry to have taken up your time."

"Dr Gray, I think the fact that you cannot speak, and that you react this way, is the greatest tribute I have had tonight."

She decided to look anywhere but in his direction.

He slipped a card into her fingers. "I must mix, and bear with the adulation. But if you still feel this way in half an hour, this is my room."

He turned to go, then turned back.

"Let me be perfectly clear and honest with you, Dr Gray. I like sex as much as the next man, and I am not above a casual dalliance. But be assured that I am not thinking of this as an easy way into the pants of some star struck fan, soon forgotten. I think that your feeling this way is as much a tribute to yourself as it is to me."

7. Ancient History

"You *what?*"

"I had sex with Dr Harlington. *The* Dr Harlington."

She had just arrived home and had been undressing in their bedroom when the words just spilled out, like some great achievement or revelation that would not be contained.

Trevor stared at her. "I… well, I guess he's a guy like any other. But Christ, I'm impressed. He can have anyone, and you got him, right under the noses of an entire delegation of luminaries. Wow. Dr Harlington. The Time Lord himself."

The outline of Harlington's achievement, and what could be done with it, had by now been released to the public. It took little time for the media to anoint him with the title of Time Lord.

She smiled, tossing her panties into the dirty clothes. "His DNA will be on these panties. Maybe I should auction them off."

"Classy."

"That's me. All class. That's how I hook the big fish."

"How *did* you hook the big fish?"

"You sound a little too surprised. Don't you think I'm good enough?"

"Oh, I think you're good enough," he growled, raking his eyes over her now naked body. He grabbed her and she squealed as he threw her on the bed. "If you're good enough for the Time Lord, you're good enough for me. If he had you, I'm keen to be next in line. Talk about one degree of separation. There's something ridiculously horny about sharing, um, *that* with a Time Lord."

"You bastard!" she said, wrapping him in her legs and twisting so she was on top of him.

"That's if *I'm* still good enough for *you*, Wonder Woman."

She sighed. "I suppose after having sex with a god that having it with a mere man *is* a big step down. First let me check," she said, reaching down between his legs. "Hmmm, strange, how gods and men are so much alike."

He laughed, and twisted her over on her back. "Well, let's see how much alike we really are!"

~~~

Vickie had flown to the Machine facility for the opening as one of the Important People, but her physical presence was not required for her actual research. That's what physicists and technicians were for. They would target and collect the data and send it to her; she would tell them what she needed; all her work could be done from the comfort of her own workplace far away.

At odd moments she would look up from her work and wonder what would have happened if the Protectorate had decided that she should work at the facility. Would she and Harlington have repeated their union? She thought not. That night seemed as if it should stand alone, an immaculate achievement, to be observed and honored but remain forever singular, forbidding the commonplace of repetition. She was happy that any temptation was so far away. Mortal men were enough for her.

She was in charge of the entire historical project. There were a number of side projects of interest to the Protectorate that would be handled by others under her ultimate control, but the main one she would be doing personally.

The event that defined their history was poorly understood. The Protectorate dearly hoped to understand it, knowing that the more they understood the better armed the world might be to prevent a repetition.

Nobody really knew how the War had started. The Americans blamed the Russians; the Russians blamed the Americans; within those broad areas of blame, some blamed the Government, some blamed a rogue commander, some blamed men gone mad under the pressures of impending war, some even blamed accidents. But between the incompleteness of the record, the deliberate fog of propaganda and the more random fog of war, it was all speculation with little certainty.

Vickie aimed to fix that, and she faced the prospect with delight. *Perhaps I shall achieve my own brand of divinity after all, and prove worthy of the night I shared with a god.*

The incredible energies that fed the Machine were not without price. The Machine could not be run too often. Each time it had to be checked, recalibrated and if necessary repaired. Alignments had to be precise within a small margin of error. If an instability developed the Machine might be damaged, possibly beyond repair, at the least costing days or weeks of lost time. And for all that the Machine could pierce the barriers of time, those who used it were carried along in time's inexorable flow, powerless to add or remove a second of it.

There was also a reason why the staff worked on site, beyond ensuring maximum reliability of information and instant feedback of results. It was unlikely that an error would do more than damage the Machine. But the possibility remained that a greater breakout of its immense energies could occur. Nothing concentrated the mind more than being at ground zero of your own mistakes.

The heart of the Protectorate was kindness and altruism. But it protected that heart with teeth of steel.

So it took a while. In addition to the War investigation, there were the lesser but still important historical projects, technical monitoring and improving of the equipment, and purely physical experiments.

But slowly the story took shape. At first Vickie probed times and places that the records they did have indicated may have contained clues. She then followed the clues or tried again. Iteration after iteration they approached the truth of the War.

Finally she knew.

The Russians had placed nuclear missiles on the island of Cuba, near the United States of America. Vickie was no military strategist, but even she could see that was clear provocation: no doubt some ill-conceived bargaining chip in the mess that was international diplomacy in the Cold War, a mess still little understood.

The USA felt it could not ignore or allow this, so in order to show its displeasure and prevent further provocations or indeed outrages, it blockaded Cuba with its warships.

The Russians, of course, thumbed their noses at the Americans, attempting to bypass the warships with their submarines.

Neither side wanted war. The Russians feared the Americans and did not trust their stated intentions of peace. The Americans feared the

Russians and did not trust theirs. Neither could back down and show weakness, fearing the other side would press its advantage, and that allies would weaken and enemies be emboldened; that the end result of any show of weakness was surrender or war. Enough men on both sides remembered the folly only decades earlier of appeasing an enemy who talked peace while plotting war. They could hear the talking but only guess at the plots, and they dared not be taken for fools this time.

The world stood at the brink. Neither side would move into war; neither side would retreat into peace. It would only take a spark to blow the whole thing up.

Then the spark struck. The Americans detected a submarine trying to run their blockade, deep under water. They tried to force the submarine to surface by peppering its location with depth charges. The Russians in the submarine assumed they were under attack, which meant they were already at war. This submarine was armed with a nuclear torpedo, and it attacked. Most of the American fleet was obliterated.

The Americans responded with force. So did the Russians. And that is how the War began.

She looked at her report. She had finished it with what could become the iconic photo of the death of the Old World: a nuclear fireball rising from the center of the ruined US fleet.

Looking at it made her sick to the stomach.

You crazy, stupid, irredeemable idiots.

It was all just a ghastly mistake. They had played with fire and it had turned on them. *What possessed the Americans to drop depth charges on a nuclear armed submarine?* She realized that they mustn't have known. *But they knew the Russians had them. What possessed them to run such a risk?* Perhaps they believed it had only normal arms. Then they would not have feared an attack from it. *On what a small thing can the death of a world hinge.*

But the world had not died. It had been wounded grievously but had not perished. And the Protectorate had grown out of the ashes, charged with never allowing such a thing again. She felt a swell of pride that in her own small way, she was helping in that noble quest.

Most people would have stopped there. The story was clear and logical. Every step of the disaster was mapped and every step made sense, each in its own crazy fashion. Every step that led them to their doom. There was no more to be said.

If she stopped now, no doubt the Protectorate would be satisfied. They would act on the knowledge as best they could, if there were any way to act on the death of a billion people due to a mixture of stupidity and bad luck. Neither were susceptible to being outlawed.

But Vickie was intelligent and thorough. The Machine was hellishly expensive to run, and she knew that after her report its work on this project would be terminated. But the story did not satisfy her. Perhaps there was no more to learn, but if she stopped now she would never know for sure, and she would forever doubt and regret.

She composed a message to the operators of the Machine.

8. One Man

A ping in his ear announced an incoming call, the tone of the ping telling him it was someone on his prequalified list of callers. He clicked the earbud to accept the call.

"Dr Harlington?" a female voice asked.

"I am he."

"It's Vickie Gray here, Dr Harlington."

"Oh, good morning, Vickie. You have called me Ravan on at least two occasions, Dr Gray. You do not have to be so formal."

"I feared it would be an impertinence, given those occasions."

"Nonsense. I am happy to be reminded of it."

"Thank you. Ravan."

"That's better, Vickie. Now that the informalities are over, what can I do for you?"

"I have finished my investigation into the start of the War. Before I submit it to the authorities, I thought as a courtesy I should tell you my basic findings. They are quite fascinating!"

"Why, yes. Everyone is interested in the War. It is quite a scar on the collective psyche. But wait a minute while I return to my office."

Once there, he transferred the call to his office system, and he saw her looking at him from across her own desk.

"So! You have results! Please tell me."

"First, I managed to trace the original trigger for the war," she said, proceeding to tell him the history she had deduced.

"I see. Quite tragic. But you said 'first'?"

"Yes. I almost left it there. But then I wondered about the

47

individuals, and I decided the story wouldn't be complete without a bit more insight into their decisions. A finer grained view of history, as it were, in a unique case. And such insight may well be useful in its own right."

"Their actions seem almost inevitable in the circumstances they faced, but yes, I see. And what did you find?"

"It was even more tragic than you could imagine. I must confess I wept when I discovered it."

"Go on."

"Some Russian submarines, like this one, were armed with what they called their 'Special Weapon', a nuclear torpedo. It seems that if they were unable to receive instructions from their government, then a nuclear attack could be launched if both the Captain and the Political Officer on board agreed it was warranted. On that submarine, both the Captain and the Political Officer were convinced that war had begun, and believed they should attack."

"Well that is what we expected, surely? We know from your original findings that the submarine was under attack. These were military men, who made the standard decision for military men. It would be unusual, and uncommonly lucky in this case, to encounter one with a greater flexibility of mind and, shall we say, more prudent wisdom. While tragic, yes, I don't see that we have learned much more, merely confirmed our obvious deductions. Though in itself, that must have interest for theoretical history, of course."

"So you might think. But this submarine was different. There happened to be a third man involved. Because he was in command of the entire flotilla of submarines, on this one vessel he had to agree too. He was not convinced. The other two finally convinced him, but he had been wavering, and as far as we can tell from analyzing their conversation, almost vetoed the attack."

"Oh my God! It was that close run a thing?"

"I'm afraid so. If he hadn't been there the attack would certainly have occurred. But he was there, and he nearly prevented it."

For a few seconds she remained silent.

"Ravan, the whole damn war came down to one man. One man. Of course many men were involved: the Americans, the Russians, all the way down to the US fleet commander who decided to drop the depth charges, to the Captain and Political Officer. All playing their part, all pretty much following an inevitable script. But one man could have stopped it, and he almost did. He almost did, Ravan!"

She stared, not at him but into some space only she could see, before continuing in a leaden voice.

"But he didn't."

~~~

The man sat nervously, holding his hat in his hands, in great danger of squeezing it into shapelessness.

He was successful enough in his profession, a linguist who had a great ear for languages. He had even been retained recently on a mysterious government project, in which he had helped adapt an auto-translator to understand some archaic Russian conversations, recorded on a rather patchy video. He had wondered where the historical relic had come from, but it had been made clear to him that such questions were best not asked at this stage, and all would be addressed at the right time. He had of course now heard of the Time Lord and his Machine, and that had prompted excited imaginings on the recordings' origins. But he knew not to wonder or speculate when so instructed, and thus had kept his thoughts to himself.

He had never been invited into high circles, and frankly he liked to keep it that way. The higher you were drawn into such circles the further you had to fall, and the more people were happy to kick you off; and he liked his modest, safe life. He had a profession he enjoyed, a wife he loved, children he adored, and enough money to live well. He sought no more from life.

Yet here he was, in a reception room to which he had been summoned by Dr Ravan Harlington himself. His suspicions as to the provenance of the videos firmed up under that fact, as did his fears of why he would be summoned. He wondered what secret project Harlington could want him for now, and why Harlington wanted to see him in person. He hoped it was a new secret project, and not something he had done wrong on his previous secret project.

He was not a brave man. In his mind bravery was a noble quality, but one best observed in others.

Finally the receptionist looked up. "You may go in now, Doctor."

He stood nervously, still mangling his hat, and nodded his thanks. When he didn't move, she smiled and pointed to the door. "That way."

"Er, yes, of course. Of course."

He entered timidly, and saw the Time Lord himself, sitting at a desk.

"Come in, Dr Stavanski, come in. Sorry to keep you waiting,

something came up that I had to deal with immediately."

"Certainly, certainly, no problem at all, sir. I am at your service. How may I assist you?"

"Why, I would like to learn how to speak Russian, Dr Stavanski. Mid Twentieth Century Russian. I understand you were recently involved in a project where you excelled yourself in the very dialect I am interested in. I think you're just the man."

"What is your interest, may I inquire?"

"You may not. The fact of my interest is all you need to know."

He nodded. "I understand. But do *you* understand? It takes months, often years, to become fluent in another tongue. If your need is urgent, perhaps you should retain me, or some other, more directly?"

"Perhaps I misspoke myself somewhat. I fully intend to use a real-time translator. But they are only as good as their training, and I need you to train the device so its translations and accent are as accurate as possible. And I need to know the basics so I can use the translator most efficiently. You have already shown your competence in adapting such a machine to understand the language, but there was no need for it to go in the other direction and speak it. Now I have a need."

"But I don't understand, sir. Nobody, outside of a few experts such as myself, speak the language any more. Its modern descendants are quite different, as different in accent and idiom as say modern English is from the language of Shakespeare. I can understand your interest in understanding the spoken language, since you have found some old recordings. But why speak it? There is nobody to speak it to."

"True, true, Dr Stavanski. But I could also ask why do *you* speak it? It interests me, as a challenge, and kind of a hobby. Sometimes a man feels like a new challenge, no?"

Stavanski stared at him briefly. One possible, or rather impossible, use flitted across his brain, but skittered away with the rapidity of a forbidden thought in a nervous man. Then he nodded again. "Of course, sir. I did not mean to pry. I am, as always, at your service."

9. Reset

When Ravan had first heard the verdict from Vickie Gray, he was appalled. *No wonder you wept,* he'd thought. *All that blood, all the death: on the wavering head of one man.*

He had been silent for long moments.

"Vickie," he had said slowly at last, "I have a suggestion to make, and a request."

"Certainly, Ravan. I value your opinions."

"Your finding raises some interesting theoretical questions in my own field, and I would like some time to study them. If I'm right, the results will round out your findings rather well. So may I suggest you submit your original draft, without the extra information on the pivotal role of your third man? Once I have my results, you can add the complete story to your final report."

"Oh! Well... maybe," she replied dubiously. "Might that not be better as a later commentary?"

"Of course it's entirely up to you, but I think the result will be worth the wait. I think there are aspects of that final piece of the puzzle that could be... misunderstood... if presented without some more exact science. It shouldn't delay your final submission unduly. They will want to read a first draft anyway. Most of your findings are in the original story, are they not? You can just say that we are working on some additional aspects to complete the picture."

She nodded, still looking a little dubious but apparently swayed by his reasoning. "Yes... yes... if you think so. I must say that I've been fascinated by the results, but thinking about how I got them makes my head hurt. I shall do as you ask. You're the quantum mechanic."

~~~

Alone in his office, Ravan had sat back, feeling the sweat under his armpits despite the perfect cool of the air. When he had heard her conclusions the first thing he had felt, after the vast if impersonal pity, was a wordless certainty that she must not relay those words to the Protectorate.

On the heels of that certainty came another: that he must not alert her to its importance either. She was ambitious, he knew that. And ambition can lead to betrayal. He did not think she would betray him: the night they had spent together, and the depths of character which had led her to it, would not allow such venality. But perhaps he was a fool and her words on that night had just been a game, the same way his were today: not the feelings of a soul laid bare, but a mask over a shallow desire for the trophy of bedding a famous man. He could not risk it. More, there may have been other listeners: the Protectorate was ever alert for forbidden thoughts, and even he might not be immune from their oversight.

The last thing he wanted was to shine a spotlight on that which he sought to hide. So he had chosen his words with care, and would have to hope it was enough to disguise whatever truly lay behind his dread certainty.

Now he stared at the certainty, seeking to find that truth himself.

The first layer of the onion was a simple one, and it took little introspection to arrive at the answer. The very question brought up images of a wild-eyed student speaking of dangerous thoughts, and his own attempts, when first he started on this path, to deflect any suspicion that the past could be changed. *Attempts so successful I almost believe them myself.*

But as soon as he thought it, he looked at his own inner vision, appalled.

Who would think anything could be done? Who could imagine they might divert the great forces of history, the sum of so many interlocking and often unknowable influences? But what if the fulcrum rested on one man, and what tipped one way could be tipped the other? That to change history, this once, might not need the powers of a god, but just the smallest push in the right direction?

It was insane. He knew it. But the siren call of the hints he had seen in the equations, suppressed even in his own mind, would not let him go. For he could not let go the image he had seen of a mushroom cloud rising above what had moments before been a peaceful sea, nor escape the images in his head of over a billion dead.

I will do nothing, he assured himself. *I dare not assume such a responsibility. I will simply prepare, and see if it is possible. Perhaps then I will take it to my masters, and trust in their wisdom. I am just being prudent. Thorough. I will not act upon it.*

He wondered why he felt the need to keep telling himself that.

The whirling in his mind stopped again, caught on another point, like eddying seaweed washed to and fro by the sea but pinned by a rock. *But even if one were to try,* he thought, then stopped, grimly amused at the defanging of his own thoughts. *At least have the honesty to name the players, Ravan. Yes, even if I were to try, risking my career, if not my life, if not the world: am I really risking anything, or was I right all along? And it truly cannot be changed?*

He sat still, trying to impose order on the confusion in his mind. *On the small scales we act at now we cause local changes, but the wave functions are repaired by equal and opposite forces: stresses created by the conservation of energy shaped by the changes themselves. Perhaps that is true at all scales. Perhaps we cannot change decisions made in the past. Or if we did change this one decision, maybe all we would achieve is the same outcome with a slightly different immediate cause, and the only effect that would ripple through to our age is a slightly different report from Dr Gray, of no consequence to their future or our past.*

He leant back in his chair, staring into space for long moments.

And if we stop this disaster, if the War never happens: then what? Perhaps the next month, or the next year, there would just be another one.

Then he thought of the mushroom cloud, and the billion dead.

But I could give them a chance. They could have peace in their time. Perhaps having come so close to the brink, they will learn what we learned without having to fall into the abyss. And if they do not learn without disaster, maybe our race is doomed to learn only from it. Maybe I cannot save the human race, because we don't deserve to be saved. Peace in their time is all that is in my power to give. I can only hope that they know what to do with it.

If I can even give them that.

~~~

Had some judge pronounced a verdict on the people of his age, Ravan Harlington would not have been declared the most superlative of them.

His beauty was irrelevant, and perhaps would even cost him some points for daring to contaminate him with its impertinence.

His intellect was relevant: not that brilliance was an end in itself, and had Ravan treated it as such he would have been disqualified; but that brilliance could bring boons to his fellow man. And indeed Ravan had applied himself to do just that.

But chief among the criteria would have been his character. If he was not the best among men, certainly he was one of the most exceptional. For what the Protectorate cared for most was empathy. What the Protectorate made sure was inculcated in all youth as key to their education and personal development was empathy and caring. And in these things Ravan had few peers and fewer superiors.

The Protectorate was founded on a philosophy that to a past world would have appeared a strange syncretism, born in the collision of the ideals of the West with the traumas of the War. The rugged individualists of America's birth and the intellectual champions who followed them would have called the Protectorate collectivist, built on the ideal that the community was all, and the individual nothing. But the Protectorate would have called them wrong.

The Protectorate valued the individual. That is why an ambitious woman like Vickie Gray would bother being ambitious, and could be so without the soul-eroding contamination of hypocrisy. The ambitious, at least those who earned the arrogance of their ambition, could hope for rewards commensurate with their talents. If one gave great value to society surely society should give great value in return: especially when the equations of such trade meant that society could never repay more than a fraction of the value it had received. And if those capable of such gifts knew that the greater they applied their gifts the more fabulous their rewards, then surely that would encourage them to greater and greater heights, lifting all of society with them. Gifts were valuable only if they were applied, and then they were invaluable.

But the Protectorate was born of contradictions. It needed ambition but feared an ambition that might serve dark desires or fears. How to stop this, its founders had wondered? How to reward ambition that did good, without enabling its darker side? They had a solution. If those in power, whether it be political, economic or social, had true empathy for all people, then of necessity they would serve those people. Whatever talents and ambition might circle it, if at the core of their being lay empathy, then they would not seek their own advantage at the price of pain to others: they would feel that pain too keenly in their own souls. The Protectorate needed no laws to stop men plunging their own hands into a fire or a knife into their own breast: they would gladly stop themselves, and fight any who tried to force them to do it. And what prophet would urge their disciples to kill the unbelievers, and what conqueror would lead their armies to invade the world, if they felt the terror, pain and grief of their victims wailing inside their own soul—and what armies would serve them, feeling the same?

And thus the Protectorate taught its children that empathy was not only the highest virtue but also the surest sign of a healthy mind.

If the Protectorate erred, still their error was close enough to the truth to succeed. They did not try to suppress the individual. They did not try to tell people to bury their own loves and desires for the contradictory sake of others' loves and desires. They did not tell people to sacrifice themselves for society. They told people to live for their own joy: but to feel the joys and pains of others as well. Able to feel no joy if it were at the price of another's misery.

In the philosophy of the Protectorate there was no conflict between the good of society and the good of the individual. An individual could only achieve his or her own good by being rewarded for doing what was good for others.

It is true that all people are fundamentally the same, so that none deserve to be sacrificed to the ambitions of others, and none deserve to succeed by means of destroying others. It is true that in a society of people seeking their own good, nobody needs to be sacrificed and all can gain. Perhaps the way to achieve that is not through empathy: perhaps simple justice is a better way. But it is the way the Protectorate chose, and it worked well.

If Ravan had all his beauty and all his brilliance but insufficient empathy, he would never have risen to the peak he reached. The Protectorate would not have allowed it. The Protectorate did not merely attempt to imbue empathy in its children. It measured and sifted it. Without it Ravan would have become a valued and useful lower-echelon physicist, his talents contributing to society but never achieving heights of his own. He would have been happy; perhaps wishing for greater glory than he could reach, perhaps in the darkness of his heart begrudging those of lesser intellect who soared above him; but forever cut off from power. In the absence of enough empathy, the Protectorate had decided, power was too dangerous a thing to grant or unleash.

But Ravan had always excelled in empathy scores. No doubt his education had helped, but it was also his natural aptitude. He saw himself in other people; he knew they felt joys and sorrows in the same way he did, and more: he felt them keenly. Perhaps not quite as keenly as his own, for who can feel a burn in another's skin as intensely as one's own? But he could no more watch another's pain than ignore his own, nor could he see another's joy without feeling their happiness in his own soul and being glad for it.

And now he sat, staring at the deaths of over a billion souls. Now he sat, unable to fully grasp it, yet unable to resist its enormity.

And now he sat, mere weeks after his conversation with Vickie Gray, knowing he could save them all.

So now I know. I can do nothing. I can pass the decision to the higher reaches of government. Or I can act.

He considered his options. He felt as if he stood under a spotlight, under the eyes of a billion dead, the eyes of the billions more left behind to suffer and to mourn, and knew he could not do nothing.

And if I pass this decision to others? What will happen then? They will not act. They will be too afraid, it is their nature. They will choose, and as they must take the science on faith, not knowledge, then fear of acting will set their choice. I can tell myself it is my duty to pass the decision to them. But that is just a coward's way of choosing to do nothing.

He could feel himself being drawn to an inexorable result, like a ship caught on the edges of a whirlpool it lacked the power to escape, and felt icy terror of what must come.

But if I save them, at what price? To change history is to wipe the present from existence.

He stared at the horror of it, feeling fear that it would swallow his very soul. *So to save the world as it was, I must wipe out the world as it is. But the billions suffered in pain and fear and grief, and their horror still reverberates today. And I can save them, and there will be no pain or fear or grief then, and no pain or fear or grief now. We today are the inheritors and beneficiaries of their agony, and can we hold our own existence as our excuse to let theirs end in such a way? And perhaps we will simply come to be in another form. A better form. But will it really be gone? How can it not have been, when it has been?*

He gazed into his own past. He remembered a scene when he was a young boy, crouched in a field, intensely studying a flower and the blue butterfly shimmering upon it. Being comforted in the folds of his mother's dress, the bruises and cuts from a fall throbbing. The shyness, fumbling and too rapidly overpowering ecstasy of the first time he had slept with a girl. That memory led to another, of the unexpected and strangely immaculate meeting of bodies with Vickie Gray on the night of his triumph.

More than a meeting of bodies, it had been a meeting of souls, and so his thoughts jumped to her soul, feeling her life beating in his arteries as he felt his own. She also had lived her youth, her joys and her pains. A lifetime of actions and feelings, sifted by time and memory into the unique consciousness she now possessed, the unrepeatable person that was Vickie Gray. Those joys included the one shared with him when their world lines so briefly intersected, and the longer term union with her husband, a braiding of two world lines scattering an infinity of threads to who knew where. Her husband too was the sum of a lifetime of thoughts and happiness and sorrow. And so on, forever, to their friends, their parents, their lovers, a whole network stretching throughout the world today, reaching back through the centuries and millennia past, and forward into the unknowable millennia ahead.

All those people of past centuries lived. But they no longer exist, not even in memories, except for a few fragments held in living minds and dead recordings. Yet they existed. Yet now they do not. Perhaps now they will never have. But how is that different to them now?

If I do this the people of the past are no more dead; if anything they are less dead, if that has any meaning. The people of the present will feel no pain, no sorrow, no terror and no loss. But all those billions then will be saved.

He looked at the images of spacetime manifolds summoned by equations: images and equations his great mind had itself conjured and understood. *And here I am, now, the heir of the past, a living mind, remembering the life that brought me here. And then it will never have been. And yet it is, and was. The sharpness of its existence cannot be denied, so how could it never be?*

His mind tried to chase the contradictions, but they led in circles, never to a resolution that made the slightest sense. *It is so, I know that. But how is it possible? To be yet never have been?*

In his mind's eye he looked at the images he had conjured, knowing the answer lay within, and came to a realization.

Smythed if I know.

10. Show and Tell

The incoming call announced itself as from Dr Ravan Harlington. Vickie Gray's eyes were tired and her head was fuzzy after a morning of hard thought, chasing an idea that would not allow itself to be fully apprehended; but now both eyes and mind cleared with anticipation.

"Good morning, Ravan," she said with a smile when she accepted the call. "This is an unexpected pleasure. What can I do for you?"

"Good morning, Vickie. I thought you would be interested to know I have completed those investigations I told you about. The results are remarkable, truly remarkable."

"Why, that is excellent news! Thank you for calling! What can you tell me?"

"I think you deserve to see it rather than just hear about it. I should like you to fly here. Tonight. Then I can show you in the morning. You don't want to miss it."

"Why…" she said, looking at the time, "It is a bit late but I guess I can do it. Is it that important?"

"I think it is very important, yes."

"I'll be there."

Good. Each in our own way we began this, didn't we? It seems fitting that we are both at its end.

~~~

By the time Vickie landed at her destination it was dark. She'd assumed that Dr Harlington had arranged for transport to her hotel, but was surprised to see the man himself standing there waiting for her.

"Why, Dr Harlington!" she cried. "Ravan, I mean! I didn't expect such personal service!"

He smiled, "It is my pleasure, Vickie. It was rather rude of me to insist on your presence at such short notice." *Too risky to delay, and I owe you this much.* "I owe you some compensation."

Under his smile she saw something else, some intensity or even pain, but that made no sense. She imagined it was just the hour, and the excitement of whatever he wished to show her in the morning.

He drove her to her hotel, where she had already been checked in, and escorted her to her room. She opened her door then turned to look at him in farewell, and she was again struck by the strange intensity that seemed to hold him rigid, like an electric current coursing through him. She remembered her thoughts on the immaculate singularity of their night together, that it could never be repeated.

Hang that, she thought savagely as she grasped his forearm, and with neither apology nor explanation pulled him into her room and slammed the door shut with her foot.

He had said nothing, with only a faint look of astonishment on his face as reaction, and she stared at him with a touch of defiance. *Tell me you don't want me, and go. Tell me I am a fool, and I have lost my chance at whatever revelation you had wished to honor me with, by throwing your honor into the gutter of my desire. Or laugh at me with that ironic smile of yours, to tell me I was one of your casual flings, unworthy of another when you can have many younger and more nubile than me.*

But he said none of those things, just remained standing, his look of astonishment vanishing into its previous intensity. But before, the intensity had been focused on some vision of his own. Now it was focused on her. She faced him fully and squared her shoulders, ready to endure his rebuke. *Or take me now, without words, with nothing but the act, of and for itself.*

As if he had heard her thoughts, he grasped her roughly by the shoulders, and she felt her defiance crumble under his strength. He pulled her to himself, asking no permission as she had not asked it of him, and kissed her. He pushed her away to arm's length and looked into her face.

Then he pushed her to her bed.

~~~

When Vickie woke, lying on her back, she could vaguely see the ceiling and its light fittings, in the grey morning light shining dimly through the blinds of her room. She turned her head and saw Ravan, his face in profile to her. His eyes were also open, but he was staring at the ceiling. Something about his eyes and the set of his mouth sent a shiver of fear along her spine.

"Ravan? What's the matter?" she whispered.

He turned to her, and for a moment it seemed he gazed at her as if he had forgotten who she was; as if the passion of last night belonged in somebody else's memory.

"Nothing," he whispered, but she quailed from the look in his eyes. "Nothing is more important than this, now," he added, and he reached out, ran his hands from her cheeks down her neck and down to her naked breasts. She groaned and threw her leg over his hip, drawing him to her. Then his words became true and nothing else mattered for a long while.

Afterwards they lay together, limbs still entangled, her breath soft and panting on his chest. *It is fitting that our last time is with each other,* he thought. *Will you forgive me when you know? Will you understand? Or will you curse my memory and damn the pleasure we have shared? Will you even know? I cannot tell you. I cannot ask forgiveness. I can only do what I must, as must we all.*

When he was able to speak, he touched her cheek. "We should go now. The cafeteria at the facility is open all hours. Let's get breakfast there. Then you can see what you need to see."

She stretched luxuriantly and smiled, sighing. Many replies came to her head, some witty, some ironic, but all that came out was, "OK."

He rose and dressed, and she followed; they could have showered, but for some reason neither wanted to wash away the residue of the other. They drove to the facility in silence. It was as if nothing more needed to be said, or should be said. What they had done, and where they were going, were enough.

They ate breakfast in the cafeteria. As she was sipping her second coffee, he stood. "You finish your coffee. I'll run along and set things up. Follow me in about five minutes. Here's a pass, it will let you into the Machine Room."

She smiled and watched him go.

~~~

When Vickie arrived at the Machine Room she was confused. It was only dimly lighted and she couldn't see Ravan anywhere. Then she looked down at the stage where the great forces gathered to create the wormholes, and was surprised to see him standing there.

He turned his head to stare back up at her, and called out, "Stay where you are. I'm nearly finished down here. When I'm done, keep your eyes on the screen there. That's what I want you to see."

She nodded, wondering. The Machine was on and she saw the telltale signs of a wormhole already created, though as yet nothing showed on the screen. She was surprised he was there so near its presence: surely the risk of leaking radiation was too high? He was wearing an apron or toolkit around his waist, and if she didn't know better she'd have though he was holding some kind of gun. On his head was a helmet that extended an armature beneath his mouth. There was a small black controller on a bench next to him and he looked at it as if uncertain.

Perhaps I am wrong. It may be history cannot be changed, and the tensions that repair the world on the small scale will repair anything. Perhaps I will be unable to achieve what I seek, or if I do the rules of causality will induce some other disaster with the same effect. In any case I have cast my own die. Whatever happens to the world, my own time ends here.

She saw him look up at her again and she wondered why he stared at her with such a strange intensity.

I leave you as my witness. If I fail then you will see my failure, and our world will be wiser for it. But if I succeed, will you even know it? What will you see? Your youth, our first night, last night: surely they happened. Yet they will never happen. You, me, all we have held dear, will be erased from eternity.

He reached for the controller and pressed a button, and the number 6 appeared on the display. A second later it became a 5. Ravan looked around for the last time at the space housing his greatest achievement, before his gaze returned to her as if in silent homage or farewell. "Goodbye, Vickie," he said as the counter reached zero.

The pinpoint became a sphere, eight feet in diameter: blacker than night, black as nothing, filling the space where Ravan had stood. She gasped in horror, wondering what unimaginable disaster was unfolding, wondering if that terrible blackness would expand to destroy the world.

Then it was gone and the stage stood empty.

She stared at the scene of the disaster, unable to believe it. She noticed that the tiny wormhole still seemed to be in existence. Then she looked at the display and gasped again. In it she could see the Russian Commander, the man who might have stopped the war: and there facing him was Ravan.

She swayed on her feet, then fell into one of the chairs facing the screen. *It is I. I who have done this. We always thought history was a vast manifold, continuing on its way no matter what rocks we might throw in its path. I did not know we could visit the past. But you knew. And it is I who showed you what to do there.*

Then she slumped back and watched the fate of her world unfold.

~~~

Vasili woke suddenly, a faint sheen of sweat on his brow testimony less to the heat than to the dream that had awakened him. But when he tried to grasp the dream it danced away from him like the shimmer of a mirage, and was gone.

He sat up on the narrow bunk in his cramped cabin, stretching the kinks out of his muscles as best he could. Then his eyes widened, as a sphere of blackness limned with an aurora-like sparkle appeared. Then his eyes widened even further, if that were possible, when the sphere vanished and in its place stood a man.

Vasili was unable to move. *I am still dreaming,* he thought. The man was dressed in some unfamiliar fashion and was holding an object pointed at his chest, as if it were some kind of gun. *But no gun I have ever seen. Wake up, Vasili!*

Then the apparition spoke, in accented but understandable Russian. What the accent was Vasili could not have guessed. There seemed to be an odd disconnect between the movements he could see on the man's face and the sounds that issued from the object covering the bottom half of his mouth.

"Do not fear, Commander, I have no wish to harm you. This," he said, waving the object he held, "is merely to prevent you from doing anything foolish. To remove any doubt you might cling to as to its nature..."

The man moved the gun slightly so it no longer pointed at Vasili, then there was a soft hum, upon which six metallic darts embedded themselves in rapid succession into the metal wall next to his head. Before he could react, the weapon was again aimed at his chest.

"As you can see, this is a gun, even if it doesn't look like any you are familiar with."

"Who are you? What do you want?"

The man moved forward, and Vasili automatically leaned backward. The man placed what looked like a block of dark glass on his desk and stepped back. With his other hand he took yet another object out of an apron he wore, but pointed this one at the block of glass. "Watch," he said, pressing a button.

Vasili gasped and jerked back. An image had appeared above the glass. More than an image: it was like reality; like looking at a three dimensional scene within the confines of his room.

"What magic is this?" he cried.

"Watch," ordered the man again, pressing another button on his device.

Vasili watched. He would have watched even if the man had not held his strange gun on him; even if the man had said nothing.

He saw, as if he were a bird soaring above a real scene, a marine flotilla sailing on the sparkling blue waters of the Caribbean. At its center was an aircraft carrier with the insignia of the USA. He saw the carrier, and most of its attendants, obliterated as a terrible flash and then an even more terrible mushroom cloud rose above the formerly peaceful sea.

He saw other missiles raining down on military bases, on cities. He saw scenes of rioting, of starvation, of death. He saw visions of skulls, miles of skulls in fields of bone. He saw the skeletons of dead cities on the shores of lakes of glass.

When it was over, he saw an unmoving image of the mushroom cloud rising over the Caribbean.

"What... what is this?" cried Vasili.

"It is the future of your world."

"Why are you showing me this?!"

The man pointed at the mushroom cloud. "It is you who caused it."

Vasili stared at him, thunderstruck, the feelings of his dream returning. "Who are you? Why are you here?"

"This is your future. It is my past. The past of my world. A billion dead. The destruction of your own country. Decades of suffering, beyond the power of any to know or bear."

"You say I caused this? *I?* Are you here to kill me then?"

For the first time the man appeared to smile, though it was not a happy smile. "That would be counterproductive."

"You are making no sense!"

"Then I shall explain. Today, in a little while, the Americans above will find you. They will drop explosives around your position, trying to force you to surface. Your Captain and Political Officer will believe you are under attack. They will want to launch your nuclear torpedo. You will agree."

He pointed to the mushroom cloud. "This will be the result. All the rest will follow. *All the rest.* Hundreds of millions will die. All told over a billion lives, now and in the decades to come."

The man stared at Vasili, and Vasili's soul quailed at the sight. "You are not at war. The Americans only want you to surface. If you fire your torpedo, you will start a nuclear war."

Vasili turned grey, and looked like he was about to throw up.

"You're lying! This is some kind of trick!"

The man smiled again. "You do not believe that, Commander. You do not believe that your American enemies have the ability to make weapons like this," he said, waving his gun, "Or machines that can show such movies and images," he added, pointing it at the three-dimensional tableau still floating in the air. "Most of all, you do not believe they can walk through a hole in spacetime into your room in a submarine hundreds of feet under the sea."

The man looked at him, daring him to object. "If you did, I think that when the Americans knock on your door, you would rush to the surface to surrender as fast as your submarine could get you there.

"So accept what I say. Accept that I am a man from the future you created, and I am telling you the truth. That I know it is true, because it is the history of my world. A world whose fate is now in your hands, even more so than it was before: for now you know the truth. Now, if you launch your weapon, it will be in full knowledge of what you are doing.

"I know this is a burden you did not ask for, Commander, but I pass it to you now. A thing from the future cannot long endure in its own past, only the things it does will. If you make the right decision I will no longer be, for I will have never existed. Even if you choose to ignore me, still I cannot remain in this existence much longer."

Vasili could only gape at him. "You're mad..." he whispered, but all the man did was gesture to his evidence. "Or I am mad..."

The man shook his head. "You are not mad, Vasili. Madness would be to launch a nuclear torpedo at the Americans."

Vasili continued to stare at him, unable to speak. He looked at the mushroom cloud still floating impossibly in the air of his cabin, and he knew what he would do.

Then the man was gone.

Vasili rushed to where he had been, but there was no sign he had ever existed. He spun to his desk, but the glass slab was also gone. The darts were no longer in the wall. *Surely I am mad! Or I was dreaming!*

But then he looked more closely at where the darts had been, and six deep narrow holes were drilled in the metal, where no holes had ever been before.

Vasili put his head in his hands.

"*Blya!*"

~~~

Far in the future, a woman watched this tableau, reading the automatic translations as they floated under the scene. She stared as she watched a new history unfold, too stunned to fully appreciate its meaning. But slowly, her mind grasped a glimpse of its full import.

So this is why you wanted me to be here. To share in the end of our world. To judge you? To forgive, or condemn? Or is it to condemn me? Or just to see?

She knew why he had done it; even understood it, though the visceral terror of an animal clinging to life gripped her.

But there was nothing to grip on to any more. No ledge or crack to cling to that could save her. Save anyone she knew.

Oh my god, what have you done?

It would have been the last thought she ever had, had she ever existed to have thoughts at all.

~~~

Vasili rose and left his room, his head continuing to spin. But as he walked he straightened his spine, forcing his usual military bearing back into his reluctant bones and tendons. *Perhaps you are mad, but you are still a man. And if you are not mad, you must not appear so, lest you lose more than your life.*

Then as he walked the first boom and rattle sounded, and he knew the enemy had found him, and he knew it was all true. *So now I go to meet my destiny, and hope I am worthy of it.*

When Vasili entered the room, the captain and political officer stood in greeting and respect, but said nothing. He looked slowly from face to face and knew their thoughts. Beneath his own trademark calm, icy currents swirled in the darkest reaches of his soul. He knew what they would say. He knew what he would say when they did.

But they had to say it.

"Report status," commanded Vasili.

"Still nothing from Command," replied the Captain, "and we are now under attack."

"No word from command after all these days," added the Political Officer, unnecessarily voicing their thoughts.

Vasili gave them each a hard stare.

"We are not under attack. Can you not tell that these are small charges, not intended to sink us, but merely intended to tell us we are discovered? The Americans have found us. They want us to surface, nothing more."

The Captain replied angrily. "And how can you read the Americans' minds? I do not think dropping explosives on us is an act of peace! If they want us to surface, it is merely to make us an easier target! I say launch!"

"I concur," added the political officer.

"Comrades, we need cool heads, not hot metal. I know what you think and why you think it. But do you really think that the Americans would do this if they suspected we had a nuclear torpedo with which to smite them? And if they did not suspect it, and we are indeed at war, that they would hesitate to destroy us once they found us? No. We are not at war. We are trying to run their blockade and we have been discovered. That is all."

The argument went for some time, the Captain and Political Officer expressing their conviction that their duty demanded action, unable to understand how Vasili could be so unmoved by their plight or their reasons. He looked like a man who was sure, though how he could be sure they could not tell.

"I cannot agree to an attack, but I understand your fears," he said at last. "I suggest this. Load the torpedo and prepare it for launch. Then surface. If I am right we will find there is no war. If you are right the sole purpose of the Americans is to expose us, the easier to destroy us without risk. They will have miscalculated. We will have time to launch. They will destroy us, but at the last we shall reach out to take them with us."

He looked at the two men. "If we launch now, we are dead anyway. This way, perhaps nobody will die."

At last, the men agreed. When their ship breasted the surface, they looked around at the enemy.

"What is that noise?" asked the Captain.

Vasili laughed, a laugh of vindication and release. "I believe they call it 'jazz', Valentin. I think the Americans wish to reassure us by having their band play us a song, which they would hardly do if we were in the middle of a war."

The submarine was sent on its way, its mission a failure, running back to Russia with its tail between its legs, humbled and ashamed. On the bridge, the Captain's face was red with shame and anger. "Failure! Failure! Now we must face the consequences."

But Vasili merely smiled, and in an unexpected act of informality clapped the man on the shoulder. "Be of good cheer, my friend. I think they will understand. Surely it is better to be sent on our way with a slap on our rump, than to be the men who destroyed the world."

Part B:
Pachmeny's Stars

And summer's lease hath all too short a date:
Sometime too hot the eye of heaven shines...
And every fair from fair sometime declines,
By chance, or nature's changing course, untrimm'd.

Shakespeare, Sonnet 18

---

11. SEEKING TO MAKE BETTER...

The world still swayed on the edge of the gulf, but now it did not fall. The fate Harlington had feared did not eventuate. Slowly, slowly, heads cooled, until at last the crisis was over.

The men of the carrier group went home to their families. The world continued on its way. Cities did not burn; radioactive clouds did not sweep across the land; the millions of dead lived on, not knowing. Beyond a few people in Russia, nobody knew how near disaster had come.

The American President was assassinated, victim of the same clash of ideologies, only this time manifested in a more personal madness. But on that scale people always died, and most of life went on. The decade that began in fear became a decade of love and flowers, though cynics may have thought it more lust and dirt. Many died in other wars, but these were regular wars; worse than many in the past, perhaps: but not ones to destroy the Earth.

The world did not know how close it came, and did not learn its lesson. The Russians learned a lesson, but it was how poorly armed they were compared to the Americans. All they wanted was to catch up. The doctrine of Mutually Assured Destruction would not work if the other side's destruction wasn't assured. And while it looked like madness, surely it was safe, because who would be so mad as to risk it? After all, had not the world teetered on the brink, and survived?

So the years went by, as the missiles and bombs became better and more numerous, each side too afraid of the other to dare do otherwise. Wise heads knew this was foolish and small steps were taken backwards, with hotline communications and treaties; but never enough to truly reduce the threat. It was never enough, because too many feared that it was only the threat that kept them all safe.

~~~

The man sat at his desk, watching the displays on the electronic panels arrayed before him. He sipped his coffee, bitter and black, its black bitterness alleviated only by the two spoons of somewhat gritty sugar dissolved in its depths.

Had he been asked to name the defining aspect of his personality, and had he cared to answer, he would have said 'phlegmatic'. Someone less inclined to be charitable may have said 'unimaginative'.

Neither trait had been obstacles in the path his career had taken to its current heights. As heights they were not spectacularly lofty, but he did not mind. He was as phlegmatic about his own career as he was about life in general. As long as he had some degree of respect and sufficient pay for an adequate lifestyle and a supply of vodka—for those occasions when he was allowed to drink it—he was content. Had he been more ambitious or imaginative, more fired by a desire for heights, perhaps he would have reached them, but they would have been on different peaks entirely.

For one prime requirement of this job was to be phlegmatic, bordering on the comatose. A man of more average humors would not have survived it. No man who felt its weight on his shoulders could bear its pressures for long, and worse, nobody watching him could tell when the resulting fissures would crack into an implosion of ruin. Only a man with a personality off which the pressures ran like water could stand under them. If ever he should feel that he needed to bear those pressures, by definition he could not bear them. Only someone who could look at the screens and dials with clarity and detachment, then go home to his family as cheerfully as any office worker, could do it. No Titan, no Atlas, could do it, no matter how strong or grimly determined he was to bear his load: only a man who stood calmly at watch, heedless of the rain and pain running off his skin.

Even less desirable was imagination. A calm evaluation of evidence was critical. Seeing more in the evidence than was there could be disastrous. Imagining the possible consequences of his decisions, even more so.

The man took another sip of coffee, less than a minute after the previous one. Such an acceleration of his usual rate of imbibing was the only outward sign of the added levels of stress in the last week. The man noticed it himself, and sat back to ponder the source of his alarm; his watchful eyes never leaving his displays.

Hundreds of people had died in the flaming wreckage of a passenger jet only three weeks before. Some man like him had made the call that had then rippled upward through the layers of responsibility, then rippled back down, ending in a finger that had pushed a button that had launched the missiles. The West, of course, protested: all those innocents lost, for no reason. The man smiled cynically. They would say that whether it was true or the jet had been crammed full of spies. He shrugged. A tragedy, yes. But nobody, least of all him, would ever know the truth of it: whether the ultimate cause was the West probing the Motherland's systems and resolve and being bloodied for it, or the same cause as so much other tragedy, human error. Perhaps some good would come of it. Perhaps those hundreds of lives were the price of the West learning that his country's systems and resolve were not to be challenged, whether the probe had been deliberate or not. Maybe in the long term the result would be greater peace and fewer deaths.

But in the short term, tensions were higher than normal. They had already been high due to the anti-Soviet chest-beating engaged in by the American President, and now they were worse. Other than his slightly elevated rate of coffee consumption, this did not affect his attitude or his job. It remained what it always was, whether it was a time of peace and rapprochement or under the clouds of threatening war. The enemy could attack in either, whether hoping to exploit a drop in alertness, or out of their own dark fears or ambitions.

In any case he would be ready. Then he would go home and live his life until the next day. As he had done in the last weeks of tension and the years before that.

Those thoughts rippled over the surface of his mind, then the disturbance vanished into his habit of smoothly calm watchfulness.

He would not have been human, however, nor capable of doing his job, if he was immune to all alarm. And so he sat up straight and frowned at a flashing alarm from the panel. This is what he had been trained for. He bent forward to examine the data.

His eyes widened. The early warning system was reporting the launch of a single intercontinental ballistic missile from the USA. Surely this was a false alarm? Would they really think one downed jet justified a pre-emptive attack? If they did, why launch only one? A lesson? One base or city for one jet? Then the system reported a second launch.

His brain went into overdrive. If one false alarm was possible, so were two. Or perhaps the loss of one jet was not enough for the West to launch *all-out* war; but if downing that jet was Mother Russia showing her resolve, the West would show its disapproval and its own resolve by hurting its enemy with a limited strike?

He knew he had less than a minute to decide, and drummed his fingers on the desk. Overall, he felt that it was probably a false alarm, some glitch in the satellites or systems. If he was right, no harm done. If he was wrong, two missiles were bad but there would be plenty of retaliatory strike capability remaining, and the USA would learn an even more painful lesson.

But then the system reported more launches, perhaps as many as five additional missiles beginning their short trajectories into space before plunging down his throat. The launches were still few, but escalating, and he had already delayed. Perhaps that was the plan: uncertainty, leading to delay, so by the time a response to the escalating attack was mounted, their response would already be blunted. His duty was clear. He would have to report his conclusions and leave it to the politicians to decide on an appropriately measured response. He punched in his codes and sent his message: up to seven nuclear missiles had been launched toward the USSR.

The generals who received this message knew that so few missiles would not cripple them, and wondered what it meant. They feared that it meant the start: a probe, followed by more. They knew the doctrine of mutually assured destruction; the only thing worse, in their view, was one-sided destruction. They decided to show the West a lesson of their own. They would not respond with all-out war, but with their own measured response.

On the tail of a strongly-worded diplomatic response to the USA, NATO and the United Nations, the Soviet Union launched their own missiles: ten to strategic targets in NATO, another ten toward the USA.

Both sides had their own phlegmatic, unimaginative officers analyzing the output of similar systems. Both were shocked by something that could not be a false alarm but made no sense. But nor had the downing of a civilian airliner made any sense.

The one thought echoed in many heads.

May God forgive us.

Then the West launched its own attacks.

The seven launches had not been real. These were, and soon after nuclear fireballs began to blossom over bases and cities in the West, an even fiercer hail fell on the Soviet Union.

The Soviet leadership and command structure fell into disarray. But they had launched their doomsday weapon. Not a super bomb, but a missile designed as a fallback if the leadership was put out of commission.

After all, how else could Mutually Assured Destruction be assured?

The doomsday weapon was designed for one task and, not receiving any coded messages to desist, it duly sent out its own commands. The entire remaining Soviet nuclear arsenal was launched at the West.

12. The Concord

The world would have survived a nuclear war at the time of the Cuban Missile Crisis two decades earlier. There were fewer, less sophisticated missiles then, with much less ability to bombard one continent from another within mere minutes. Mankind would have been bloodied badly, but recovery would have taken mere decades, or at worst centuries.

This time it was not so fortunate. Too many cities were destroyed, too much infrastructure lost, too much radiation released, too much death unleashed. Some tried to hold on to the treasures of the past: in regions held grimly by the remnants of armies or civil authorities, in isolated communities hoping the weather the storm devouring the world, or in hidden retreats. Most fell before the year was out.

Again, dust and soot blocked the sun, cooling the earth: only worse this time. Again, armed forces once sworn to serve and protect turned to rule and pillage, competing with other armed groups driven by desperation: only worse.

Still the world held on by its grim fingernails, and with luck it might have recovered.

It was not lucky.

In eons past the Earth had been warm, ruled by vast forests inhabited by giant amphibians and insects. Over millions of years both the continents and the climate shifted. By the time the ancestors of humanity were looking at the world with the first glimmers of understanding, the world had entered a period of instability.

For untold millennia, the world danced uncertainly between

warmth and ice. For long stretches it enjoyed relatively warm periods in which the great ice sheets were banished to the poles, and most of the globe was bathed in sunlight, warmth and life. These alternated with other long stretches of bitter cold, where sheets of ice miles thick marched toward the equator, gripping most of the world in an embrace of deathly cold. And for hundreds of thousands of years as the ice came and went, the ancestors of humanity continued to eke out their existence with tools of wood, bone and stone.

When the last of the great ice ages ended the survivors of the human race were ready, having at last achieved a level of sentience and skill, perhaps a gift from the ice itself, that primed them to take over the entire world. And take it over they did. The entire history of the race, from agriculture to metals to science to space to the war that destroyed them, took place in the mere eleven millennia of warmth since the final retreat of the ice sheets.

Yet the Earth remained uncertain. The climate was subject to many factors: the Earth's orbit and inclination and the activity of the Sun. Life also had its say. Many thought that the Earth was peculiarly lucky, orbiting in a narrow 'Goldilocks Zone' where the Sun was not too close to bake it and not so far it would freeze. Yet in the absence of certain heat-absorbing gases such as carbon dioxide, the Earth would have been a snowball; too much and it would have become an oven. Life had removed much of these gases from the atmosphere into its own bodies and remains, but also released some. Colder and warmer periods still came and went.

People had only just begun to understand what caused the great ice ages. They had learned that small changes in the amount of the Sun's heat reaching Earth could tip it from one state to another; and that once started the ice sheets would not easily surrender their rule. Their blinding white reflected sunlight too well, banishing the sun's warming rays back into space.

And the world had entered a cooling trend. Scientists had not been sure whether the trend was real: it is hard to see a small signal in the presence of larger fluctuations that are poorly understood. But underneath it all, it was as if the Earth wanted to cool. Yet it struggled in its desire, for the gases released by humans as they dug up then burned enormous quantities of fuels, fuels that had held the Earth's carbon locked up for eons, had spread like a thickening gossamer blanket over the globe.

Had mankind not fallen, it would have been only a few years before they started worrying that their own activities would cause the opposite problem. They would begin to fear that the carbon dioxide produced by their mighty industries would add to the warming blanket of the atmosphere until the Earth became too hot for them: that in escaping the ice of a natural progression, the human race must suffer in a heat of their own creation. Instead of ice they would die by fire.

But their mighty industries were now ashes. And worse, literal ashes: the dust thrown up by the explosions and burning of the cities dimmed the sun. The Earth had already been overdue for its next ice age, but perhaps mankind's warming effects would have prevented it. And since its birth the Sun had been growing slowly hotter: maybe that would have made the difference even without humanity's burning of fossil fuels. But it had been on a knife-edge. Mankind hadn't known it and even if they had, they were now powerless to stop it.

And so the Earth began to cool.

Winter was a little longer. Snow and ice covered a little more area, then stayed, their bright white reflecting the Sun's energy away into the darkness of space. The world cooled a little more. As the air became drier and the vast pumping of carbon dioxide and other gases had all but ceased, a little more heat could escape through Earth's thinning blanket. Slowly, but at an accelerating rate, the summers got cooler, the winters got colder, and the grip of the ice expanded.

By the time the immediate effects of the war were over it was too late. Crops failed. People starved. The survivors faced famine on top of the rest. And famine led to war, as if there had not already been enough war. Still people struggled: to hold on to whatever remnants of their glory they could; to fight off those who would destroy them; just to live.

And meanwhile the ice continued to grow, seeking to restore its dominion over vast reaches of the planet, like it had millennia ago before the first birth of civilization.

Those parts of the Earth not covered by ice were colder and less productive. It was the final straw. Populations crashed. As had happened so many times before in humanity's distant past, bands of warriors and invaders swept the lands, driven away from their own land by seasons too poor to support them, or towards the mythical lure of fabulous wealth elsewhere.

What remained of civilization finally reached its fatal tipping point.

For years it had held on in shrinking beacons of hope, slowly sliding toward the abyss. Now the abyss claimed it, and what was left of the human race fell into barbarism; from barbarism, into chaos; and from chaos, into a world lit only by fire.

For millennia the world was held in the grip of the ice, and mankind lived much as it had in the previous ice ages: as small groups living off the land as best they could. Then slowly it began to warm again. Life became easier; populations grew; slowly people were able to reinvent agriculture, and small towns grew, linked by networks of trade and kin.

Much had been lost of the ways of the Ancients. In many places nothing was left except mysterious rubble; in places, lakes of glass where few dared to venture, for they were cursed. In other places the remains of their cities still stood, tall dark towers, crumbling with age, but still reaching pathetically toward the stars their owners had once dared to attempt. The Ancients had left few clues; but there were some, and slowly their descendants began to learn.

On the continent once known as North America such knowledge was highly prized, and slowly the towns organized themselves around Farmers and Hunters as the majority, Artisans who were fewer but possessed special and prized skills, Defenders as elite fighters, and over all of them the Sages. The Sages were the wisest of men and women: those with the vision to see and understand.

If one were to compare the developing land with forgotten times past, what it was most like were the city states of ancient Greece. However these people had a different history, that brought with it an almost racial memory of the perils of war. They had a different mix of technology. Most of all there were fewer physical barriers to separate peoples, and consequently stronger ties of trade and kin. So the scattered city states were more cohesive than those of past times and stronger for it. They grew naturally into a confederacy, and while remaining fiercely loyal to their own cities they were also loyal to the whole, which became known as the Concord.

Civilization has always had to contend with barbarians, and this one was no exception. Sometimes the barbarians broke upon the shores of the Concord and swept away what they could, leaving death and destruction, but not so much that it caused more than local pain, soon smoothed back like the sands. Other times the invaders were stronger, and the Defenders from nearby regions joined together and struck back, driving them away and more often than not pursuing them to their deaths. By such means the Concord, rarely interested in its own wars of conquest, widened its range, members and power.

Sometimes, it faced greater dangers.

13. PRAXIMAR THE MIGHTY

Praximar the Mighty sat in his tent, a luxurious bearskin at his feet and two of his favorite concubines by his side. They may have been his favorites but they, and the rest of the luxuries he owned, were a mere surface pleasure, without power to distract the thoughts in his great mind.

He had not named himself the Mighty. That title had been bestowed upon him by the fierce band of men under his command; a band that had become a horde.

For years, times had been good in the North. Perhaps too good, for now the weather had become colder again for season after season, and the expanded population found itself struggling for food. This was not unusual in the North. Usually the hungry hordes turned on each other, seeking to acquire land and food from their neighbors, until a new balance was reached. Often, those further south would also turn their avaricious eyes on the rich lands of the Concord. Though the risks were great, the wealth that might be found there was a temptation resisted less often than it should have been, something that many a powerful chief had lived to regret or more often died regretting.

This time was no exception. What was exceptional was Praximar. The third son of a minor chief, he had always known that his fortune must lie within himself. Such men had little trouble gathering bands around them, for there were numerous other second and third sons with few prospects among their own families, and many simply driven away from their ancestral lands by lost battles. And there were plenty of aspiring leaders like Praximar happy to accept their fealty.

There have been many men who have sought war; not so many generals who have excelled at it. Fewer still could aspire to the status of an Alexander or a Caesar, military geniuses whose exploits had survived millennia until the world had lost its memory. Praximar had never heard of these men, but he was their equal.

His strategies and tactics were innovative and savage. First he crushed and absorbed competing bands in his home territory. Feeling secure in his power, he sent an emissary to his father the chief, suggesting that Praximar had proved his worth and earned his own title to the chiefdom. His father was impressed, but not that impressed, and sent his own army to assert his authority over his disrespectful and rebellious third son.

Praximar became chief shortly thereafter.

His ambition did not end there, nor did his genius falter, and he rapidly extended his dominion. Then he turned his eyes to the south, considering.

Because the world had become colder the Concord knew there would be trouble from the North, so they were worried about attacks, and destruction, and death. But they were not worried about the survival of the Concord itself. Barbarians had attacked many times in the past and been repulsed. No doubt they would do so again. As always the Concord would be ready. The Defenders polished their weapons and their alliances, and began to recruit young men who imagined they were eager for the dangers of battle.

Praximar was bold but he was not foolish. He knew the Concord was a dangerous enemy, with deep reserves and unknown strengths. He would attack, and measure the enemy like a hunter encountering a new and dangerous form of prey. He would stab and they would bite back. If at any point they proved too strong he would withdraw. If not, perhaps one day he would rule them all.

He attacked in the east, where the forests were denser and the Concord less closely knit. When Defenders came he drew them into a trap and routed them. He gave the Concord no time to gather a response, but began to sweep through the country, taking city after city.

The barbarian attackers were usually concerned only with plunder, and would take what they could and more often than not destroy what was left. They approached their raids as bandits, keen to steal then carry their gains back to their safer homelands. Praximar had bolder plans.

The Sages were in many ways a mystery to him, with alien thoughts and motives. But still they were men, and it was not long before Praximar's method for dealing with them became established.

Some Sages were brave and unbending. They would never join cause with a murdering barbarian. These would be made to watch the spectacle of their daughters being raped by his ugliest soldiers and their sons being put to the sword, before their own heads ended up displayed on spikes outside Praximar's tent.

If a Sage were more amenable, his daughters would join Praximar's harem. If that were not the fate their fathers had dreamt for them, at least their lives would be ones of relative peace and comfort, and the only man who would impose himself upon them was Praximar and the occasional honored ally. His sons would join Praximar's horde as servants, perhaps one day to rise to high positions. The Sage would remain in his city as Praximar's vassal, his loyalty guaranteed by his hostage children.

Praximar made sure that these alternative fates were well known to all the cities in his path.

And now Praximar sat in his tent, pondering the next day. Until now the cities he had conquered or looted had been relatively small and isolated. Now he was entering richer lands, and finally a large force of Defenders had managed to collect itself and barred his way. He had received the reports of his scouts and spies, discussed the matters with his generals, and now sat alone with his thoughts and his concubines, seeing the lay of the land and the enemy in his mind's eye, weighing and calculating.

Finally he had his strategy. He nodded to himself. It was good. As usual with a foe of equal or greater strength, it was based on deception and meeting strength with deflection, and weakness with a deadly thrust.

He snapped his fingers, and a servant hurried in bearing wine and fruit. He began to eat and drink, as his concubines began to work their arts upon his willing flesh, and smiled.

~~~

The battle was going well.

One wing of Defenders was withdrawing in good order, but they would soon find it was either rout or death. Another wing was advancing against desperately crumbling opposition, but would soon find themselves doomed. Praximar was heading down the center toward where the cusp of the battle would lie. Then his ever alert eyes noticed a movement high in a nearby tree and his head spun to examine it.

Hidden among the tree's leaves, a Concord archer lay in wait. He was one of several arrayed around the field of battle, hoping for the chance this man now saw: the vicious barbarian general Praximar, striding arrogantly into range of his crossbow.

It was an improved crossbow designed and constructed by a Sage from far to the south. While somewhat slower to arm, it delivered its finely crafted metal quarrels with unparalleled force and accuracy. It was a new invention, difficult to make, and few could be armed with it yet; but the emergency of actual defeats at the hands of this barbarian had seen the ones they had rushed to the front lines. The Concord had risked its best marksmen with a weapon it hoped would put an end to the threat cleanly, and suddenly here was this man's chance. He moved the leaves aside to give himself the best aim. The damnable killer must have had the eyes of a cat, for he instantly turned and looked straight at him. But he was too late: the man fired.

Praximar wore armor. He was a man of bold courage, but not stupid courage, and he knew the vagaries of war. But his armor could not withstand the force it was struck with this time, and he looked down stupidly at the deadly metal shaft protruding from his chest. Then he fell over into the dust.

The archer's quarrel had not penetrated his heart. But it had penetrated his lungs and nicked an artery. Within minutes, Praximar the Mighty lay dead, his blood soaking into the soil of the land he had sought to conquer.

Within an hour his horde were in retreat, demoralized by the loss of their mightiest general, facing an army energized by the same event.

The Concord was never threatened so closely again. Wars still sometimes happened, as had been humanity's curse through the ages. But times were improving, knowledge was growing, and civilization continued the slow process of clawing back its place out of the wilderness, taming both the forests and the barbarians.

As it grew fat in peace and prosperity, as had happened in far forgotten ages there was exploration, development, conquest and discovery. Great centers of learning sprung up around the seats of the most revered of the Sages, as humanity began its halting steps back onto the path to science and technology. Then finally it began to follow that road toward the achievements of the Ancients themselves.

14. Variables

According to legend Achilles, the mighty hero of the Trojan War, had been offered a choice. He could choose a life of quiet, the life desired by most men, and reach an obscure, forgotten but contented old age. Or he could choose a life of glory, outshining his fellows but never returning home.

A star is granted a similar choice, though in its case the choice is given to it: by the size of the giant molecular cloud from which it forms, and by the complex dynamics of that stellar nursery as the star and its siblings begin their long journeys from dust to glory.

If by the time the cloud has dispersed they have gathered too little of the cloud to themselves they may not ignite at all, and be condemned to wander the eternal dark as dim rubies, with nothing but the dull heat of their contraction to mark their passing.

Gather some more gas, and when they condense to sufficient density the nuclear fires of fusion will light, and they will shine like beacons in the cold night that stretches for unimaginable distances around them. With not too much mass they will be red dwarves, glowing like embers, far dimmer than the Sun that warms planet Earth but still beacons in the sky. They burn slowly, so despite their low mass they are the Methuselahs of the universe, continuing their slow and steady burn for hundreds of billions of years, perhaps even to the end of the Universe itself.

More mass still and they will shine with a blinding glare, warm enough to nurture planets far from their boundary, long-lived enough for life to appear and thrive in their heat and light. Such was the Sun around which planet Earth revolves. Eventually these stars too will die, expanding to become red giants that devour their planetary children. By then, 10 billion years or so after their birth, perhaps any life they nurtured will have found a way to escape its fatal nursery.

But start with eight, ten or more solar masses, and the star will blaze in a glory as bright as it is short. After perhaps only a few million years, having burnt all its fuel it will collapse and explode in an outpouring of energy that can outshine its entire galaxy. Such a star can never live long enough for life to arise under its glaring brilliance; but the ferocity of its death could destroy life around other stars, even as far away as fifty light years. Ironically, the ashes of its death will seed space with the metals that later life might depend upon.

Fortunately, no star that bright exists close enough to Earth to be a danger. The nearest would be a sight for people to be amazed by and astronomers to study, with a short-lived frenzy matching that of the star's final song, comfortable in the assurance that no harm would come to them, only knowledge.

But there are other ways for a star to die. Small and obscure, white dwarf stars abound. Some have companions. Some of those companions are close enough for the white dwarf to feast on matter drawn off from them, siphoned through a straw of gravity onto the dwarf's surface. Enough of that stellar feeding and the mass of the white dwarf can exceed a critical limit, beyond which runaway nuclear fusion will ignite. The star, that could otherwise expect a long life of slow decay, will briefly match its larger cousins in the fury of its detonation.

Even rarer might be two white dwarfs, engaged in a dance that could last an eternity, or perhaps end in a merger of death.

There are no such stars known near Earth.

But stars move. And thirty millennia is a long time.

~~~

Pachmeny was bored. She knew a Student was not the equal of her Sage, but why did that mean she had to do rote work that a trained monkey could do? Yes, it was the way of the world and every Sage had once been a Student too. In Pachmeny's view that did not excuse it. Surely if her Sage had suffered through the same process he should have been less, not more, likely to inflict it in his turn.

How did we ever get out of the caves—twice, she grumbled in the privacy of her mind, before sighing and turning back to her work.

Her Sage, Shemsak the Exact, studied the stars. For all her grumbling, Pachmeny knew she was lucky to be his student, and that if a trained monkey could do her work it would have to be an exceptional one. Shemsak had made his name, and achieved his own Temple in the sprawling grounds of the great center of learning that hosted it, by conceiving, designing and building a way to electronically image starfields at unprecedented sensitivity and resolution, an advance that had spawned many lines of investigations into the cosmos. But the inconstant air above them shimmered and shivered, distorting the light from the stars, even if the telescope were on a remote peak far above the fog and dust of the Earth. The Sages wanted more, and bent their noble heads to the task.

Pachmeny's age had not had a space race. There had been nothing to press resources into such a quixotic quest as sending men into the cold hard vacuum of space; nor even the more prosaic quest of sending machines there. People had imaginations and brilliance, but these were pressed to other concerns. Nor had this age had a mad dictator bent on conquest at the right technological time, whose lusts would help push rockets from toys to machines powerful enough to pique the interest of those with more peaceful concerns.

In another age men might have put a telescope into space, far above the dance of the air, where the cold pinpoints of starlight could fall unwavering onto one of Shemsak's devices. Men in this age thought of it too, but the task was too hard and the expense too high for too uncertain a return. So they found other ways.

In other areas their technology was advanced. They knew why the starlight juddered and that if they could measure it, they could distort a mirror to correct it; they had the technology to achieve both. And so on a high mountain they built a giant telescope, able to measure the distortions in the atmosphere above and ripple its mirror to send the errant light beams back on the right course, into the most advanced Shemsak Detector ever built.

As the great machine came online many astronomers hardened their elbows and jockeyed for access to its data; some succeeded. But none could begrudge Shemsak being granted the greatest share of the bounty that had sprung from his great mind.

He sought students to come under his wing, to extract what treasures they could from the vast storehouse of raw knowledge now under his command. Pachmeny was brilliant, but like a star in a galaxy of other stars, who could measure her worth? Others appeared to shine brighter, and perhaps they were.

Or perhaps they had merely flown higher by being launched from a greater peak. Pachmeny's family were not poor but nor were they notably wealthy, mere ordinary merchants in one of the lesser clans. So Pachmeny had been educated, but not in one of the greater schools; nor had she been taught by the greater tutors, whose brightest students were the most eagerly sought.

But still she had done well enough to be seen, so now she found herself in her little domain, on her little project, delighted beneath her grumbling. She did not really compare herself to others, except perhaps in her darker moments when she wondered what justice there was in the Universe. Then she would remember that there was none; that if she sought justice, it would have to come from people. She would have to earn it. Even then, the justice might not come, but at least the fault would be theirs for failing to see, not hers for failing to try or do.

One of Shemsak's diverse interests was variable stars. Pachmeny's project was to refine the analytical engine which pored over the images with a speed and precision no mere mortal human could match. But nor could it match the judgement of those mortals. There were many sources of variation between the images: asteroids, meteors and comets crossing the heavens at speeds from a crawl to a flash; clouds or even flying things dimming images; eclipses by planets or moons; and the optical correction that made the whole thing possible could not be perfect, as distortions of the air were not uniform. Pachmeny's task was to divine signatures of the different distortions so that they could be excluded from the analysis, or perhaps shunted to other departments whose interests they might pique. Once perfected, if indeed that were possible, the machine could then work its tireless magic hour after hour, day after day, offering up to its masters only those gems worthy of the attention of their august minds.

Human flesh was not so tireless, and Pachmeny stretched, yawned and rubbed her eyes. A grumble from her middle told her that she was hungry as well as tired, and she was tempted to ignore the flashing light indicating an analytical anomaly. *Just one more, Pachmeny. Then dinner, a show and party all night.*

The Esteemed Shemsak's fame had bought him five-image series from many parts of the sky, on the theory that five would simultaneously help them weed out spurious differences while giving better data on true variations. So now Pachmeny called up the five different views of the tiny area the analytical engine had flagged, running them in a loop to help her eyes spot and evaluate the pattern.

Curious, very curious, she thought. There were two objects, each a bright point of white, very close to each other and engaged in some kind of slow cosmic dance. The tags noted that these particular stars had never been catalogued. That was not surprising: they were so dim that until this technology had been developed it was unlikely anyone would have noticed them, especially when their backdrop was an arm of the galaxy teeming with anonymous pinpoints of light, many far brighter to the eye than these.

I dub thee Pachmeny's Stars, she thought, amused at the notion that anybody outside the rarefied atmosphere of astrophysics would ever hear her name, let alone the name of her stars. Then she frowned. There was something odd about the pair, something she couldn't quite put her finger one, and she leant back to think about it.

Her specialty was not stellar dynamics, but she was sure there was something wrong with what she was seeing. Her eyes widened at the thought of what it was and what the answer might be; but she could not be certain. She had to take this to Shemsak, but she would prefer to give him a story she could be more certain of.

She wasn't an expert in dynamics but she knew someone who was, and the grumbling in her stomach changed to a tingling somewhat further down when she thought of him. He was another student, a few years older than her, several miles above her in reputation. And while his habits were not rigid, he was not one of those obsessed people who would work without eating: to the contrary, he knew that his ability to think fell rapidly when he was hungry. So at this time of night he was usually to be found in the precinct cafeteria.

Two rats with one rock, she thought happily, rising from her chair.

15. THE ABBEY OF THE CAVES

Not much had survived of the Ancients and their knowledge. That they had lived was certain from the ruins that dotted the Earth. That their knowledge and power exceeded that of the present age was clear from the nature of those ruins and the mysterious objects found therein. That their wisdom had failed to match that knowledge and power was evident in the fact of the ruins.

Nobody knew exactly what had happened to them. Most believed they had destroyed themselves. Certainly the old myths said so, speaking of fire and ruin rained down from the heavens by gods angered beyond reason. Some of the myths assigned the blame to the Trickster, the evil god who led men to their doom by appealing to their hubris and playing on their fears.

For millennia men had avoided the most blasted of their ruins, especially the Glassy Plains. There were many legends of men seeking forbidden knowledge, or even more forbidden power, who had been brave or foolish enough to explore there; who had been cursed by the spirits of the dead, so their hair fell out, their eyes bled, and they died.

It was not until mere decades ago that the Sages had discovered that the legends were true, and why: the strange elements that radiated a power as deadly as it was invisible. From that clue, they had discovered that these elements were not entirely the creation of the ancients: that some natural minerals possessed the same power, albeit far diluted; that the elements responsible could be purified.

As in every age since the harnessing of fire and the taming of oxen, men had hungered for the powers from nature that could amplify their own far weaker ones. So it was not long before they learned how to harness this power too. Nor was it long before they knew what else could be done with it: that as fire could cook a meal or burn a city, so the nuclear fires could power a city or destroy it.

But they knew what had happened to the Ancients. They knew that if even the Ancients could be ensnared and destroyed by the Trickster, then the people of this age were no safer. Nuclear weapons would never be developed in this time.

The knowledge of the ancients had been long lost. Except for some scraps, anything recorded on paper had decayed to nothing over the millennia of neglect. If they had stored their knowledge on other materials that too was long gone. Perhaps some of the mysterious boxes and circles had once held it; but if so, no one knew how they might be read.

Since before the Age of Sagacity there had been one exception. A cult dwelling in the deep caves of a mountain had for untold millennia kept preserved, by painstaking copying from generation to generation, fragments of the works of two great kings, or perhaps prophets, Newton and Einstein. The accuracy of their copying was preserved and attested by what the priests claimed were the original pages, now faded almost to illegibility, yet good enough to confirm the accuracy of the copies. The claim was supported by the fact that the pages were preserved between sheets of glass so smooth and pure that surely they must have come from the Ancients themselves.

But nobody knew what their words meant, let alone the mysterious symbols and squiggles that accompanied them.

~~~

Timmony was feeling cheerful. He had finished school, doing well enough to be accepted by one of the Sages as his student: not one of the greatest Sages, to be sure, but an eminent one nonetheless. Timmony was from a wealthy family; not one of the greater clans but great enough; his family not one of the wealthiest, but wealthy enough that Timmony could look forward to a life free of worry over mere matters of the flesh.

He, or at least his family, could also afford to pay for long travels. It was not unknown for the wealthy to substitute money for ability; however Timmony had not bought his studentship, but earned it. He was a bright, ambitious young man, interested in physics, the science of how the world worked. But unlike some of his fellows, who had a focus on their work such that they barely noticed the rest of the world, Timmony was interested in many things: not only science but history, the arts, and even religion. And he loved a mystery.

He had read of the Abbey of the Caves and their holy Relics. Few outside the Abbey had ever seen them, and none of the visitors thus blessed had been allowed more than a brief glance at these treasures, let alone the right or time to copy their contents.

One, a reporter for a cultural magazine, had asked the Abbot why, if the Relics were so important, the Abbey did not want to share them with the world. The Abbot had merely smiled and replied cryptically, "The Abbey must preserve the Relics until the world deserves them."

"Then what must the world do, to deserve them?" the reporter had asked.

"It is written that when one comes who will understand one, then must he be given the other."

"Do you know what they mean?"

"Only that they hold the secrets of the Universe."

Ever since Timmony had read the story, he had been intrigued by the mystery behind the Relics and their legendary link to the Ancients. So now, near the end of the year of travel he had granted himself between the hard work of school and earning his place with a Sage, and the years of even harder work under that Sage which he knew were to come, he found himself facing the hard, metal-clad wooden outer door of the Abbey.

The Abbey did not forbid visitors, but nor did it encourage them. No powered vehicles were allowed, even if they could have navigated the narrow, winding path climbing up the mountain from the city on the coast, now so far below. Timmony knew that the arduous ascent was one test of any who wished to enter, and knew there were more to come. He raised the heavy bronze ring on the door and knocked.

When the ringing of the bronze had stopped and its echoes long faded, he did it again. And again. Finally a small hatch in the door was slid sideways and an aged face peered out.

"Yes, my son?" it asked.

"I wish entry, Father."

"There is little here to interest a young man, my son. Old rooms filled with old men, or young men old in mind. Go back to the town. There you will find drink, and food, and women to please you."

"Thank you, Father. But I have a lifetime to do that. What I seek lies within."

"What do you seek here?"

"I study the secrets of the Universe."

The hatch slid shut, and Timmony feared he had failed some test and his journey was wasted. But some long seconds later, the door creaked open and the old man beckoned him in.

"Thank you, Father," he said, as the man closed and sealed the door behind him. He looked around at the courtyard he found himself in. Besides the wall he had come through, it was surrounded by three other walls, each with a number of heavy doors, all closed. There were windows but nothing was visible through the heavy drapes masking them, except the flickering of a light or candle behind one not fully drawn. The courtyard was deserted and looked surprisingly untidy, with small drifts of leaves and twigs scattered over it, and in one spot an even larger branch had fallen.

The man noticed his gaze but made no comment, except to say, "Someone will come to see you." Then he went through the nearest of the doors, Timmony heard the distinct snick of a lock, and he was left alone.

He stood there for five minutes, waiting, but still nobody came. He noticed a broom leaning against a wall, and smiled, *As if they wish it to be clean, but cannot find the...*

He picked up the broom and began to sweep.

Half an hour later the courtyard was neatly swept, the debris gathered in buckets, and Timmony leant on his broom, his brow now beaded with sweat.

A door opened and a man dressed in black robes with the golden circlet of an Abbot on his head came out, looking around in approval.

"You are a man of the mind, yet not afraid of servant's work."

"Here, perhaps I am but a servant."

"But that is not why you came. What secrets of the Universe do you expect to find here?"

"I am a student of the Universe, soon to be a student of a great Sage. I have heard about your holy Relics, that they contain the wisdom of the Ancients, but none can understand them. I crave your indulgence to allow me to see them. To see the words of the Ancients with my own eyes."

"Do you think you can understand them?"

"No."

"Then why do you wish to see them?"

"I love all knowledge, and they are a Truth beyond measure even if I can merely see it, not understand it. But who knows what the gods may grant the humblest of men?"

"Then come, my son."

The man led him down corridors and stairwells, deep into the earth. Finally he stood before one of the relics, the one with the strange characters 'NEWTON' inscribed upon them. He gazed in wonder at the strange curves and symbols it held.

Then something tugged at his mind. *Impossible! How can this look so familiar? I have never laid eyes on such wonders before.*

The symbols were different, their patterns strange. But there was something about their form and arrangement that was eerily familiar. Then he gasped in wonder.

What had gripped his young mind and sent him on his course into the world of physics was when he first read about the discovery, made by a great Sage many years ago, that the force which pulled rain from the sky and held his own feet to the ground was the same force which caused the moon to circle the Earth and the Earth to circle the Sun. The theory of gravity had transformed men's understanding of the world, and was one of the things that had started the Age of Sagacity. It had transformed young Timmony's mind.

And now he saw its equations, in another form written by a hand long dead, but those same equations nonetheless, in the Relic before him.

He swayed on his feet, and the Abbot rushed to hold him, lest he fall upon the sacred Relic itself.

"My son! My son! Are you ill? Some feel the pressing of the walls around them, is that what ails you? Come, we will depart!"

"No…! No…! It is… these are… this is…"

He stopped, staring wildly, at the Relic, at the Abbot, at his inner vision.

"My son?"

Timmony breathed heavily, forcing calm upon his nerves. He turned to face the Abbot. "Father… I think I know what this is!"

The Abbot just stared at him.

"This, or part of it, is the Law of Gravity. The attraction between all matter. The science of the Ancients!"

The Abbot stared at him for long seconds. "Then come with me, and see what you can see."

He led Timmony into the next room, to a similar relic bearing the inscription 'EINSTEIN'. Timmony stared at it. He could tell it was like NEWTON, written in the language of mathematics. But it was a far more complicated mathematics, one that struck no bell of familiarity in his mind, one whose meaning he could not guess at.

"I'm sorry, Father. I can tell it is similar to the other, some kind of mathematics of science: but I can neither recognize it, nor divine its meaning."

The Abbot nodded slowly, as if Timmony was merely confirming the long known. "That is all right, my son. Come, stay with us a while. Rest, and eat. Perhaps one of our Sisters will find you favorable for this night; indeed, once this tale is told, I expect you might have to choose among the applicants."

~~~

Timmony spent a month at the Abbey, the rest of his holiday forgotten. His days he spent in discussions with the Abbot and the Brothers and Sisters of the Abbey; his nights he spent continuing those discussions, while enjoying all the hospitality the Abbot's cooks, vintners and Sisters were pleased to offer him.

He learned much about the Relics; thought he recognized more of the knowledge recorded in NEWTON. But the works of EINSTEIN remained opaque.

Finally the Abbot called him into his office. "You would make a fine Brother, Son Timmony. But I can see you are of the world not of the Abbey. And you will do more for us by returning to the world than remaining here, for one day you will become a great Sage. So now it is time for you to go. These are our gifts to you."

Timmony looked at the bound sheaves of paper the Abbot handed to him, and then into the Abbot's eyes in wonder. "This is… everything!" he cried.

For he held in his hands the finest copies of all the works the Abbey held of Newton and Einstein.

The Abbot nodded. "As it is written. So take our gifts and depart. You will always be one of us, and our doors will always be open to you."

Timmony bowed low to the Abbot.

"Thank you, Father. Truly, I desire to stay. But as you have said, I must follow the higher Truth and that is to learn more, that I may one day understand all of these. And that I can only do in the world. But may I stay one more day, to say my farewells?"

"Of course, my son. One day, or two, it matters not. It matters only that you are the one we have waited for."

~~~

If Timmony was the one they were waiting for, he thought they had waited in vain. The find made him famous; even his Sage, who had been tempted to dismiss ancient relics as a distraction at best or superstitious nonsense at worst, was persuaded to change his mind by the interest generated by the relics and his student's part in their liberation from the Abbey's crypt.

But while Timmony and others made progress in linking some of the equations and even the words in NEWTON with known science, much of it remained mysterious; and nobody could understand EINSTEIN.

Then came the find of the millennium: an ancient, hermetically sealed safe. Inside were a few trinkets, along with six books that looked like they had been written for children: richly illustrated, two obviously simple stories, the other four apparently about the life, times and science of the ancients. The books were extremely fragile but intact; evidently whoever had sealed the safe had done so with some kind of inert gas. Perhaps someone, in the last days of the Ancients, hoping against hope that they could make some knowledge survive. When it had been sealed, its gems had no doubt been treasure and the books practically worthless; now nobody cared about the gems, but the books were a treasure beyond measure. With their simple language and accompanying pictures, and their sheer quantity, deciphering the language of the Ancients had now become possible.

Many Sages, and many more amateurs, rushed to the task. So many that in the field of the Ancient Language the lines between Sage and amateur became blurred. They deduced simple nouns; they deduced what were verbs, adjectives and adverbs; they gained a rudimentary but growing understanding of Ancient grammar. Some of the rules of grammar and spelling made little sense, and many debates raged about the finer points. There were some clues that, as in the modern age, there were other languages besides the one in the books. But if there were they would remain a mystery that might never be solved.

Combining this knowledge with evidence from many sources, including theories of the evolution of modern languages, the possible ways in which the multiple combinations of letters could actually be spoken, and the Abbey's pronunciation of the relics NEWTON, EINSTEIN and their various other ancient incantations: they even gained a rudimentary idea of what the ancient language sounded like.

Had one of the Ancients heard their attempts, he or she might have stared at them in mystified astonishment. But perhaps they would have been able to puzzle out some of it.

With this new understanding of language, Timmony and his colleagues took a fresh look at his manuscripts. Fortunately they were written in the same language as the books, and they began to divine their meaning. The words helped explain the mathematics, and the mathematics helped translate the words. Soon even EINSTEIN began to divulge his secrets.

By this time Timmony was a notable Sage in his own right with his own students. One of them was a particularly brilliant young man, with a fast and creative mind, a talent for advanced mathematics, and an interest in celestial mechanics. In what would prove to be an inspired insight, Timmony already suspected that since the showpiece of NEWTON was his 'Theory of Universal Gravitation', the showpiece of EINSTEIN might be a more advanced development of that. So he suggested that course of study to his new student, who leapt onto the idea like a barbarian onto a stallion.

16. Arragath

That student's name was Arragath, and at the moment he was chewing distractedly on a bun stuffed with hot minced cow, lettuce, tomatoes, beetroot and pickles in a savory sauce. *The complete balanced diet,* he thought, when he bothered to think about his dinner and the glass of cold, frothed flavored milk that accompanied it.

He was staring into nothing when the direction of his stare was eclipsed by a young woman, another student by her clothing. He vaguely recognized her; was sure he had chatted to her on occasion, though he could not remember what occasions. His work was his passion and he did not really care about other people.

It was not that he disliked them, just that neither their existence nor their opinions were central to his consciousness. He was complete in himself.

Sure, he had friends, or people like friends, with whom he would meet and eat and chat; even play, on those occasions when his brain needed rest, or perhaps room to rummage around in his subconscious. Sure, he sometimes indulged in physical pleasures with women, but what meeting of minds there had been had not reached the delight of their meeting of bodies; and while he might sleep with them once, or twice, or even a few times more, none approached the meeting of souls which could have led to a more permanent union.

But tonight he hoped the girl would drift out of his gaze as quickly as she had drifted into it, like two asteroids briefly passing, barely influenced by each other's presence. Then she smiled and asked if she could sit with him.

Pachmeny had been relieved when she had spotted Arragath sitting on his own at a table by the window. If she hadn't found him she would have done what she could, and faced Shemsak tomorrow with whatever she had—the only thing worse than telling him a half-baked theory would be hiding a theory from him once she'd thought of it. But if Arragath would help her, all the better. So she walked up to him and smiled.

"Hello. Do you mind if I join you?"

He looked at her, and she could tell from the look in his eyes that he would rather she didn't. But she knew that despite his coldness, which some interpreted as arrogance or malice, he was beneath it all both fair-minded and curious. She hoped his curiosity about her approach would defeat whatever he was thinking about.

After a moment he nodded. "Sure. Why not?"

She noted that he didn't ask her name but nor did he greet her by it, and she wondered if he remembered or cared. "Hi, Arragath. I'm Pachmeny, we've met before."

"Yes. Hi Pachmeny."

She sat down and started wolfing down her own food, at a pace that looked calculated so that she would finish around the same time he did. Arragath occasionally studied her as they ate, wondering with a single quantum of curiosity why she would sit there and not say a word, just eat at him.

He glanced around, noting that the place was far from crowded at this time, which was later than the peak dinner period. "Did you want something?"

Maybe I want you, she thought, but decided against saying it. *Don't play games and don't bug him off by being too coy. Or you surely* won't *get him, now or ever.*

"Yes. But I'm also hungry, and you're eating too. So it can wait."

But she betrayed herself. As she was finishing off her meal, she could contain herself no longer, and started speaking around the food still in her mouth.

"I've found something interesting. As in weird. But I'm not sure. I'd like to get your opinion. It's on celestial mechanics."

Arragath gave her an interested look, then downed the last of his milk with a sucking sound as he vacuumed the dregs through his straw.

"Oh? What is it?"

"I'll have to show you."

"Sorry Pachmeny, I know I don't look busy, but I am kind of occupied on my own stuff. Ask your Sage tomorrow. I hope you're not trying to impress him or her with my work."

"No! I mean, I don't want to go to Shemsak with a half-baked idea, but I also find it exciting enough I want to be sure in my own mind first. Can you help me? Please? It won't take too long. If it's nothing, it's nothing. If it's something, I'll give you full credit for your part, believe me."

Arragath sighed, tapping his fingers in a complicated rolling pattern, as if her request were a question of higher mathematics. "I'd help you if you'd thought to bring it with you, but did you say Shemsak? That means you're a bit of a detour for me. So sorry, not tonight."

"I'll pay you."

Arragath looked surprised, looked more closely at her. "I think I'm richer than you are, Pachmeny. I don't think you can afford me." But at least he finished it with a faint smile.

"I think you'll find it interesting enough to be worth your while. How about if you help me, but it's nothing, I give you a gold Hawk for your time?"

His eyebrows went up a notch. "You'd really give me a Hawk just for helping you with a puzzle in celestial mechanics? You'd better be careful, or people will think you're weirder than I am. But my time is more precious to me than your money."

"What if I offered to sleep with you if it is a waste of your time?"

He looked even more surprised, but could not tell from her expression whether she was serious or he'd better avoid her in games of bluff. Then he laughed, a short, sharp exhalation. "I cannot tell whether that means you are supremely confident or just trying a very roundabout way to get me into bed with you."

What possessed me? Gods of Fire! But when you have the wolf by the tail...

She smiled, hoping it came across as mysterious. "Some people say you're arrogant. Perhaps they are right!"

"Do you think you should insult me when you're asking for my help?"

"What makes you think I intended it as an insult?"

He looked at her speculatively. "You are a strange person, Pachmeny."

"Is it my turn to be insulted?"

He smiled. "What makes you think I intended it as an insult?" he said in the manner of a quotation. "All right Pachmeny, you win. I am intrigued. I will help you, if you grant me the right to choose which if any of your offers I take in recompense."

She hoped the sudden quiver of flame in her lower abdomen didn't show in her eyes, as she replied ambiguously, "Thank you, Arragath. I am sure it will be worth your while."

So they finished their meals and left together, heading off to Pachmeny's work space.

"Watch," she said when they arrived, directing him to her viewer. "These five images were each taken a month apart. See how the two faint stars move relative to each other? I'm not going to prejudice you with what I think, but don't you think it's odd?"

Arragath studied the images, repeating the playback several times. He pursed his lips as he did so. "Get me something to write on," he said. "What's the scale on this thing?"

He sat there for a few minutes, taking measurements, doing some calculations. Then he stared into space for a long minute, and looked back down at his work, as if rechecking it. Finally he looked at her.

"Damn."

"Damn?"

"Damn. They're too fast. Either they're both much heavier than they look, so their gravitational field is stronger than it should be, or they're crazy close. Celestially speaking, I mean. To have that orbital speed, at that angular separation, they must be only eight, ten light years away, maybe less depending on exactly how big they are. Hellfire! How come nobody ever knew about them before now?"

"Would you notice them against a starfield that dense when they're that dim? Especially before we could make images this sensitive and sharp? I'm not even sure they'd be visible. And I don't know that anybody would notice them if they weren't moving like that."

"Yeah, yeah," he said. Then he stood up, as if unconsciously, staring into space with excitement in his eyes. He looked down at her. "Wow. OK Pachmeny, you win this one. This is big. They must be two dwarf stars, two white dwarfs, orbiting close to each other, practically in our own back yard!"

She couldn't help herself. She reached up her hand to his face and touched him on the cheek. *You idiot,* she told herself when his face jerked at her unexpected touch. *Now is not the time.*

But apparently now was the time, for Arragath put his own hand over hers, and the look in his eyes took on a different intensity.

"About that offer..." he began.

She pulled his head down and kissed him, and the night became perfect.

17. The Stars Above

Pachmeny woke early, her body tingling from the aftermath of the previous night. This was not the first time she had experienced intellectual excitement, nor the first time she had spent the night with a man, but it was the first time both had melded together into such perfection.

Arragath was still asleep, still holding her body in a gentle embrace, and she bathed in his warmth and the regularity of his breathing. Then he woke, and she felt a gentle start, as if he had been surprised to find himself holding her. But then he mumbled "good morning, Pachmeny", and he kissed her neck. She could tell that he had a particular type of good morning in mind, and so she eagerly turned to join his embrace. *Ah, young men,* she thought happily. *Even you, my dear Arragath, who can seem so cold and austere, have the same passions. And for now, at least, they are mine.*

~~~

Afterwards they ate a companionable breakfast, during which their thoughts and conversation returned with a vengeance to the more intellectual discoveries of the previous night. Then they headed off together to see Shemsak.

Shemsak was a busy man, and though he took his responsibilities to his students seriously, sometimes those responsibilities had to wait. But when Pachmeny, in whom he had seen a spark of something beyond what the dry figures of her schooling might predict, arrived with the stellar Arragath in tow, only a true emergency could have stopped him making time for them. Especially when they both came bathed in a glow implying they had news of startling import. Either that or signaling they had just had sex together, but they would hardly come here to tell him that.

"Good morning, Pachmeny," he said, "And you, Arragath. What would bring the two of you to see me, especially when Arragath's own Sage Timmony is not with you, and has not advised me of your visit?"

Arragath bowed to him. "Our apologies, Esteemed Shemsak. But this is Student Pachmeny's discovery, and yours. I merely helped with her calculations."

"Please call up these slides, and play them in sequence," asked Pachmeny, handing him a printout of the reference numbers.

Shemsak did what she asked, then looked up at them in surprise. "Curious. What is your interpretation?" he asked.

"I haven't done a full analysis," Arragath replied, "only a quick one when Pachmeny showed me this; and no doubt you and the Esteemed Timmony will want to get together on that before anyone else is told. But according to my calculations, this combination of luminosity, separation and relative speed is only possible if we are looking at a pair of white dwarf stars in tight orbit around each other, about seven light years away. With any luck, we have images of this same part of the sky from another point on the Earth's orbit and can confirm that distance more precisely by parallax measurements."

Shemsak nodded. "Yes... yes. As you say." Then he looked up at them again. "Remarkable! Truly remarkable. Well done, both of you! Especially you, Pachmeny, for seeing its importance so quickly. I will discuss this with Timmony. Meanwhile, Pachmeny, you can collect all our images of this region and do more analyses; and Arragath, you can refine your calculations based on that... then, well, we'll see what we see!"

The two bowed, turned and left. Unconsciously, Pachmeny reached out and took Arragath's hand. Shemsak saw and smiled in amusement. *Right on both counts, it seems.* But then his smile faded and his face took on a haunted look.

Enjoy your triumph, children. And hope it is a triumph, and not the death of us all.

18. SUPERNOVA

Six months went by during which the scientific world, or at least its astronomical corner, began to buzz with the news of such a nearby and thus readily studied phenomenon. The buzz even leaked into the general media, and 'Pachmeny's Stars' became stars in the public mind, dragging Pachmeny along with them.

She had no time for that. She was happy in her work, ignoring the fame except as it helped her work; happy in her relationship with Arragath, which had transformed almost seamlessly from a night of passion to something deeper and more lasting.

The only oddity was Shemsak. Sometimes Pachmeny thought he was jealous of her success, though that made no sense. It never occurred to her that he could be jealous of her relationship with Arragath; which was probably a good thing, as that was the last thing on his mind. He was nothing but supportive of her and her work; gave nothing but his blessing to her union with Arragath. Yet too many times she would catch a glimpse of him alone at his work, a look almost like fear on his face. Other times she would catch him looking at her, as if staring at his own death.

Then one day he called them into his office.

"Shut the door," he commanded.

Then he waved to the chairs before his desk. "Sit."

They looked at each other. It was rare that any student was invited to sit before a Sage; a breach of protocol, almost, except in cases of exceptional success or failure. Their success was too old, and had not invited a seat when it was new. So they sat, but on the edge of their seats, looking at Shemsak nervously.

He looked back, folding and unfolding his hands, as if he were even more nervous than they. In his prime he had exuded power and confidence; now, only six months after their discovery, it was as if his greatest success had drained him. He looked almost haggard, and when he finally spoke, they could detect a distinct quaver in his once firm voice.

"Pachmeny. Arragath. You must know how proud I am of both of you. But now I must tell you some of my own latest work. I was working on this even before you discovered the stars that now bear your name. Then, I was not sure. Now, I am. Or perhaps I am coming to you, Arragath, as Pachmeny did that night. Perhaps I am wrong."

He was silent for a while. Then he spoke again.

"You are familiar with the theory of exploding stars?"

Pachmeny nodded. "Yes. When a giant star runs out of its nuclear fuel it can no longer support its own weight. But in its collapse, it triggers a fusion explosion beyond understanding. It tears itself apart with a violence that rivals all the output of its home galaxy. Even today we can see the remnant glows of supernova explosions thousands of years ago."

She paused and Arragath added, "I too know the theory, but I do not see your meaning. There are no such stars anywhere near Earth. They cannot hide for they are too bright. Even behind clouds of dust their presence would reveal itself."

Shemsak nodded. "No, there are not. But there are other ways a supernova can be caused. A white dwarf star, drawing mass from a companion red giant, can add enough mass to its core to trigger a collapse, with the same result."

The mention of white dwarfs piqued Arragath's interest, with a subtext of fear. But he replied after a moment's thought, "Interesting. But a red giant is also too bright to hide, and there are none of them close enough either."

Shemsak looked at them, and suddenly seemed older, as he added softly, "A white dwarf feeding off a red giant companion... or when two white dwarf stars combine."

"You aren't saying...?"

"I am. Pachmeny's Stars are not only close to each other, they are in an unstable orbit. I do not know why. Perhaps they are in a cloud of gas and friction is causing orbital decay; perhaps some other nearby star perturbs their orbit; perhaps that Einstein physics Arragath is working on has something to do with it. The effect is small, but their orbit is highly elliptical, and Pachmeny B comes very close to Pachmeny A at its closest approach. So it only takes a small effect. As white dwarf stars they are both very dense, and so despite their tight orbit, little material is transferred between them. Until they get too close. Then they will merge, or enough material will be stripped off Pachmeny B onto Pachmeny A to achieve much the same thing."

"When?" whispered Pachmeny.

"I cannot yet say. Years, I fear. Decades, I think. Centuries, I hope. They may already have done so. We will have no warning. Once critical mass is reached the collapse is extremely rapid. One day they will look as they do today, invisible to the naked eye, filling the days and nights of astronomers. Then one day their light will fill the sky. They are too close. Even thirty light years would be too close, though maybe some would survive the holocaust. Seven... seven is too close. They will sterilize every part of the planet their radiation hits. They will destroy the layer of ozone that protects us from the Sun's ultraviolet light. We will all be dead. I imagine that simple life will survive, hidden away from the worst of it. But the ecosystem will collapse. The Earth will become a desert."

"What... what can we do?"

"Nothing can stop it."

"Then... why tell us? Why tell anyone? Perhaps we would all be better off not knowing! Living our lives and our hopes, our dreams: never even knowing when they end."

"Now you know the burden I have borne."

"I do not think I can thank you for sharing it. I can neither help you bear it, nor bear it myself."

"No. I am sorry, Pachmeny. I have come to think of you as a daughter, and it tears my heart apart to do this to you. But I must. For there might be a way out. The way is neither easy nor guaranteed; perhaps it will merely add suffering to pain. But can we ignore the one hope of the human race, by shutting our eyes to escape our own pain?"

Pachmeny looked at Arragath, tears pricking her eyes. *We had such hopes, you and I. Our careers, our children, our legacy. Now there is nothing. Could we even have children now, knowing the fate they must meet? Why, Shemsak, why? I think I would have preferred to live my life until death crept up on me unseen; to strip my life and dreams from me without my ever knowing.*

Arragath looked back at her, knowing her thoughts; sharing them. Then he turned back to Shemsak. "What is the hope you see?"

"You, of all men, know what we have been learning from the work of the Ancient Sage Einstein. There is more to space and time than meets the eye. We cannot escape the death of these stars. We have not yet managed to escape our own planet, let alone flee tens of light years ahead of their rage. But Einstein teaches that perhaps there is a way. Perhaps we can tunnel through space to a far part of the galaxy. Escape Earth. Maybe many, maybe only a few. Enough to preserve the race."

"You cannot be serious! You yourself said it! We have not even left our planet, yet you imagine we can build tunnels through spacetime itself?!"

"I wish I were not, but if you know of some other way I will readily hear it."

"Can we not literally tunnel? Dig into the Earth? Build shelters, protected under miles of rock?"

"Perhaps. Indeed, that is part of my plan, if 'plan' is an appropriate word for what it is. Not to weather the storm. That is impossible. The biosphere will be destroyed for millennia, if not forever. Even buried under tons of rock lined with lead, in the face of gamma radiation and the rest in such ferocity, complete protection is impossible. People would survive. But whether they could have children..." He spread his hands helplessly. "And if they could... even with nuclear power, I see no way they could survive long enough to return to a living surface that could support human life. It would buy time: decades probably; with luck, a century or two. But it would only prolong the inevitable. Soon enough all will die, having achieved nothing but the extension of pain. An asymptote to the end of Man."

"Then why consider it?"

"Because we know nothing! Except that what we don't know might save us! What I want is to set the whole world working on a solution, set up such shelters, then populate them with the best and brightest of humanity, so they can continue the work after the end!"

Arragath looked from him to Pachmeny and back. "You're mad."

Shemsak shrugged. "Perhaps. Who would not be, after six months knowing what I have known? But it is that, or roll over and die."

The two students stood, as if as one. "We will think about it, Shemsak," said Arragath. "But will anyone believe us? Even I don't believe it, and I'm an astrophysicist!"

"We will have to make them believe, or we are all dead, and with our death comes the end of the entire human race."

19. THE UNDERGROUND

It had to be done carefully. The cabal centered on Shemsak slowly grew, approaching the most rational of the Sages, the wisest of the Clan Heads and Governors.

A quiet revolution occurred. Those who would not accept it, or who appeared unstable or untrustworthy, were quietly silenced. The cabal was not yet ruthless; they could not justify to themselves killing for some greater good. Their victims were merely imprisoned, until and unless they realized that what had to be done, had to be.

The people were not informed. What was the point? Let them live their lives, as Pachmeny had wished in her own mind when she learned of it. They could do nothing to stop it and would probably make things worse: panicking, in fear or despair destroying the last hope of the human race, overthrowing governments as if governments could do anything at all, and as if removing them would hurl Pachmeny's Stars from the sky.

As far as the public knew, a major breakthrough had been made in science based on physics learned from the Ancients, that might lead men to the stars and to unimaginable wealth. That accounted for the heightened activity in the great centers of study and learning. It accounted for the large scale drilling programs into the bases of two high mountains whose purpose, the people were told, was research that needed thorough shielding from cosmic rays.

They brought in psychologists. An enterprise of this nature could not be kept completely secret; and even if it were, people were prone to make up conspiracies where none existed: let alone when they were.

So the psychologists, and the marketers, and other experts in persuasion, set about discrediting or redirecting undesirable rumors, while promoting desirable ones.

It was not a stable situation. Neither the mood of the people nor the economy could survive their respective departures from reality. Eventually it would unravel, and the world would explode. They did not know whether to fear or hope that the sky would explode first.

Then they turned their minds to the selection of people for the shelters.

~~~

An hour ago, Sage Kuchalki had been intrigued about why she had been invited to a mysterious meeting with the Head of her Clan and a famous physicist, a field far from her own. Now she just sat there, aghast, wishing she could turn back time and refuse the invitation.

"Is this some kind of joke?" she asked weakly.

"I'm afraid not, Sage Kuchalki."

"We're all going to die."

"That was always going to happen, I'm afraid."

"We're all going to die at once. Everyone. Forever. Any time now."

"Yes."

"Yet you want me to tell you how to breed, what? A race of supermen? So they can discover some kind of superscience before they all die, so they can escape to God-knows-where light years away?"

"Yes."

"It can't be done."

"What?"

"Any of it! You're mad. Totally, irretrievably mad!"

"That would be preferable. But you've seen what we know. You might not be a physicist, but you are a Sage. I think you know that we know."

Kuchalki rubbed her temples. "You do realize you've ruined my day. My life. Gods of Chaos. Why did you tell me?"

"Because we need your help."

"So you don't know when this is going to happen; it might happen tomorrow or next century; but you're rolling the dice to breed a bunch of people smart enough to solve the problem before or after it happens?"

"Yes."

"You're mad."

"We've covered that already."

"Totally, irretrievably mad."

"Desperate. We see no other hope."

"Yes. Quite. Quite so. Yes, of course I will help you. If I can."

She sat there for long minutes, thinking. "All right. We know all about selective breeding. Domestic animals have changed a lot over time as farmers have selected them for desirable traits. Usually they do the obvious, choosing their best specimens for breeding. So in principle, yes. Maybe. Unless humans have already hit their maximum possible intelligence—unlikely, perhaps, but possible—then in theory we could selectively breed from the highly intelligent. But what farmers have done they have done over centuries, millennia. You're talking a generation, at best two, before we run out of time regardless of what we do. Unless this supernova is further in the future than you think. How likely is that?"

"Possible. But not likely. I wouldn't want to stake the future of our species on it."

"Well, there you have a problem. It is called 'reversion to the mean'. If you breed two highly intelligent people, or two people who are elite in any field, you usually get children closer to the average of the population. You don't get better geniuses. The reason is that traits like intelligence are complex, based on many genes, and worse, their interactions; and to muddy it more, also on the environment. It is the particular combination that gives you your genius. But mix two geniuses together and you get a random combination. Usually not as good. Maybe if you could do your breeding program for centuries you'd get somewhere. But one or two generations? Good luck."

"But it is possible? With lots of different geniuses in the pool?"

"You could get lucky. But nobody has ever tried. More likely you'd get a bell-shaped curve much the same as the general population, but moved upwards to a higher average intelligence. But a higher maximum? Maybe. I'd say don't count on it, but I guess you have to. Or maybe you'll have enough time for even a bunch of natural geniuses to get the job done."

"Could you advise us on the best details for such a program?"

"I could, as much as anyone could. It won't be an exact science. But we could make educated guesses. But I'll never know if I succeed, will I? None of us will ever know."

"Probably not. But at least we will have tried."

"How much... latitude will be allowed? Hell, I'm not going to sugar-coat this," she added bitterly, bitingly, as if blaming them for ruining her day. "How much force will be allowed? Are we going to drag husbands screaming from their wives, and vice versa? Put them in pens and tell them who to mate with and on what days, like so many prize cattle? Cart away their defective children in the dark of the night?"

"Sage Kuchalki," replied Arragath wearily. "You are right to ask that. If we are brought to the point where our only practical course is something so immoral that at any other time we would recoil from it in horror, then perhaps our race does not deserve to survive. But here we are, impaling ourselves on the horns of just that dilemma. If we act morally, do we doom the human race? Then how can it be moral? But how can the measures you mention be moral? I do not know. I hope we can do what we must. I fear that we *will* do what we must. But if I must sell my soul to save the world, then I am not sure I have the courage to do either: to sell my soul or doom the world to save it."

"Perhaps instead of a geneticist you need an ethicist."

Then she paused, and looked at him strangely. "Or perhaps you have answered your own question," she added slowly.

"What do you mean?"

"You speak of being practical. You speak of breeding from geniuses. Perhaps it is not practical to stake the fate of the world on an army of geniuses who hate your guts for what you have done to them."

He gave her a startled look. "Quite so... quite so. But what is the alternative? Our shelters will be nuclear powered so they have unlimited energy, but still they are restricted in size, and can only grow enough food and otherwise support a certain number of people. If we start letting in not only the people we need but their loved ones, we must start keeping out the people we need the most. We do not know when the disaster will happen so we have to populate our shelters then seal them, for good or ill."

"Then I have a suggestion. A series of suggestions, if you will. If you have two equal candidates and one is single but the other is married to an unsuitable partner, take the first. Seek volunteers. The life you are offering them is uncertain, perhaps a sentence of a long, painful death instead of a short, clean one. Some will understand. Others will respond to the appeal of necessity. You fear you are willing to sell your soul for this; many others will be willing to do what they must too, no matter the cost or the pain. Both those might hate themselves: but they will not hate you; and the level of their hate will become the level of their loyalty to the ideal for which they sold that which was most precious to them. It is terribly cruel, but the cruelty is not yours: it is in the stars.

"Those who are left, choose: perhaps there is no compelling reason to take them over others more compliant. And if they are: do not forget what I said about reversion to the mean. It cuts both ways. Just because someone isn't a genius doesn't mean they don't have the seeds of genius within them. And remember that we are speaking of the partners of geniuses: chosen for a reason, containing some spark of their own that would attract even a genius. So assuming the numbers are modest, as I believe they will be, I think you should keep your soul and let them in. They are insurance against our ignorance: an additional pool of genes we did not choose, our wildcard if you will. Besides, someone needs to maintain the facility, tend the crops and feed the babies. This takes at least some of that off the plate of your geniuses, who have more vital work to do."

~~~

So above the ground Sages and their students worked tirelessly on the problems of advanced physics, while below the ground two mighty shelters took shape. To the world they were introduced as the Twin Advanced Science Facilities, fabulous temples of mysterious science that were the subject of breathlessly excited commentary and speculation.

Within a week, everybody just called them The Eggs. They were built with ovoid shells to gain maximum thickness from the amount of material that could be diverted to their construction. Deep underground, inside their thick shells, the delicate instruments within would be protected from interference by cosmic rays from above and lesser natural radiation from below. Through their thinner underside, their deep location also gave the best access for secondary research into the core of the Earth beneath. Built a world apart, they gained the longest possible baseline for experiments peering into the most distant reaches of the cosmos.

The Eggs promised a brave future for humanity. A team of the finest minds on the planet had been assembled to develop unheard of technologies from a remarkable scientific advance only recently discovered and still kept secret by the Sages. Inevitably, conspiracy theories also sprang up around them. These were tolerated, even encouraged, by the authorities. To the world, the conspiracy theories were an escape valve and entertainment, becoming a kind of mental flypaper for any suspicions buzzing around the cultural atmosphere. The few who took them seriously had no power to act on their beliefs, and like such people through all time were content to preach without acting, themselves generally living as if their theories did not touch the reality of their lives.

To the Sages, they were Eggs in more than shape, the precious embryos laid by a doomed race in hope of future rebirth.

They had been afraid to put all their figurative eggs in one basket in case some disaster wiped one out. If they could they would have built hundreds, but with their limited resources and time they could only build two. They were under mountains on nearly opposite sides of the planet relative to the plane of Pachmeny's Stars, so that they would not both bear the full brunt of their fury when it came. Even the width of a planet was not full protection, but perhaps it would be enough that if the nearest fell, the farthest would survive.

The two shelters were connected by communications cables in case the cross-fertilization of minds helped advance their science. Nobody expected the cables or radio links to survive the storm, not across half the planet, but they had to try. The shelters received the most advanced nuclear reactors with the safest, most passive design, with enough fuel for hundreds of years. They installed the most carefully and simply designed life support systems, and the most advanced scientific equipment; with enough machine tools and raw materials to hopefully cover any contingency.

The plans changed somewhat. The leaders chose the most brilliant minds among the Sages and their Students. But they also had a lottery. The Eggs, the people were told, also provided an opportunity to study the best ways for a few people to survive in isolation for long periods. Hints of space travel, possibly of generational ships slowly inching their way toward the stars, drifted into the public mind via rumor and speculation. Applicants, the people were told, had to be highly intelligent, resourceful, and have no ties: to be willing to leave the world behind and spend who knew how many years inside the Eggs cut off from communications. There were many applicants, more than enough to round out the genetic pool being passed to the future.

Construction proceeded at a breakneck pace. After only five years they were largely completed, and after another two they were ready.

Pachmeny and Arragath went to see Shemsak. He rose and embraced them both. They were fortunate, or cursed, depending on your perspective: both young, both brilliant, and both intimately involved from the start, they had been chosen for one of the shelters.

"Goodbye, Esteemed Shemsak," said Pachmeny, breaking protocol by hugging her former Sage. "I wish you would come with us. We could use your mind."

He looked at her sadly. "Goodbye, Pachmeny. Don't worry about me. This is a young person's charge, not one for elder Sages like me. I will be here for you, whenever you need me. Until the end of the world."

She took his hand, tears in her eyes, and held it to her breast. "Goodbye, Shemsak," she whispered.

And then they were gone.

Knowing what the future held, they had already had a child of their own. They knew that the genetic program had priority over personal interests: that perhaps no future children would be of them both. But they could live with that. They could live with each other giving or taking the seed of another, for the sake of the race, to buy a future. For they would always be with each other. And at least one child they carried into the future with them would be theirs, and it was enough.

20. BARONAK

The night was cold, its clammy fingers caressing his skin and reaching into his soul. He knew the night was no colder than any other, and that the chill lay in his soul not in the air. Or perhaps the climate system too was finally failing.

He knew he had little time remaining. His own parents had been gone many years now, and he would soon be following them into whatever night had already taken so many others before and after them. When he was young he had faced his life with fire and passion; knowing one day he would die, as all men died, but hoping that on that day he would look back on his life and feel the pride of a life well lived. As if some judge, be it the gods, the universe, or his own conscience, would pronounce the words 'Well done!' over his life, and thus give their sanction to his existence.

But somehow the years had passed into shadow and were gone, and he sat looking back at them unable to give them sanction, yet unable to see how he could have done better. *Perhaps all who feel their end coming look back at their life and feel its sum. But whatever they feel, be it the flame of triumph or the ashes of defeat, have any come so close as me to the cusp between the two, and failed so utterly?*

The work that stood before him was not his alone. Out of the many brilliant minds who had labored within the Egg, maybe someone could trace the paths that led to this final solution if they cared to try. Perhaps Baronak had been the key: certainly the condensation of the formulae into their essentials that glowed at him from the screen was his. But it did not matter. All that mattered was the solution.

116

And that it was too late.

Decades ago, in its last gasp humanity had built two precious Eggs and cast them into the future, hoping that one day those within would learn how to tunnel out of their shells onto a new world. Of the other one nothing had been heard since the Fury. At first they had hoped that it was merely a failure of communication, not unexpected. But as years had passed and turned into decades, and their own communication technology had improved, still no whisper had been heard, and they had long given up hope that it remained.

Perhaps it had, and those within it had escaped to their own destiny, unable or unwilling to communicate with this Egg, but still carrying humanity's future with them to the stars. Or perhaps they still lived on, laboring as Baronak labored, living on a dying hope. But most likely they had perished and this Egg held all that was left of the human race.

And so his parents and their generation had carried the lone surviving Egg, the precious package now passed to Baronak and his generation in their turn. Their ancestors had done their best and could not have done better. But nobody knew all the details of what happened inside a supernova, or all the effects the hellish brew it emitted would have on a nearby planet or its biosphere. The other Egg had succumbed. This one had been damaged: not fatally, at first not even inconveniently. But the damage was done, and as the years went by both the delicate bodies inside and the systems keeping them alive decayed and degraded faster than hoped.

So now Baronak stared at the essence of the solution, hoping to feel hope while seeing in it nothing but doom. The solution was not what they had expected, and contained in itself the seeds of its own peculiar type of tragedy. It also held hope. But the twisting of spacetime was not without cost. Vast amounts of energy had to be concentrated to bully the laws of physics into giving up what they did not want to surrender. And the power plants were no longer capable of providing that amount of energy. They had done the experiments; calibrated the energies; refined the equations. Perhaps there were other solutions: better ones. If he were younger, with the brain he had as a youth, he might have found one. If the power plants were younger, perhaps they would have found the energy.

He looked at the mighty twin achievements, both mocking him for his and their own inadequacy. The equations, startling in their power, deadly in their effect: just scrawls on paper, with no agency to achieve either. The experimental apparatus, with its eldritch powers, backed by unimaginable energies: both no doubt would seem like magic to past generations, but were too close to death to reach either far or long.

He felt as at the end of a long relay race, where many had fallen along the way, yet the golden egg was still borne along its path. And now it was he who held it, and finally he could see the end of the race in the distance, but he no longer had the strength to finish. He would struggle until his lungs burned and his heart struggled for release, until he too fell, and this time there would be no others.

If only there was another to whom he could throw his precious egg, then he could collapse at last into peace. Not in victory, but at least knowing that someone else had shouldered the burden, so hope may yet live.

He sat still, held by that thought and his earlier one. *There is not enough power for much, but perhaps there is power enough, if only I can find where to apply it. Perhaps I can find a place to stand, and move the Earth. But who can I find who might understand, and how can they even know they need to understand, in the time they will have?*

Then for the first time that night he smiled, though he saw death in the equations. *I just need the right time, the right circumstances, and the right frame of mind. And I think I know where to find them. I just need to remember. Remember my youth.*

21. THE MESSAGE

Baronak looked at the equations, as he had done so many times before. They danced mockingly before his brain, jeering at his failure to understand.

Or perhaps there was nothing to understand. Perhaps they were all doomed.

His own father, the great Arragath, had done much of the work to develop these equations from the hints of the Ancient Sage Einstein and his own insights and talents, fed by all the talents of first the world and then the Egg. For ten years after his parents and thousands of others had been sealed into the Egg, the world above went on; it had now been another twelve since communication with the outside had ceased, with nothing but a storm of static as witness to its fate. And so the world had ended except for the two enclaves built by men, now cut off from each other, possibly forever; each hoping the other had survived, hoping against hope that one would achieve the dream bequeathed to them: not fall to the doom prowling the wasteland that was once the vibrant greens and blues of planet Earth.

Unlike too many of their fellows Arragath was still alive, still working. But Baronak, his first child, born before the Egg and now twenty five years old, had proved to be everything the planners had hoped for. In the genetic lottery he had combined not the average but the best of his parents; his was the mind of generations.

There were many others of great genius in the generation born around and after the Fury, and they too struggled with the tortured equations of spacetime and their elusive hints of burrowing through the fabric of the universe. Perhaps they would see the solution. Baronak hoped so, because he could not.

The equations of spacetime were now advanced even over the work of the great Einstein. They even showed how to make a burrow. But to keep the burrows stable seemed impossible. Spacetime folded about them, and the bigger they were and the further they went, the less stable they were. Experiments confirmed it, and so far had offered no way out. The tunnels collapsed in a flash of radiation moments after they were created. Some of the researchers claimed that to keep a burrow open would require negative energy. Unfortunately nobody could say what that was, let alone how to produce it. Some claimed that negative energy could be created via a new, exotic form of matter; but none could say what that was, either.

We're never going to get there. It is too hard a problem, our resources too small, the systems that power our experiments and keep us alive degrading by the day. Our own bodies beginning to fail us. If only we had more time.

He stretched, slowly turning his head and wriggling his shoulders, trying to unknot the tensions of the night. He was tired but too keyed up to sleep; a hollow feeling told him he was hungry. He reached over and toggled a communicator.

~~~

Geldamur frowned wryly. A sandwich and a jar of caff. Seriously?

In the genetic lottery inside the Egg, Geldamur had not won any notable brilliance of mind. But he possessed a great facility for cooking, fortunately coupled with a love of the arts of the chef. Perhaps the limitations of life in the Egg made that career difficult; or perhaps those limitations merely challenged his creativity the more, and added to his enjoyment.

In any case he loved his job. There was no real day or night inside the Egg. The automatic lighting in public areas was set to the standard day-night cycle, but nothing was to interfere with the Great Task. So depending on their proclivities, opportunities or mere insomnia, while most work was done during 'daylight hours', enough people could be found abroad at any hour that services never ceased.

If asked, Geldamur would have said that he most loved the early evening, when people were relaxing and socializing and really appreciated an inspired meal. But the variety of his life was also something he loved, and whether he was assigned to breakfast, lunch, dinner or night shift, he enjoyed the challenges of meeting whatever requirements he was rostered to meet.

Unless they ask for sandwiches.

He grinned and set to work. *Let's see if I can give The Great Baronak the best damn sandwich he's ever eaten.*

There were a number of students scattered around the cafeteria. They were studying, reading or watching entertainment, but like many people they were also here to serve the Great Task in whatever manner was asked of them, and if they were here but not eating it meant they were available for any tasks Geldamur might require.

He caught the eye of one of them, a young woman who'd had her nose in a notebook but chosen that moment to remove it and glance in his direction. He did not know her well, as she had spent most of her time in another section and only recently started frequenting this region, but he had seen her around and chatted to her once or twice.

"Can you deliver this to Baronak, Jennara?" he asked her. "His room number is printed here if you don't know where he camps."

"Sure thing Geldamur, right away," she replied, scooping up the tray and heading to the bank of lifts.

~~~

Baronak had forgotten about his sandwich until his thoughts were dragged back to the mundane by a gentle knock at his door.

"Enter!"

A young woman came in, bearing a tray and the unmistakable air of 'Student', an air possibly unchanged since the time of the Ancients.

"Yes?", he enquired.

"You ordered a sandwich and a jar of caff, no?"

"Oh. Oh yes! Sorry! Just put it down here. Thanks, er…?"

"Jennara."

"Hi Jennara, pleased to meet you," he said, clasping her forearm in formal greeting with one hand, while reaching for his sandwich with the other then taking a large bite. "Sorry," he muttered around his mouthful, "now it's here I'm a bit hungry."

He looked at the sandwich in surprise. "Hey, this is the best damn sandwich I've ever eaten. Maybe I'm hungrier than I thought."

She looked at him critically. "You look more than hungry. You look completely done in. I think you need sleep more than that jar of caff."

He smiled ruefully. "Probably. But you know how it is. I can't go to sleep with these equations bugging me. Problem is, that means I might never sleep again."

She favored him with a look of disgust. "Well at least relax a bit. Here," she ordered, "sit back and eat your sandwich. Let me work my arts."

She had wondered if he was one of those prickly types who would order her out for impertinence, but he took it with good humor, rolled his eyes and obeyed. "Yes, Mom," he murmured.

As he lay back in his chair she began to massage his shoulders and neck, and she heard him groan with relief as the knots in his muscles began to unwind.

"You're good at this. I'm not normally one for massages, but I might change my mind."

"Shush. Stop talking. Stop thinking. Just relax."

He leaned back further, relaxing into the chair, and sighed.

"I'm allowed to sigh, right?"

"Shush!"

He shushed, and allowed himself to drift, letting his thoughts loose to drift where they would too.

Then he noticed with some surprise, since he had not been thinking of her in that manner, that while her hands were succeeding admirably in their task of relaxing his upper body, his lower body was reacting in its own, different way.

Jennara had not been thinking in that direction either, but she could not help noticing his reaction. *Probably been a while for him, carrying the world on his shoulders and on that remarkable mind of his.* She felt an answering tingle from her own body. *Been too long for me, too, come to think of it.*

He knew she had noticed when her hair brushed his cheek, as she leant over to say in a soft but hoarse voice, "I think you need more than a sandwich and a massage, my Sage."

She paused before adding, "I think I would be happy to provide it."

The Eggs were designed with enough space for psychological comfort, but private offices were no larger than required for their purpose. As he spun around to stand up, his elbow brushed against a small pile of papers on the edge of his desk, scattering them onto the floor.

"Sorry! My fault for startling you!" she said, bending as if to retrieve them.

But he grasped her arm and looked down at her. "I have a more urgent task for you. If you meant what you said?"

"I surely did."

He had a cot in his office, as nightly researches were far from uncommon in his life. They moved toward it, undressing each other with abandon as they went, then they fell on it in a tangle of limbs.

She was surprised by the violence and speed of their passion. *It really has been a long time for him*, she thought, when thought found a way to express itself. Fortunately for her, the speed was compensated by the violence of it, and her own nerves screamed their approval, so by the end of it she too lay gasping.

"Oh, Baronak," she murmured, holding him, but there was no reply, just softly even breathing. She opened her eyes, and saw that he was already asleep.

"Jennara's Stress Reduction Service, open for business," she whispered, then she too was asleep.

~~~

Baronak woke a few hours later, the slightly brighter hue of the strip lighting around the floor indicating early morning. Jennara was still asleep beside him, but he somehow managed to gently disentangle himself from her without waking her, before covering her with a blanket.

He quietly padded across the floor to his desk, picking up the scattered papers from last night. One of his habits was to jot down random thoughts and ideas on pieces of actual paper, which he would examine at leisure later in random order to see if some otherwise hidden thought or connection would reveal itself. He had gathered this sheaf early the previous evening with a view to such an exercise but then never got around to it.

He was surprised to see a single piece of it still on his desk. *I could have sworn that wasn't there,* he thought. He glanced at it. It was clearly his handwriting, yet it was strangely wavering, as if written in great haste or fatigue: perhaps it had been a sudden insight at the end of too late a night, hurriedly scribbled in an exhausted hand and then forgotten.

He took a closer look, and gasped. *But this… is this what it looks like?*

He skimmed the entire page almost in one glance, before going back over the equations with greater care, staring at the strangely twisted equations and their peculiar transformations, as if the answer might emerge from the warped spacetime they represented.

There were no diagrams of what the equations represented, just the symbols; but a mind like his, looking at the equations, could see the diagrams in his head. *If this is right, then… but if this is also right, then…?* *Impossible! And yet…*

He put the paper aside and fired up his computer.

Spacetime he thought. *Maybe I've been looking at this wrong. Maybe… no. What good could that do?*

He sat up straight, startled by his own thoughts, as the thought from earlier in the evening echoed again in his mind.

If only we had more time.

~~~

Jennara sat up and yawned. She glanced over at Baronak, who was back at his computer, seized either by uncommon dedication to his work or a more commonplace desire to ignore her. *Well, good morning to you too!* She knew that many men's eyes were dark with interest and passion in the night, but having achieved their pleasure, in the morning they wished only that you would vanish quietly and forever. She figured he was one of that standard type.

Not that it matters, she thought with a shrug. *I'm a grown woman, and I got at least one thing I wanted.* So she quietly began to dress.

The sounds of a person rising from bed and dressing no doubt reached Baronak's ears, but somewhere between there and his conscious mind they got lost, until finally he heard a quiet "Good morning" and sensed a presence standing behind him.

He spun around in his chair.

"Oh!" *Are you still here?* Jennara heard. "Good morning." *If you are, I suppose I must be polite. We did after all just sleep together.*

His eyes looked as if he weren't even seeing her, which only reinforced the cynicism of her mental translations.

"I'm feeling like some breakfast, but I have to finish this." *I never finished the sandwich you brought me, so why don't you fetch me something else to eat, since you're just standing there?* "How about you go down and order breakfast for two, and I'll join you in about ten minutes when it's ready?"

His last sentence somewhat derailed her translation, so after a second's pause she replied, "Oh! Um, sure. That'll be nice." *Slick, so slick.* "Um, what are you working on that got you up so early? You must have had only about four hours sleep."

She rested her hands on his shoulders as she said it, hoping he would not flinch. Some did.

"A new direction. It's weird. One of the papers I knocked over last night... well, one that didn't get knocked over, I guess, caught my eye. And it was... fascinating. Here, take a look."

He reached for the piece of paper, but it wasn't there. "Huh. That's funny. I'm sure that's where I put it." He rummaged around a bit. "Huh. Weird. Where'd it get to? Oh well, doesn't matter. I'll show you later."

She could tell he was already drifting away from the world of flesh and blood into some higher realm of mathematics, so she stepped back and quietly slipped out of his room. Glancing back as she eased the door shut, she could see he was already immersed in his computer, apparently having already forgotten she existed. *See you soon. If you remember. At least for that I have an ally in your stomach.*

<p style="text-align:center">~~~</p>

Geldamur was still at work when Jennara came down for breakfast.

If he had noticed that she had not returned last night, he now could not have said whether she had or hadn't. There was nothing remarkable about it. Even students sometimes slept.

But when she asked for breakfast for two, mentioning Baronak's name and asking for 'whatever his favorite is', and the man himself duly joined her, he smiled to himself.

Geldamur was somewhat temperamental, a trait not uncommon in those of his profession. In the circumstances of life after the Fury, in him it was also accompanied by a certain streak of melancholy. So in defense against the melancholy, he liked to see people find happiness where they could: especially if they found it in a meal prepared by himself, but wherever else they found it too.

This is what life is, is it not? he thought as he gazed at them enjoying their breakfast, while displaying the subtle signs of a more personal shared intimacy. *A pleasure here, a piece of joy there, a love gained in the night. In the midst of whatever other tragedies we may endure, it is the accumulation of such joys that life is made of, and that let us bear the rest.*

Then another call for food came, and his mind turned from the contemplation of the infinite to the contemplation of breakfast.

The lovers continued doing both.

"So did you find your piece of paper?"

"Huh?"

"Did you know you say 'Huh?' a lot?"

"Oh! Sorry!"

"You say that a lot, too."

125

"Huh?"

"Oh, shush! I said, did you find your piece of paper?"

"No... but it'll be somewhere. Doesn't matter. I know what it said. If I wasn't so hungry I'd be back there working on it now."

"Sorry."

"What for?"

"I interrupted your sandwich last night."

He grinned at her, then intoned in a solemn voice like a Sage extending a special favour to a Student, "I forgive you."

"Thus I know I am truly in the presence of greatness."

"No, seriously, you were right. I needed the relaxation and I needed the sleep. And what went between. Gave me fresh eyes. And who knows, if I hadn't knocked over those papers, I might never have gotten around to noticing that one piece of paper on the bottom that was left on the desk."

She nodded, "So what's it all about?"

"A new way of looking at spacetime. If those equations are right, and I think they are, then they might open up a whole new world. Unfortunately it might not be a world we'll like. But progress is progress. Reality is what it is."

"Painful knowledge is better than blissful ignorance?"

"Usually. Blissful ignorance has a habit of sneaking up on you and ruining your bliss. Knowledge lets you know what to do. Gravity sticks you to the ground, whether you know what it is or not. But science can let you fly when nobody could before."

"Do you think," she asked speculatively, "that all those people who died, you know, in the Fury, that if they'd been given the choice, they would have chosen knowledge over ignorance?"

Baronak rested his chin on his hands and gazed at her, or perhaps through her. "I've asked my parents the same thing. You know my mother is Pachmeny, the one the stars were named after? She says sometimes she wishes she herself never knew what was coming, that she could have just lived her life and died without even knowing it. But then she says she's glad they knew. Well, not glad, but at least it meant they were agents, not just victims. Someone had to take on the burden of knowing, if anything were to be saved.

"But for the rest, what could they do? Nothing. The knowledge would have ruined their lives to no benefit. Perhaps they were wrong, the Sages back then, to keep the knowledge secret. I don't know. All I know is that I hope I am never called on to decide over the lives or deaths of others, but if I am that I have courage to do it and the wisdom to do it rightly."

She nodded slowly, drinking the remainder of her caff.

He finished first and stood. "Well, speaking of such matters, the equations won't solve themselves. I must be off."

She smiled at him, waggling her fingers in farewell. "Of course. Thank you for your time, I know it is precious."

He turned to go, then looked back. "If I call on you again, will you come?"

She answered softly, "If you call, I will come."

22. The Way

Baronak began to work feverishly.

The equations were difficult, the lines of thought they opened tantalizing in their hints but reluctant to give up their full secrets.

For a little over a month he worked on the problem alone, chasing his vision down paths of higher mathematics only he could see, wondering if any of it was real.

Occasionally Jennara would visit him, bearing gifts of food and morsels of conversation. Sometimes she would find him stretched out in an exhausted sleep, and she would cover him as he had done for her that first morning, before silently slipping out. Sometimes she would see his eyes burning with excitement, and their lovemaking would seem to burn like the Fury itself. But other times his eyes were haunted, and those times were increasing. She wondered why, but when she asked he would not say.

Finally one day he sat before his computer, looking at what he had found. It looked terrible, but right. *But is it real, or have I created a mirage?*

There were many experimental facilities. Baronak did some calculations, then the next day he modified one of the experimental rigs according to his findings and set its target. There were dangers he dared not risk yet, not when he still knew so little. So he would not be able to see his results. He did not have to: his instruments would tell him the truth.

He turned on the machine, tuned the great energies that twisted spacetime, and in the center of his apparatus a small point of light appeared. He looked at the readouts of its detectors then applied more energy. The point of light grew to an impossible blackness surrounded by a circlet of auroral light, about a quarter of his finger's diameter. He counted: one, two, three.. ten heartbeats. The circle was still there. He dialed back the system and turned it off, and the circle vanished.

He resumed breathing.

He pored over the data from the sensor array, comparing it to his equations. He repeated his experiment with some variations, again being careful to avoid the most obvious dangers.

A week later he went to see Pachmeny and Arragath.

~~~

"My son," greeted Pachmeny, holding out her hand to him.

"Mother, Father," said Baronak, bowing then kissing their foreheads.

They had aged beyond their time, his beloved parents. Both were still bright of eye and keen of mind, but the toll of years had worn them down. Whether it was the stress of their task, the unavoidable toxins in their closed environment, the higher radiation they suffered, or old damage from the Fury, their bodily systems were degrading faster than they should have. *And now perhaps I can save us. But at what cost?*

"You look exhausted, dear Baronak. Are you eating enough?"

"You no longer need to nag me, Mother," he replied with a smile. "I have gained a friend, Jennara, who has made it her mission to ensure I eat and sleep occasionally. The nagging is in good hands."

"I am happy for you, son. But you said you had found something important, Baronak? It is sweet of you to come to us with it, but you know that you have long surpassed us in the science of Einstein."

"Your thoughts are always valuable. But it is more than that. What I have found is dangerous. Extremely dangerous. If our straits were not so dire, I would probably run from it, not carry it to you."

Pachmeny and Arragath glanced at each other. Dilemmas like that were no stranger to them.

"Speak, beloved son. We are always here for you."

"To build a burrow is possible. That we already knew. To build a burrow through spacetime to a distant place, large enough to be useful and persistent enough to complete the journey, is impossible."

He saw the fading of light in his parents' eyes, but the residue of hope remaining: for they knew he would not tell them this if it was all there was to tell.

"It is impossible because it requires negative energy. For all the advances we have made, understanding its nature and harnessing its power is far beyond us, if it exists at all. We have come this far by grace of the effort, lies and sacrifices you know more than any. But we can go no further. Perhaps one day it will be possible for people to understand it and walk to the stars. But we have exhausted our power. Our world is dying, and we lack the strength to reach our goal. We are finished. We are out of time. We may have decades left to us but no more. Even decades are not enough when each year erodes our power."

He looked at them for a few moments in silence.

"But there is another way to look at the equations. I cannot find a way to burrow to a distant space, but I have found a way to burrow to a distant time."

His parents gasped. "You mean… time travel? Back in time? How? How can you do that without violating causality? Surely to travel back in time, and act in your past, is to destroy your own present?"

"Now you see why I came to you with this."

"Tell us all."

"We need negative energy to build a useful burrow across vast distances of space, and we have no idea how to do it. But the very paradoxes of travelling back through time provide their own solution. Burrowing back through time in itself produces something mathematically akin to negative energy. A burrow through time produces its own reinforcement, as it were. The length and size of the burrow are no longer limiting over spans of tens of thousands of years."

"And beyond that?"

"It is a curve, not really a bell-shaped curve but something similar. Too short a time and there is too little negative energy equivalence for a useful burrow. A day is too short. For a week, we should be able to achieve a small burrow with a limited life. Too long a time and the potential causality violations begin to overwhelm the effect, and the burrows become increasingly unstable again. Between those extremes, the further back you go and the wider the burrow the more energy you need to open and maintain it, but it remains stable long enough to be useful."

Pachmeny and Arragath stared at him, trying to absorb the enormity of what he was saying. Finally Arragath spoke.

"But the Earth moves through space, both around the Sun and

carried by the Sun and Galaxy through the vastness of the cosmos. If we can burrow through time but not space, what is the purpose? The burrow would open into the vacuum of empty space."

"Space is not absolute: space, time, matter and gravity are intertwined. The burrow is anchored in the Earth's gravity well. The further back in time we go, the more we can wander from our geographic point of origin, but as far back as the Death of the Ancients itself, no more than around the surface of the globe and a few thousand feet in elevation."

"But that itself increases the causality problem we started with," objected Pachmeny. "If the burrows ended up far away the potential for causality violation would be almost eliminated. But going back into Earth's own past? How can you do that without violating causality? What stops you doing something that will alter the future to stop you doing it, creating a time paradox?"

"That isn't a problem on small scales. While some have speculated that the time invariance of quantum equations means causality is an illusion, in fact it is the opposite. The wave equations repair themselves, like a rubber band returning to its original form after being distorted. You could say that reality and causality 'snap back' around any quantum-level breach caused by our burrow."

"How far can we push that?"

"I do not yet know. But my preliminary calculations are that we can view the past safely. That is not surprising when we already know viewing the past is inherent in the finite speed of light, and brings with it no genuine paradoxes."

"But this is different, surely? To observe the past through a burrow, are you not stealing information and radiation from that past, so that whatever it would have hit is no longer hit, thus changing history?"

"It is the rubber band again. The effects of absorbing energy, provided we minimize them so they are small compared to the wash of quantum events they are embedded in, do not affect the future. We cannot actually steal radiation from the past, but if we absorb it, it is replaced by random, incoherent radiation from our present. Thus we absorb information from the past while transmitting none from the future; while the net energy in both is conserved."

"If that is true, what good does it do? It sounds like you can do some fiddling at the quantum level, but whatever effect you caused will not persist. So you couldn't even send information, let alone objects."

"My equations indicate that we can send macroscopic objects back through time. But they will last only so long as they do not cause effects which cannot be snapped back by compensating distortions in the quantum wave functions. In other words, when reality is inexorably set on a new course they will cease to exist. In a sense they never existed. Also there is a time limit. The equations are too complex for more than an approximation at this stage, but I estimate that the maximum persistence is about half an hour, and certainly no more than an hour. Their very presence affects things and the causality tensions steadily build up; again, the object will cease to exist because it never existed, or was never sent back."

"But how does that preserve causality? If the object changes history so it never existed, how did it exist to change history? We are back to an insoluble paradox."

"I have been thinking about this. Let me lead you along the path I have travelled.

"We know that light is a wave, but where its photons are absorbed is random. Those photons are not particles, though mathematically we can treat them as such for many purposes of calculation. Their reality is that only quanta of light energy can be absorbed or emitted, so any such absorption or emission must become localized to the point where it occurs. The light energy itself spreads through spacetime as a wave until and unless it is absorbed."

He looked at his parents, who nodded their understanding.

"Now consider a wave equation, looking forward in time. All outcomes are possible: we can only predict what might happen as a matter of probability. The possible and probable do not become actual until they occur. Mathematically the wave function collapses, much as the wave itself collapses. Until then we could say that all possibilities exist in a virtual future, until the future becomes the present and then the past."

He glanced up and his parents nodded again, albeit less certainly now.

"What happens if we travel back in time is not a causality paradox, but a causality loop. If you were a god standing astride eternal spacetime looking at the structure of reality, you would see a loop from a virtual future curving back to change the course of history, so that what was once a virtual future now becomes reality, while the former reality becomes virtual. What that actually means is beyond my comprehension. But that is what the equations tell me."

His parents looked at him in stunned silence. Finally Pachmeny spoke again.

"I will not insult your intelligence by telling you this is impossible, much as I would like to. But how sure are you of all this? One can see many things in equations, only to find that some factor you haven't taken into consideration prevents their reality. Just as we found with our theoretical hopes of burrowing through lightyears of space."

"I know, because I have done it."

The room was silent for long seconds. Finally Pachmeny said softly, "You risked a causality violation?"

"I figured that if nature allowed it, it would be allowed, and the worst that could happen was failure. But I was careful. I sent my burrow two years into our past, long enough for modest stability of a tiny burrow but short enough to minimize any changes to the timeline, and to a time when I knew nobody would be in the laboratory to see it—since nobody did.

"But I did it. The sensor results confirm that it went back in time; and the stability and size of the burrows I could maintain matched the equations.

"And that is why I am here. That was as much as I dared do on my own. But to do anything useful I need to do more. Much more. At the risk of snuffing out our own existence. I could not make that decision alone."

"But again: what justifies the risk? From what you say we can't use this to escape into the past, for we would vanish before the day ended."

She stopped with a gasp. "Or are you saying we can escape into the future, to some point thousands of years from now when life may again have covered the Earth above?!"

He shook his head. "That is what I hoped. But it doesn't work. The burrow needs to go back through time in order for the negative energy to hold it stable. Going forward produces no such tension and cannot be done. At least, if it can be done the answer is not in my equations."

"So you have discovered something amazing, but it does not help us? We can neither go sideways through space relative to Earth, for the burrows cannot be built; nor forward through time, for the same reason; nor backward into the past, for the release of causality paradox would destroy us soon after we arrived?"

"No, it does not help… us," he replied slowly.

"What… what do you mean?" asked Pachmeny softly.

"Imagine if what we have achieved today had been achieved hundreds of years ago? Or thousands? And they knew what was to come? Centuries more for the combined intellect and resources of a world to study the problem? It would give the world a chance: a chance to find the route to the stars. A chance to escape the fate of our world."

"But…"

"But. We would cease to be. I would never have been born. You would never have been born. Nobody in our past from soon after the resetting of history would have been born.

"It is a death sentence for you, me, for everyone we have ever known and ever loved. A death sentence for billions, stretching over thousands of years.

"We seek to save the world. But to do so, we must destroy our own past and our own present."

Pachmeny knew her son, knew what lay in his eyes. "And still there is more, isn't there?"

He nodded. "Yes. We have one shot. One shot only. Once we do this we cease to exist. If we fail to buy the world time it is all for nothing. Perhaps those who replace us will do a better job. But there is only one thing we know: *we* know an answer. We do not know that those others will find it. I was lucky to find it myself. We can decide not to do this and hope we find a better answer before the end. But if we decide to do it we must choose carefully. We must get it right the first time, for that is our only time. Or we will have destroyed our world as well as ourselves, and possibly any chance for our whole race."

23. ONE WEEK

Baronak sat in his laboratory, watching the space above a bench surrounded by an array of probes and sensors. For once Jennara sat beside him. She had been with him at the start, even been instrumental in that start: she deserved to see this with him.

One week. In a week I shall do the experiment that may kill me. Let us see if I shall have the courage.

The space they were watching appeared to shimmer, then a light-rimmed circle whose center was blacker than night appeared there. A small piece of paper, no more than the size of his thumb, fell from it onto the bench and he bent forward to see it, being careful to stay well outside the experimental zone.

On it was written a single sentence, *And now the future meets the past.*

He had not yet decided what he would write.

The black circle vanished but the paper remained. He picked it up and examined it more closely. *An object from the future. Just one week in the future, but a week reverberating through time.*

Quickly, he put the paper down on another benchtop with its own array of sensors and waited, studying their outputs. After a few minutes there was an uptick in radiation at all wavelengths he was monitoring, as if virtual particles were giving their lives to send him a message. Then the paper was gone and for a moment in its place was a blackness without end, then it too was gone.

Baronak and Jennara stared at where its ghost had been for a long time.

They came back to the laboratory the next week, where he wrote the message on a piece of paper. He turned on the machine, and they watched as the titanic energies unleashed made the air glow and shimmer like the images of the Northern Lights from a long ago Earth, before they opened a burrow to last week and sent the paper back.

They stared at each other, the thrill and the dread filling their eyes. He held her and kissed her. "And so it begins."

He collated the sensor readings from this end with those of the week before, and again went to see his parents.

~~~

"You have done it," Pachmeny said when he entered. "Show us."

He spread out the results for them to see, then explained.

"Today I sent back that piece of paper with the message. Last week I received it. You can see they are the same. You can see the stability of the transfer and the inherent instability yet persistence of the object back in time. It can be done."

"What about the causality violation? I know what you said before, but this is different. What if, having received the paper, you decided not to send it, or to write something different on it?"

"Then I would have changed the past, and the message would be as I then had written it; or there would have been no message, and I would not be here telling you I had done it. The original would have come from an alternative, now virtual future. It is the same. It does not matter how an object from the future changes that future. Whether I choose to fulfil that future or change it makes no difference. By the time we got to this point of me showing you my results, the message sent and the message received would be the same."

"So what do we do now?"

"Now we need to tell the others. We could not afford for them to forbid these experiments, for that would be our doom. But now we can answer their fears, or at least answer them well enough. And now we need them. We cannot do this alone. We need to discover not only where to go but what to do when we get there."

"They will be working for their own deaths."

"As are we. If the best and brightest of what remains of the human race cannot find it within themselves to achieve the one hope of humanity, then perhaps we do not deserve to live. And it is not as if the reality we are changing is one truly worth fighting for. The lives of everyone outside the Egg are already gone, and our own time comes upon us soon enough."

"Still, the desire to live is strong. Perhaps this should be another secret, revealed only to those we can trust."

"The secret will not stand, and if it is discovered before time, we might not survive their rage at what they may well feel is betrayal."

Arragath sighed. "I wish I could say they would be wrong. All right. Any fears of arbitrary unknown causality violations will be allayed by the experiments you have already done, which were certainly allowable under our Charter. High stakes are our way of life. As for the rest, it is research, not action. We will not be doing anything risky until we have learned much more. Those who wish to help will help. Those who wish to pursue other hopes are free to pursue them. We do not need to decide until the decision is forced upon us. That will take some time."

"At least we still have the time," added Pachmeny. "Much as I fear what we are about to do, I sometimes wake up in a sweat at the fear that you could easily have discovered it too late. That we would have had the answer, or the hope of an answer, in our hands too late to use it."

Baronak cleared his throat, looking uncomfortable. "About that… I don't think it is actually a… a coincidence. Or luck."

"What do you mean?"

"I have been thinking about it. I worked out the solution when I looked at a transformation of the equations I had done, which gave me the clue that the essence was spacetime, not space, and that I should look at the time component."

He stared at them, his eyes dark with something that looked like fear, but wasn't. "I had written them down one night when I was tired, and they just got buried. Or so I thought. But they were radical; radical enough that when I saw them again I had to follow them to their end. Radical enough that there is no way I could have thought of them one night then just gone to bed, no matter how tired I was. Let alone forgot what I had done."

He swallowed, his throat suddenly dry. Then he continued.

"I do not remember writing them."

They stared at him.

"Not only do I not remember writing them, but I have never seen that piece of paper again."

"Are you saying…?"

"Yes. Nobody could have taken it. Besides myself only Jennara was there, and she had neither opportunity nor motive to remove it. I remember clearly putting it aside, but when I reached for it to show her, it was no nowhere to be found."

"Then…?"

"Yes. I think after who knows how many years, how many decades, we discovered the solution. But by then it was too late. Maybe there weren't enough people left, or we were all dying, or the power plants were too weak to do more than send a scrap of paper back a few decades. It must have been me who sent it back, as it was in my handwriting, though weak. I would have been cautious. So I chose a time I remembered when I could send it back without my seeing it arrive, but when I knew I would still see it soon enough afterwards, notice it and realize its importance. I would certainly have remembered my first night with Jennara, and realized it was the best opportunity I would ever have. Not so early I would fail to understand, not too late to develop it to fruition, and at a time when I was working on this very problem."

He paused. "I have no proof. All I know is I have no memory of thinking of those equations, and their origin has vanished as if it never was. I think my future self was unable to do anything with the discovery. So he passed it on to his own past."

24. Emissary

Not everyone in the shelter was happy with their proposal; not everyone was happy that it had been taken as far as it had without there even being a proposal.

But they were intelligent people and they knew why they were here. If they feared death, they knew their deaths should have been years in the past, had they or their parents not been saved by moving into the Egg to do the very project that might now erase them from reality. They also knew their history. If Pachmeny, Arragath and Baronak had acted in secret in order to follow the only solution they could see: well, exactly the same process was why they were now breathing.

Some thought the plan insane and refused to have anything to do with it. Others thought the plan had merit but hoped for a better way. But a clear majority agreed to its necessity, while delaying the final decision until all knew what that decision actually entailed. They all knew that no good choices would be available.

And so the thrust of most work in the shelter moved toward a way to repair the past, in order to buy as much time as possible for people they would never know and who would never know them.

The problems were immense. Before they could start they needed some idea of what to start on. Baronak called all the group leaders to a meeting to clarify the issues.

"All right," he said, "here is where we are now.

"We know we can send objects, even a person, back through time. Our goal is to send one or the other back to some point where they can do something to save the future. There are all sorts of possibilities.

But what we know is that the more we change then, the more we alter the future and the more we risk making things worse. Our problem is we simply don't know enough, and we don't have the time to find out enough to be safe making radical changes. Earth as a home that can nurture mankind is already gone. We will be following it soon enough.

"Our first risk is time. We have run out of time to solve the problem of escaping the supernova. And the more time that passes, the more our equipment degrades and the more our own bodies degrade. We must act soon, and decide sooner.

"But our biggest risk is that we can only do this once. We can't try one thing, look, evaluate, then try something else. Once we change the past we will no longer be here to try again.

"Against that, our biggest advantage is that before we change the past we can safely spy on it. We can do that at a self-repairing quantum level, so mere spying will not change the future.

"However our spying is limited. There is much we do not understand and problems we don't know how to solve. We can send our burrows through time, anchored to the gravity well of Earth, and peek around at any location on Earth. But not all times and spaces are available to us. Spacetime is complex, and parts of it are inaccessible to the precision of our technology, or the amount of energy we can apply, or both. And the equipment cannot be run continuously. Between probes we must recalibrate it, and also allow the disturbed quantum spacetime to recover. So we can't learn just anything we want to. We can't go everywhere and we can go only a limited number of times.

"We are also severely limited in what we can do, which constrains what is worth learning how to do. Anything we send back will not last long in the past. We cannot send a library of all our knowledge back to the start of our re-ascent as a technological species: even if they could read it, and knew what to do with it, it would be gone before they could read or copy a fraction of it.

"So all we can do is send a person back: an emissary who is not passive, but active and reactive. A person who can do enough in the limited time they have to change the future. And not just change the future—that is guaranteed. But change it in a way that makes things better.

"We cannot project enough power into the past to shift the great forces of history. But if we can find the right point, a cusp upon which the future turns, then we have a chance. We cannot be time engineers, but we can be time surgeons. Able to make one small incision: small enough that it is within our power, but big enough in its consequences to save the world."

The room was silent.

"That is all for now. Take this to your people and discuss it. Any questions, you know where to find us." He gave a faint smile. "We aren't going anywhere."

Over the next weeks the arguments raged. Even those who opposed the program on principle joined in on a debate too interesting to ignore.

The essence of human beings, our distinctive feature that distinguishes us from all other animals, is our ability to think. With that come the intellectual pleasures of problem-solving in our own mind and intellectual debate with other minds outside it. Inside our minds our own opinions are undisputed king; outside it are many other kings. Yet when our king essays out on his battles it is rare that he is defeated: usually returning victorious or bloody but unbowed, at least in the court of our own mind.

It is a curious phenomenon of evolution that traits evolved for survival can, in the course of time, become a drive in their own right, no longer inherently linked to survival. And thus the need to eat becomes the pleasure of high cuisine, sought even after the needs of survival are met. Thus sex becomes an end in itself, even past the age of reproduction; even if the one you love is sterile; even if, for some, your lover is the same sex and your copulations incapable of producing a child. Love, evolved as the handmaiden of sex, is now a supreme value in its own right.

And so the fascination of the problem drew most of the population into the argument, even though whatever they did their doom was certain; even though the better their solution, the sooner that doom might descend upon them.

The most obvious solution was to prevent the Burning, the disastrous war that had destroyed the Ancients. The Burning had set humanity's progress back by tens of millennia. If it had not occurred, who knew what powers mankind might now possess? And if the powers of millennia of uninterrupted scientific progress were not enough to save mankind, then nothing was.

Hope began to grow in the collective consciousness of the people of the shelter. An ironic hope, as none of them would be its beneficiaries, but hope nonetheless.

A hope that would be dashed.

"I only wish it were possible," Arragath told the assembled crowd. "But we have seen in their ruins the scale of the war that claimed the Ancients. How could we hope to prevent it?"

"So we give up?" cried a voice from the back. "All this, all we have endured, all that we have done: and we give up, because it is too hard?"

Then Baronak spoke.

"I agree we should not give up. Must not give up. But we cannot stop the Burning."

He looked around the crowd, seeing their eyes watchful upon him.

"Even if we found the power to turn aside ruin at that scale, still we could not stop their war: because it is beyond our reach. The war was nuclear. Nuclear energy is fundamentally a quantum process. Such concentrated power as unleashed during nuclear explosions disturbs the quantum foam that fills spacetime. The war of the Burning disturbed it too much. It created instabilities, that like our own burrows propagate through time. We have tried, but we cannot create a stable endpoint during the war or for months before or after it. And if we cannot create a stable endpoint, we cannot open a burrow.

"At the times we have been able to reach there is tension in the world but nothing special, no more than there had been for years. No drumbeats building to war. Its origin is lost in a fog we cannot penetrate.

"The barrier is not absolute. If we had higher energy levels available, or more advanced and precise technology, I believe we could send our burrows even to the center of the war. The equations allow it. But we do not have it. Now, we can never have it. We are out of time."

First there was silence; then a low murmur, like an ocean restlessly surging against a shore. Finally someone gave voice to their mood.

"Then what can we do? If we cannot stop the Burning, we have failed. Our great project is for nothing. Our lives have been spent on nothing. What would you have us do?"

Again Baronak looked around the room.

"I too hoped we could stop the war. As did Arragath. As did Pachmeny. If you feel despair now, know we have already felt it.

"But there is hope. What we lack is time. Perhaps we can create some. Not for ourselves: it is too late for that. But if we cannot stop the Burning, what if we can accelerate the rediscovery of science after it? So that instead of the mere years our people had, those who will live in our place will have decades or centuries more to find a solution?

"We have been thinking about this, ever since we found that we could not pierce the barrier around the Burning. Do not damn us for not telling you. Until two days ago our hope remained alive. For those two days we have lived with the despair you feel now. Would you have thanked us if all we brought you was our own desolation?

"No. So first we had to think ourselves. We would rather offer hope than despair."

He looked at his mother. "You all know Pachmeny. Our destroyers are named after her. I think this is properly her tale."

Pachmeny stood and, like her son, let her gaze wander over the crowd. Her friends. Some, her enemies. But all her people. All traveling with her on a dangerous journey whose stakes were the highest in the world.

"This is what we think," she said. "We must provide our ancestors with enough information to make a meaningful difference to their scientific progress.

"We can only give them simple, minimal information: small enough that we can impart it in the short time we have in the past, yet enough for one or a few people to understand, believe and act on. We cannot tell them everything. We can only tell them enough, and leverage their own actions in order to do the rest.

"We cannot send back enough of our own scientific knowledge to achieve that. Thus our own ancestors since the Burning cannot be taught. But the Ancients themselves already knew what we know, and often more.

"Therefore, we must find a way to preserve and then recover the knowledge of the Ancients faster than happened in our own history. This knowledge has to somehow survive the end of the Ancients themselves, then the millennia of the Dark Ages, in a form their descendants—people who will be like our own ancestors— will be able to understand.

"And we have to do that in a single, brief meeting between a person from the future and one from the past.

"So here is what we have to do, all of us. We already know how the language of the ancients was written. Now we need to learn how it was spoken.

"We have to find a person, or perhaps a small group, from the past who will not only believe our story but be able to do something about it.

"Then someone has to go back, and persuade them."

After much discussion, finally a consensus was reached.

And so the final generation of the human race began their last and greatest project.

~~~

Pachmeny looked up from her desk at the faint, timid tapping at her open door. Tired as she was, she could not help the smile that came to her face when she saw her visitor.

She recognized the diffident young woman who stood there. She had known her as an intelligent but deeply shy girl whose dark eyes, on the few occasions she allowed you to look into them, dragged you down into depths whose bottom was only hinted at, never seen. Pachmeny had watched her grow into a beautiful and still very private woman. But despite the mark of genius the perceptive could discern, she had not excelled in any one field. Instead she appeared content to flitter from place to place, like a butterfly who found the variety of flowers in her world too beguiling to settle for long on any one kind.

If she lacked depth of knowledge in any one field, her breadth of knowledge was unmatched. And her peculiar talent was an ability to think of creative solutions and to see connections that nobody else suspected. Thus she had been given, or more accurately taken, a kind of roving commission to go over the growing body of data from the spy burrows that had been sent back to pepper the timeline in the decades leading up to the death of the Ancients, and to follow its clues wherever she would.

"Greetings, Emmerline," she said. "Come in. Sit. What can I do for you?"

"Greetings, Pachmeny. I found a snippet of information that caught my attention. I booked some time on the Burrower to learn some more. I think I have found something. Someone."

"Explain."

"I came across a story about a man. It was not a complimentary story. He founded a new religion, one that many people did not like."

Emmerline paused and seemed to turn her gaze inward, as if trying to disassemble an idea she held in its interlinked totality, into a narrative that would make sense to another. Pachmeny could tell from her face that this was no idle exercise to her; that Emmerline felt the future might depend on her ability to persuade others of what she saw.

"So this religion," Pachmeny asked to help her out, "was it plausible? Was it successful?"

Emmerline made an ironic face. "In the world of religion, those are two separate questions. Plausible? From my understanding of it, it was one of the silliest religions ever invented, and it's not as if there's no competition there. No, I cannot understand why anybody would be as fanatical about it as many were. But whatever formula he hit on, he was either very lucky or knew a lot about human psychology. Somehow it became very successful, rich and powerful, in mere decades. So strong that even powerful enemies failed to bring them down despite numerous attempts."

Now Emmerline leaned forward, her eyes finally boring into Pachmeny's, as if willing her to follow her thoughts and to understand.

"Then I remembered those famous relics, the works of the great Newton and Einstein preserved in the Abbey of the Caves. It occurred to me that religion can generate a level of loyalty, if not fanaticism, well beyond reason. That where reasonable men might doubt or waver, men of faith can maintain their belief not only beyond what is reasonable, but against reason itself. I wondered whether those relics would have been preserved at all over all those millennia if they had been left in the care of reasonable men seeking reasonable goals, and not entrusted to a cult hiding in the mountains.

"If that was all, I would have run with this idea in other directions. But the story mentioned something else. This was an unusual man. He wasn't the typical founder of a religion, neither mystic nor rebel priest. He was a writer. He wrote stories in what the Ancients called 'science fiction': a kind of speculative tale or fantasy based on scientific facts or theories. And he claimed his religion was based on science.

"So understandably, some of his opponents accused him of making the whole thing up. Of realizing that an idea that might earn him a modest amount as the plot of just another of his works of fiction, soon forgotten, could bring him far more if he used it to found a religion, and possibly bring him everlasting fame as well.

"But it occurred to me that such a man might be receptive to our tale. That a man steeped in both flights of imagination and an interest in scientific reality might possess the perfect combination of traits. Intelligence, knowledge, and above all flexibility of thinking.

"On its own, that isn't much. The poets and storytellers of our own history were not renowned for building monuments. But his man also had the boldness to take on the entire world.

"On its own, a religion isn't much either. They have their own hierarchy and politics. Their own faith, which can blind them to what we need them to understand and do. To subvert an established religion can fail in so many ways. To take over a minor sect is risky in so many others.

"But the two together? Here we have a rich religion, founded by a single man of imagination and brilliant boldness. Run by a hierarchy bound by layers of secret doctrine, where the higher you rise, the more arcane secrets are revealed to you."

Now she leaned forward, the palms of her hands on Pachmeny's desk. "Pachmeny, our entire theory assumes that history is not some vast, deterministic monolith. That for all the forces that drive it and cannot be turned, yet still it might pivot on one man or one action. That it is chaotic, like some say of the weather: that the chirping of a cricket somewhere across the ocean can trigger a hurricane on our shores.

"This is the man. This is the time. Maybe what we are trying is impossible. But this is our best chance."

Then she fell silent, her idea now woven complete in the air between them. She noticed herself leaning on Pachmeny's desk and straightened to just stand there, biting her lower lip in anxiety.

Pachmeny stood up slowly and extended her hand. "Emmerline, that is brilliant. We need to study some more and learn some more. But Emmerline… perhaps you have saved the world."

~~~

The crowd was silent as Salidor walked slowly up the main promenade of the public area.

Many had volunteered for this trip, but unless some grave tragedy had befallen him Salidor was always going to be the chosen one. He was a genius in a world of geniuses, and his particular talent was language. Nobody could equal his facility with other tongues, the speed with which he could grasp the essentials of another language's grammar and idioms, or his power to mimic accents.

Now he would be their emissary to the past.

Not everyone was here. Some had chosen not to see, but to spend the next minutes or hours with their loved ones, their favorite activity, or simply communing with the universe. But most were here, drawn by the same need. Displays had been set up, but there was no feed yet and they were dark except for a faint deep blue radiance.

Their eyes followed his journey toward the entrance to the prime Burrow Generator, which had been examined, calibrated and refined to as great a peak of perfection as their technicians could achieve. Pachmeny, Arragath and Baronak stood there, as silently watchful as the crowd. When Salidor reached them, he grasped each of their arms in turn; none felt the need to speak. All the words that could ever be said had been said, and now nothing remained but to act.

He turned toward the crowd and waved his arm slowly in farewell. They raised their arms in silent salute. Then he turned and went inside.

Pachmeny sat with her family, as they watched the nearest display. It sprang to life, showing the scene they knew so well, and then the meeting that might change fate. Then she could watch no longer, and for all that she had understood and planned and believed, the finality of it broke out in some last gasp of struggle, and she convulsively grasped Arragath, burying her head in his chest. He stroked her hair as she sobbed into his shirt.

Oh Arragath, my love! Baronak, my son! It is so hard. Soon we shall be no more, not now, not ever. Yet it is real. It was real. I feel you, my love; I remember it all. How can it not be real, when it is so real? Hold on, my love. Hold on as long as our breath continues. Hold on! Hold on! Hold

Part C:
Legacy

Tho' much is taken, much abides; and tho'
We are not now that strength which in old days
Moved earth and heaven, that which we are, we are;
One equal temper of heroic hearts,
Made weak by time and fate, but strong in will
To strive, to seek, to find, and not to yield.

Tennyson, Ulysses

---

25. Ron

Ron lounged in a darkened booth near the back of the bar, nursing a scotch on the rocks. It had been a successful couple of days, meeting lots of fans; receiving the adulation due to a leading author—some of the adulation more intimate than others.

He stretched his arms and legs in satisfaction, popping out the kinks. He had had enough of the talking, festivities and girls for now, and just wanted to settle into his own thoughts, lubricated by a bit of lone drinking. So he sat with his back to the bar, facing the wall and the empty red leather-bound bench under it, hoping nobody would recognize him. He felt—peculiar. For all his success he felt that there was something missing. That taking people along on his flights of fancy for the span of time they took to read his books wasn't enough. That he could do more. His words gave him power over people's minds, and the power called to him with a siren song filled with promise but empty of instruction.

He smiled at his own mood, taking another sip of the liquor, enjoying its flame, its own power to lead men to pleasure, or oblivion, or destruction. He gazed into the amber depths of his glass, as if seeking knowledge or inspiration. It stared back at him, daring him to implement the plan that had been playing in his mind for some time now. He had already essayed a probe, a preliminary skirmish to test how easily he could win the battle for men's minds. Some were well armed and easily shrugged off the attempt, like a knight contemptuously fending off a peasant armed with a shovel. But a surprising number came naked into any battle of the mind and would believe anything. But did he dare take the next step?

So he frowned when a man slid smoothly into the seat opposite him, uninvited. He studied the man sourly. Not a drunk, and not an accidental meeting: the man was clear-eyed and intent, his peculiar dark blue eyes probing beneath straight eyebrows, a slight smile playing over his lips. He looked young, yet something about him spoke of age and experience. His face was strange: a face and nose too narrow with eyes too wide and far apart; and Ron wondered what peculiar confluence of ancestry had spawned such an otherworldly appearance. Not that he cared.

"Go 'way. Look, I appreciate all you want to tell me, but can you do it tomorrow? I need some space, you know. You people don't own me. Hey, don't get me wrong, I love you all, I love all my fans! But this is my time, OK? We all need our own time."

The man smiled at that, as if Ron had made a particularly witty comment. "I won't take up any more of your time than I need to, sir."

His accent was as strange as his appearance. He spoke fluently and well, but there was something slightly off about it; as if it was contaminated by some foreign accent Ron could not place.

"'Sir', is it? Well, if you want to show your respect, how about you do it in more than words and eff off? Tomorrow, as they say in the classics, is another day. Words are cheap and peace is precious."

"I've come a long way to see you, sir, and cannot stay long. It will be worth your while to hear me out."

"Yeah? An investment, is it? Buy me another drink and I might consider it."

"I'm sorry, sir, I can't do that."

"Why the hell not? Who are you, the Christian Temperance League?"

"Nothing like that. I just don't have any money."

"Well I hope you don't think I'm giving you any."

"No, sir. I did not come here to beg. But it is funny you mention the Christian Temperance League. I did come here to talk about religion."

Ron groaned. *Great. This is the last thing I need.* "Listen, pal. You seem like a nice enough fellow. What are you, Mormon? You've got their clean-cut, intense look. But whatever you're selling, I ain't buying. Marx said religion was the opiate of the masses. Do I look like a mass to you?"

The man smiled, again as if Ron had made another witty joke. "No, I am not a Mormon, but that is as good an example as any."

"Example of what?" asked Ron, instantly regretting it. *You idiot, surely you know never to let them stick their foot in the door. Now you'll never get rid of him.*

"That some people will believe anything, even when the rest of the world can't imagine why they do."

Ron raised an eyebrow, intrigued despite himself that the man had voiced his own thoughts of only a minute ago. "You're a funny evangelist."

"Oh, I am no evangelist. Did you know 'evangelist' means a bringer of good news? I am afraid all my news is bad."

"For whom? Me?"

"For you, no. Quite the reverse, in many ways. Though whether you will come to think of it as good or bad depends on how heavily the future weighs upon your soul."

"I'm an 'eat, drink and be merry for tomorrow you die' kind of guy. The future can take care of itself."

"You are at once prophetic and most terribly wrong."

"What in hell do you mean by that?!"

"I mean the future will need a bit of help." Then he proceeded to explain.

~~~

When the strange man had finished speaking, Ron burst out laughing.

"That, my friend," he chortled with a grin, "is the best story pitch I've ever heard. If I wasn't such an honest guy, I'd be tempted to steal it for myself."

He laughed into his drink then shook his head. "Oh, boy! So let me guess. You're a budding science fiction writer, looking for a leg-up? An end run around the gatekeepers of the publishing world? Well, I have to hand it to you, after that performance, you deserve it. So sure, I'll help you, if that's what you're after."

"I do not want my story published. Ever. Just for you to do your part. Most of which you intend doing anyway."

"What do you mean by that?"

Salidor told him.

Ron just stared at him, wondering what his game was. He certainly knew too much about Ron's plans for padding out his resume. Yet all he seemed to know were hints, not the full story. And there had been no intimation of exposure or blackmail in the man's story, just a dry recital of facts. But Ron hadn't been born yesterday.

"You tell an interesting story, friend," he drawled at length. "With the emphasis on 'story'. You have to admit, it is another great plot and you spin a good yarn, but it isn't very plausible."

"Neither is the religion you will found."

"The religion you say I will found. I dunno what you're talking about. Anyway, if you know that, I guess you know whether I carry out your wishes or not. And if you want my help, maybe you shouldn't insult what you tell me is going to be my life's work."

Not that he's wrong. The whole idea was just to win that bet with Heinlein that I can go one up on the Mormons. Not that I'm ever going to admit that to anyone.

"I apologize for my poor mastery of the nuances of your language," replied Salidor. "I assure you I meant no insult, merely that you are a man of great imagination to whom mere implausibility is not a fatal barrier. But I expected you to need more. My words were merely to prepare the ground. To prepare your mind. Now I will show you."

Ron tensed as the man reached into a pouch hanging at his waist, but relaxed as he pulled out a set of some kind of goggles with a strap.

"I cannot prove what I say, but I can show you something even your imagination will find hard to explain away. Here. Examine it."

Ron took it hesitantly, turning it over, studying it. It looked like a set of wrap-around sunglasses with a strap to hold them snugly on your head. He held it up to his eyes but could not see through the lens.

"So what the hell is this?"

"Put it on so it comfortably covers your eyes."

Ron obeyed. "Great, I'm blindfolded. Now what? You going to hustle me into a car and take me somewhere to make me an offer I can't refuse?"

"Tap the right lens with your finger."

Ron reached up and felt the smooth glass or whatever it was; he tapped it and jerked back. The device had come alive, filling his field of vision with a detailed geometric design. "Whoa! What is this thing? Some kind of picture show? Some kind of tiny TV?"

"It is that, and also what you would call a computer."

"A computer? You need a truck to move one of those. You can't just slip one over your head."

"Quite so. Yet this is a computer. It is what they are... in my time.

Now watch. See what my time is like. Tap the lens again. You can also tap the left lens to pause or push down longer on it to go back."

Ron gave the button another nervous tap and the image was replaced by a photo. It looked just like a color photo: there was no flicker like on a television, no static, not even any visible dots, and he wondered what magic could have produced it. *No magic I know of, at any rate.*

The photo showed the man before him, dressed in strange garb and standing before an even stranger machine. A crowd of people stood near him, equally queerly dressed. But the strangest thing was that the man's face, which earlier he had considered odd, was not odd at all among these people.

He whispered, shocked, "Is this... is this... real?"

"Yes. Now touch the right lens with your finger for a second."

Ron did so, and nearly fell from his chair in surprise when the image began to move. And not only move, but move as a three-dimensional full color scene: he could not tell the difference from actually being there. He watched, enthralled. *I can imagine—just—that someone might have mocked up that picture. But* this? *How is it possible?*

He wondered what would happen if he moved his head. He grabbed the edge of the table reflexively as the scene moved smoothly, as if it were real and he was standing there in the middle of it.

Nor was it just vision: sound accompanied the strange movie, projected into his ears by the band of the glasses. The man was speaking, and others were responding. But the language was like none he had ever heard.

He ripped the device from his head; stared at it; stared at the man in amazement.

"Jesus Christ!"

"Watch more."

So Ron did. He experienced the peculiar combination of a room so real it was like he was standing in it, in which stood a big television with grainy images of a man walking on the moon. The moon movie had an inset of a congratulatory speech by the President of the United States, who looked disturbingly like that dick Nixon. He saw cities that looked like cover art from *Amazing Stories*, with giant jet aircraft zooming over them. Then he saw images of ruined cities, full of dark and broken towers; lakes of fractured glass; the whole horrible history of a world gone to ruin. A world of forests, ice and death.

The scene jumped and now he saw strange vehicles, strange cities, heard strange music. He saw scenes from what looked like a museum: with some kind of preserved tablets, one summarizing the theories of Newton, the other of Einstein. He saw images of the night sky, images in which the familiar constellations were distorted by time. He saw an image of two tiny stars, then a time lapse movie of their deadly dance, and what looked like an artist's conception turned into a 3D movie of the two meeting, then pouring a rain of deadly fire onto the Earth.

He tore the glasses off his eyes and let them dangle from his neck.

"No. No. It can't be! This is some kind of trick!"

"I am afraid not."

"So… what's with… what's with that final thing? The two stars?"

"That is why I am here. They are too close to Earth, and when they merge they become what you call a supernova. By the time we learn about it, it is too late. We have lost too much, taken too much time to recover, and have no defense. If we only had a few more hundreds or thousands of years, perhaps we would have known how to escape it. But we did not. We did what we could but the race of Man is finished. If any life remains at all on planet Earth it is microbes. By the time they evolve back into beings who can contemplate the stars, if they ever do, our Sun itself will be old and will do much the same job. This is our only hope. To buy time.

"It is extraordinarily dangerous to change the timeline. If not for those stars, humanity would have picked itself up from its ruin and gone on. Much sadder but much wiser. We would have lost thirty thousand years, but that isn't much on an Earth already over four billion years old. But now it is risk changing time, or die forever."

"OK, pal. So say I believe you. From what you say, our civilization is destroyed by what looks like a nuclear war. And you want me to try to preserve our knowledge to help the future. But… why that? Why not try to stop the war?"

"Nobody would believe you. You would have to give up telling people or end your quest locked away for madness. In either case your power to preserve any future at all would be negated. Frankly, I don't know how you got away with what you did get away with. If you start raving about visitors from the future giving you a mission to save the planet, you will become a laughing stock and guarantee your failure."

"Then why not leave me this device? As proof?"

"I am leaving it with you but it cannot help you convince others. It is my final proof to you, not the world."

"What do you mean?"

"You will see. Then you will believe, for you will have seen with your own eyes, and understood."

"OK… OK… say that's true. But I don't have to say why. I can devote my cause to world peace, or something! Maybe that will stop it from happening!"

"I have risked enough coming here. The future from this point is already uncertain. Please, please, for the sake of all you hold sacred, for the life of the human race: perform your mission in secret, as I asked. That way the futures we saw tracking back to this point will look the same. If you diverge from it, if you start trying to alter history for the better, you risk changing it for the worse. Perhaps the war will not happen but another, worse war will take its place. Perhaps the safe places we identified will be gone, and all your legacy with them. We can't risk it."

"But if I do anything… how much of the future will I change?"

"Consider how unlikely your own birth was: the fine tuning it took for particular men to meet particular women over the generations leading to you; not to mention the particular circumstances leading to one sperm over another fertilizing an egg at one time or another. There is a mathematics that describes this, and it basically means the future is unpredictable: tiny changes ripple forward through time until everything is changed, sooner than you might think.

"If you act in secret, if an observer from the future could tell no difference from the history of my timeline from this moment on, then you will still cause changes but they will not matter. They might not even ripple past the near singularity that strikes world history when civilization falls and nearly everyone dies anyway. Perhaps nothing will change until your legacy is rediscovered millennia hence. Or perhaps things will change but too little to matter. In any case the future of the race turns on what we do today. We dare not meddle any more than we have to, for then we risk the failure of all we seek."

The man paused, and stared into Ron's eyes. "I told you that meddling with history is dangerous. It is madness to attempt it, for you can easily make things worse than they were, and nothing but the death of all humanity would compel me to do it."

"Then why put this on my shoulders?! If you're so afraid of my small changes failing, why not have more guts? Why not jump in and change the lot yourself? Why not use your damn time machines to find out what actually caused the war, and stop it right there?!"

"We could not study the war. Our technology, great as it would seem to you, was not powerful enough to overcome the quantum disturbances caused by nuclear warfare. All we could do was hunt further away in time until we could find some other way to help the far future."

The man paused, slowly swirling his drink, before lifting his eyes again to Ron's.

"We believe that sometimes the great wheel of history can be changed by one man. Maybe not the war itself. Even if we had the power to learn its causes, I suspect the forces bringing your world's doom are too wide and vast for anybody to stop them, let alone one man with less than an hour to act.

"Then we found you. A man who might change history. So here I am."

Ron groaned and put his head in his hands. "It was all meant to be a prank, you know…"

"Perhaps your prank will save the world."

"Or perhaps I'll screw it up royally and be personally responsible for the annihilation of humanity!"

"You will do what you will, as did I."

"Speaking of you: what happens to you?"

"If you do nothing, maybe the ripples of our meeting will die out and not pass through the bottleneck of the war. Then maybe I will be pulled back to my time and will know I failed. But most likely, even if you do nothing my personal future will no longer exist. I will no longer exist."

"And yet you are here. Doesn't that prove I failed?"

"No. Do not ask me to explain the theory. Just understand that I can come from a timeline that existed but no longer does. Or will."

"Right… So this is a suicide mission? You left home knowing you would never return? Hoping you would never return?"

"The death of all I loved would not be delayed much longer. Better to save it, even if it never exists. If that makes any sense."

Ron stared at him, appalled. Finally he whispered, "And I thought this was tough on me…"

The man shook himself and stared into space as if gazing at something only he could see. "Enough. My time here is ending and you should leave. I can't be completely sure what will happen to things in my immediate vicinity when I go."

Ron stood. The strange glasses still dangled around his neck. Then he reached out and shook the man's hand. "Well, man from the future. How do I say goodbye to someone like you? I guess... if man has a soul, may yours find peace somewhere."

The man nodded and gripped Ron's forearm, leaving Ron's hand free. After a moment's hesitation, Ron gripped back. Strangely, this different farewell of another culture from another time made it more real to Ron than even the visions in the glasses.

"Thank you. Farewell, Ron. Do what you must, and take whatever joy life gives you in the meantime."

Ron backed away a few steps then stood there, unable to move further, unable to take his eyes off the man who now stood looking back at him with a sad smile. As if he had dropped his child in Ron's lap with inadequate instructions and hoped against hope that Ron would know what to do with it. And as if at the last sight he would see on Earth.

Then he was nothing but intense blackness in a faint rainbow haze, and was gone.

Ron stepped back in shock, colliding with something soft that emitted a squeak in response.

He spun around and found himself looking into the face of an attractive young woman sitting on a bar stool.

"Oh! Sorry, young lady! My clumsiness!"

"That's all right, no harm done. Say... don't I know you? Aren't you..."

"Shhh!" he interrupted, "Secret mission!" he added with a smile.

She returned the smile. "So who's your friend?"

"My friend?"

"The guy you were talking to, him over... oh! That's strange! Where'd he go?"

Ron spun to look, though he already knew there was nothing there. Involuntarily, his hand went to his neck, but the glasses were gone. He had not even felt them go. *As if... as if they had never been there.*

Shaken, he turned to look at the girl. "But you saw him, right? I was talking to some guy, right?"

She looked at him, amused. "Are you ok? Sure, you were talking to some guy. Ever since I got here, about ten minutes ago."

"I don't suppose you noticed whether I had some funny looking glasses on? Hanging around my neck?"

She frowned. "Yeah, I think you had something like that. Why?"

'My final proof to you,' he said.

Not that they are there, but that they were but now are not.

Holy Mother of God.

"You know," he said to her, "I wasn't feeling like any more company tonight, but suddenly I think the last thing I want to do is go up to my room alone."

The woman smiled, crossed her legs and leaned back against the bar. "Oh, really?" she replied in a voice suddenly more husky than it had been.

Ron felt a familiar fire below his stomach, reality attempting its rally against the unreality of the evening. "Really."

26. THE ALPHA AND THE OMEGA

Ron looked out the window of his latest country mansion, lost in thought. He had done well over the years, the lies and deceptions not weighing too heavily on his soul. *It is all for the greater good, isn't it? Doesn't that justify anything? Or was it all stuff and nonsense, with me the greatest fool of them all? The man who would be the world's greatest conman, victim of history's greatest con.*

But now he was getting old, and he could feel the aches in his bones speaking to him that his part in the saga was drawing to a close. *Will I live to see it? Will I live to see it a lie? If there is someone to pray to, please let it be a lie.*

He knew he should live to see it. His mysterious visitor would not reveal all the details. Perhaps it was as he had said, and the danger of knowing too much was a danger too far. Or perhaps he did not know himself. But he had been firm that Ron had time to prepare, time to build the plan, time to execute it. Plenty of time, but it had to be completed before the end of the year 1983. Decades away. A lifetime.

But time had passed, as it always does, with nobody able to say where it had gone or, once it had passed, how the decades stretching so far into the future could be as mist once they had gone.

And now it was September 1983, and Ron was afraid. *I do not know whether to fear that I have done it all for naught, or that I have not done enough.*

When that passenger jet had been shot down, the lives of all those people on a routine flight turning to flame and ashes, his senses had gone into high alert. But nothing had happened and he had calmed down. Yet his fear felt particularly sharp and in focus today. *Perhaps his visit entangled me with the timelines, and I can sense the coming apocalypse.*

He frowned. *Or my mind is going. The ramblings of an old man.*

He tapped the ash from his cigar into the silver ashtray on the low marble table beside him. He liked marble. The cool, elegant stone, speaking of the lives of a billion shellfish who had struggled and lived and died, bequeathing their skeletons to the ages; the mysterious swirls speaking of the titanic forces that had converted limestone to marble. A stone that men would one day dig out of the earth and then, according to their talents, turn into the *David* or a table supporting an ashtray.

More ramblings of an old man? Get a grip, Ron.

He rang a bell, and one of the servants came to him, bearing the drink the servant knew he would request at this time of day. "Stay," ordered Ron, drawing more fragrant smoke into his lungs then tapping its ash into the tray.

"Sir." The man stood, as if at ease on a parade ground, unsure of why his presence was needed, sure only that obedience was his primary duty.

"It is a fine day, don't you think, Jensen? Blue skies, just a hint of wispy cloud, with the occasional hummingbird dancing like a butterfly among the flowers?"

"Yes, sir."

"And if I had said it is a foul day, with too hot a sun drawing out too much annoying wildlife, would you have said the same?"

"Yes, sir."

"What if I wanted an argument?"

"Then I would not know what to say, sir. You do not employ me to argue, a skill in which I am sure you are my superior; you employ me to serve, and so I do. Sir."

"Don't look so worried. I just need company. I don't know why."

"Is something wrong, sir?"

Ron looked to the far horizon, the blue Californian sky temporary home to a flock of clouds. *Like this is my own temporary home. But it is good here. A good place to live out the rest of my days, if I am given them to live in peace. Yes. I think we might keep this place. I have roamed enough for one lifetime.*

"Just thinking about the future, Jensen. Thinking about finally sending down roots, here. What do you think?"

"I think that is a fine idea, sir. You will have more time for thinking and writing."

"What, Jensen? Expressing an opinion?"

"You suggested you might want an argument, sir. I am testing the waters with an opinion."

Ron smiled faintly, the smile turning to a puzzled frown at something he thought he saw in the far sky. The nearest city lay in that direction, though you could not see it from this vantage. He felt an ugly flip in the pit of his stomach. *Don't be a fool. My, you are jumpy today, aren't you?* he scolded himself.

Then there was a bright flash from the horizon, brighter than the sun, and Jensen's eyes also jerked toward the sight.

"What the *fu... hell* was that!? ... Sir?"

To Jensen's surprise, or what room there was for another surprise in the presence of the first, Ron did not look surprised, or frightened, or any of the other emotions he might have expected. He just looked wearily sad, as if contemplating some immense disaster not suddenly facing him now but known from long ago.

That there was no terror in his face sent a shiver of ice to Jensen's belly, when Ron looked at him bleakly and replied calmly but with a steel certainty, "The end of the world, Jensen. The beginning of the end of the world. Let's get into that shelter you wondered why I had built, but first: radio out Emergency Code Omega. We have little time left, so let's not waste it."

For I am the alpha and the omega, the beginning and the end.

Code Omega would trigger those assigned to the Refuges to seal their new homes and begin scanning their communication channels for intelligence on the war. As far as possible the Refuges would pool resources and intelligence; where it was impossible they would do what they could. It was an idea Ron had come up with over the decades since the Visitation, and as he sat looking at the walls of his own refuge and into the fiery liquid in his glass, he wondered.

They wanted me to leave a legacy to another future. A way to help mankind restart, hopefully soon enough to make a difference. But what if there is a better way? So I will leave them my own legacy. Maybe they won't need it, our new children. But maybe they will... maybe they will...

27. The Long Night

The war was bad. As nuclear fires blossomed over once mighty cities, and too frequently eliminated leaders of states and nations, entire countries fell into anarchy fed by power loss, water loss, hunger and panic.

The paradox of modern civilization was that for all its power and sophistication it was fragile. Enormous cities were fed by food and resources drawn to their bosoms by gossamer webs of transport and communication; the regions that fed them in turn supported by the combined brains and energies of the millions in those cities, whose bounty fed back to them over those same threads.

And most people were peaceful. They were not gunmen expecting to live by their fighting skills, but people who worked, and raised their children; protected from the few who would prey upon them by a small number of police.

The police didn't have a chance. In some places, they became or joined the new warlords. In others, they held to their duty and died.

Not all cities were hit by the mushroom clouds, but too many were, and the countryside was invaded by hordes of the hungry, who rolled over the farmlands leaving destruction in their wake. The surviving cities lost their support, or too much of it, and fell in their own ways.

It was not enough to destroy civilization. The world fragmented from nation states into city states, many often retaining a loose political alliance. But the radioactive fallout spread in plumes across the country and around the world; more people died, more animals died, more plants died, in a vicious circle spiraling down to the world's doom.

But there were remnants, many poor and dying but some, by a combination of luck, location and grit, remaining strong. Much knowledge was retained, even in some places a degree of political freedom. So the world could have recovered from its tragedy. Perhaps in only a few hundred years. It would not have rivalled the past world in numbers, not yet: but may have approached it in technology.

But fate was not finished with mankind yet. The long dance between warmth and ice, so slow that mankind had barely noticed it in the frenetic pace of their own quick generations, turned to ice.

By inches, then at an accelerating pace, the remaining beacons of civilization began to flicker and die, and the ice marched on, oblivious to their fate.

The last remnants of civilization fell, and humanity descended into its long, cold night.

~~~

No matter how softly one treads, the faint, chaotic ripples of causality cannot be denied. However careful Ron was to fulfil the entreaty from the future with minimum disturbance, still subtle changes to the timelines of men and chance flowed outwards from his actions. Most of the ripples died in the war. The few that remained continued to fade in its deadly aftermath, until finally the last filament was cut, as if by some quantum Fate wielding her scissors on the threads of time.

And so darkness fell. But somewhere, buried against time and warded against fate, the knowledge of the Ancients slept, waiting.

28. TAMORABI

How long Tamorabi stood there in the snow he could not have said. When at last he opened his eyes again he looked out at the dark forest. There remained nothing behind him but the dead past; nothing ahead of him but the death of all he loved: a world of ice and wolves. Still the dead called to him with their strange lamentation. Yet underneath that was an even stranger music.

He frowned. He had not noticed it before but it was definitely there. The wind moaning through the broken city of the gods still keened like the wailing of the dead, but there was now more. There was something beguiling about the music, as if it held not despair but hope. Perhaps the dead were calling to him, knowing what he had lost, drawing him into their chill embrace. *But is it a trap, or a homecoming?*

Perhaps others had heard the music before him, only to flee in terror from the voices of the dead. But Tamorabi heard and believed. Tamorabi's people had never heard of the sirens whose lying songs lured unwary sailors to their deaths, but they had their own legends sounding the same warning. Maybe others had heard the music and also believed, only to be drawn to their deaths. Tamorabi did not know what he believed, or even whether he now sought life or death. He knew only that the music was a third way, neither the way to old death nor the way to new: but perhaps the only way to life.

So he turned back to the broken city, and began to search for what he knew not, only that it was there.

~~~

The sun had crawled handspans higher into the sky by the time he found it. It was hard travel in here, the ground littered with the bodies of fallen giants, with traps for the unwary that could break a leg or perhaps drop a man to a deeper doom where there was nobody to hear his cries. And the music changed with the changes in the wind, sometimes stopping entirely, more often seeming to come from yet another direction; all the while mocking him with its promise, while the other voices of the wind urged him on or lamented his failure.

The wind had died to a whisper and the music had stopped when he found his way through a tangle of ruins into a more open space. He stood at the base of a tower. Like most, its higher reaches had long crumbled, with skeletal fingers all that remained reaching for the sky, or perhaps for a former glory forever out of reach. But the base had survived, still clad in the adamantine stone that had clothed many other such buildings.

Except part of the wall facing him had also now collapsed, opening the base of the tower into a cave; fairly recently from the look of the jagged edges of its ruin, less darkened by the winds and rains of the ages. The sun was behind the building and no rays penetrated its depths. He stared into its blackness, wondering.

Then the wind returned and with it the music; louder now, and coming from the cave before him.

Now it beckoned him like the mouth of death, and suddenly he felt afraid. Perhaps after all he had been drawn here in punishment for violating the resting place of the gods. But he drew up his courage and entered.

When his eyes adjusted to the gloom he saw that the stone sheath had surrounded a space largely filled by a metal structure, like a womb nurturing the precious life within, or perhaps the hard shell of a nut. He touched the metal, still partly encased in some strange material, mainly transparent, in parts crazed, in other parts gone completely. *It is like an egg, left here to hatch; laid down by the gods or their dragons as their death drew nigh.*

The music came from it. It had a peculiar structure, and when the wind blew over its protuberances it caused the music, like some enormous type of pipe or harp. Or *like a chick calling from its egg to its mother, waiting to be hatched, hoping to be protected when it does. An now it calls to me.*

He explored further and came to a large door. It too was strangely shaped, with large curved shapes over its surface, and he wondered again at its meaning. He pushed at it but it would not move.

This is an egg. It is protected from forces attacking from without. But what is within needs to get out. That is why it sings to me.

He looked again at its strange structure. *The Gods were not infallible; their dead voices tell me that. Perhaps they knew their own fallibility and feared it. They mean this door to be pulled open. So these structures are handles: one might fall, just as their towers fell; two might crumble into rust; but only one needs survive.*

He paused, his fear rising at the imminence of action. *But if this is my death, what of it? I go to meet my wife and child in the land of shadows. The wife and child I failed. When I meet them there, will they welcome me? Or will they turn their backs and curse me to everlasting shame and loneliness?*

He rested his hand on the cool metal, feeling the faint vibration of its song.

But what if it is more than my own death? What if what I am about to do is the end of the world?

He thought about the world. His life as it had been. The lives of his family. The world of his people.

A world of wolves howling in the night.

The world is already ended.

So he grasped one of the handles and pulled with all his might. But the door would not move. He tried the other handles in turn. One, weakened by age, snapped off, and he tumbled backwards onto the floor as it came free. The others held, but none of them would open the door.

He sat back on a boulder, thinking. *Why would it call to me, if it does not seek to be freed? Does the chick in the egg call before its time? So perhaps only the worthy may free it: and I am not.*

He thought about the gods, the city he was in, and how far beyond his understanding it all was.

The wisdom of the Gods far exceeds mine, and perhaps it is wisdom they demand as the key to their secrets. But for all their wisdom, they are gone: and all that is left are mortal men like me. If they were wise, they must have been wise enough to allow for that.

He examined the door more closely. There was a circular object on it, a handspan wide, that at first he had taken for decoration. The pattern on its surface was a ring of arrows pointing inwards. Unlike the rest of the door, which was made of one of the mysterious durable metals of the Gods, the circle appeared to be of fired clay.

Fired clay lasts forever. But it is brittle.
Like an eggshell.

The circle stood proud of the surface of the door. From his belt he took a hammer and chisel. *Perhaps this is sacrilege, and I bring down on my own head the wrath of the gods. But the gods can punish me little more than they have already.*

He placed the edge of his chisel against the circle where it met the surface of the door, and pounded. Once. Twice. Three times. Then on his fourth try there was a loud cracking sound, and the circle broke into pieces and fell from the door.

He looked at where it had been. But all he had achieved was a smaller circle. The part he had broken off was like the cap of a mushroom, with its stalk still embedded in the door and now flush with its surface, other than the sharp irregularity of its shattered stub. He peered at it more closely, feeling around it with the tip of his finger. The mushroom's stalk was about a thumb's length wide and fit precisely into a hole in the metal; there seemed to be a layer of some other material around it, but so thin he could not be sure.

The gods protect their egg fiercely. Yet it is an egg. So surely they want it hatched, for what else is an egg for?

He placed his chisel on the plug and pounded down. It did not crack, but on the second stroke it seemed to him that it had moved a fraction. On the third stroke it definitely moved, now half a finger joint's length into the door. He paused, gathering his strength and his courage. He struck again with all his strength, and the plug moved a whole finger's length down the hole.

A noise began to come from the hole and he stepped back in fright. Then there was a loud pop, and a wind from the gods howled into the hole, small leaves and other airborne material flying down with it into a depth he dared not gaze upon.

Eyes wide, he pushed his back to the wall and inched away from the door. Then he sat in a corner, watching the eddies of wind and dust and leaves swirling in a mad dance, as their last act before being swirled to their doom; listening for he knew not how long to the howling, wondering whether it was rage or joy. *Perhaps the ghosts of the city now return to their home. Or leave ours.*

Finally the noise died to a whistling, then to a whisper, and then was quiet. Still he sat there, afraid to move. But when nothing happened, slowly he stood and returned to the door. He peered down the hole but there was nothing to see but the darkness.

Grasping a handle he heaved with all his might, and this time there was a slight cracking sound as the door opened a short distance. It stuck, but he managed to lever it further with a branch. Its ancient hinges were well made: after this initial resistance, it took no more than half his strength to pull and push the door fully open.

At first he did not understand what he saw. The opening faced another wall of a strange, lustrous metal, with complex scenes engraved upon it. The metal wall did not fully span the space, but curved away to the left, leaving a gap opening onto more darkness. He would need a flame to light his way before he dared accept its invitation.

He stared at the engraving, puzzling at its strange images. *That image, the one partway in from the left: it looks like this city as it is now. Not as it really looks, but similar: as if the artist knew what could happen but not what actually happened.*

Then he gasped in understanding.

This is the history of the world!

He examined the engraving more closely, trying to divine its full meaning. At the left was the city as it must have been in its glory: its towers intact, people teeming in its streets, strange objects apparently flying in its sky.

Then there was a rain of fire from the sky, flames coursing through the city, unimaginable destruction. Then nothing but a few people remaining, their civilization nothing but decay until slowly, small settlements appeared on the Earth. Homes like the ones he knew. The descendants of the gods, slowly crawling their way out of the dust.

So it is true. Not gods, but Ancient Ones. Or if they were gods, then we are the descendants of gods.

Then in the center the frieze split into two. The top row continued as it was. The villages grew into towns; the towns into cities. At last, the cities began to rival those of the ancients themselves. But then some disaster came from the skies: a flame even worse than the original, bursting forth from two tiny twin points in the sky. And this time there was nothing left.

His eyes returned to where one line had become two. Joining the second line were two images: the first, a circle of arrows pointing inward; the second, a miniature of the very wall and opening he now looked upon. Then the frieze continued as the top one had. Except now the towns appeared faster, the cities even more so, finally exceeding even the ancients in their magnificence. The flame from the sky still came, but this time there was a—what? Some kind of tunnel to a new world, safe from this new horror, filled with life and trees and people.

He felt he could grasp the meaning; that he should grasp the meaning. But neither mind nor body could bear more of the strangeness. As he sat leaning against the wall he gazed upon the revelations, wrestling with their meaning until sleep claimed him.

And he dreamed again, but this time of fire from the skies.

~~~

Tamorabi woke, stiff with cold, the image before his eyes too much like the images that had plagued his restless sleep. He chewed thoughtfully on some smoked meat and hard bread, not thinking about the images, just letting his eyes and mind wander over them.

As they did he became increasingly certain. *Somehow the ancients knew their future. For all that they fell in their own disaster, they knew an even greater cataclysm is still to come. If history unfolds unaided there will be no escape, so they gave us a way out. If we take their gift our own path to godhood will be faster, perhaps fast enough that when the disaster strikes our far descendants will know how to escape it. The Ancient Ones left us this egg, so when men were able to understand its secrets they might find their salvation.*

He stared at the black opening beckoning him with its dark promise. He prepared a torch and nervously approached. He dared not go too far, not alone in this place of dead darkness with nothing but his uncertain flame to guide the way. But he needed to know.

There were more engravings on the walls, some pictures, some strange lines and patterns. But his eyes were drawn more to what was arrayed on the shelves beneath them.

It was an array of glittering objects: jewels set in gold of such intricate patterns that he wondered how any man could have made them. A tube of hard metal with smooth crystals at either end; that when he looked through it made distant things appear close.

Then he looked at the nearest of the engravings, tracing their lines with his fingers.

His tribe were not ignorant nomads. He had been taught the counting. And that is what this was: counting. The simplest diagrams were easy to understand, becoming increasingly complex until he had no idea what they meant.

But these first ones! Simple strokes: first one, then two, then three and so on. So these must be their symbols for those numbers. And this their symbol for adding two numbers together!

Then he staggered as the meaning crashed into his brain; that the jewels and gold were the least of this place's treasures. *This is a* school! *It starts at the level of a child, then leads beyond, perhaps all the way to all the wisdom of the gods themselves!*

He stood in stunned silence, looking around him. The space was indeed curved like an egg but large, his height plus half again, while three men could lie head to toe along its length. Still, surely not big enough to hold all the knowledge of the gods. But in the far wall was another door. Trembling, he approached it and studied its surface. Like the other door it was made of metal, but this time there were neither inscriptions nor handles. *The outer door opened outwards. The chick pushes out of its egg. Perhaps this door is the same.*

Tamorabi leant against the door, pushing with all his might. And as before, after a brief resistance it opened a crack. It took him only a few minutes to open it fully into the space beyond.

He thrust his torch into the gloom. He looked upon a metal cavern shrinking into the darkness. It seemed empty of treasures itself, but what he saw made his breath catch in his throat. More doors, this time like the one outside. *Not an egg. It is a nest! The Gods have left us a* nest *of eggs!*

He could not see far down the cavern nor tell how many eggs remained. And finally his courage failed him; he had none left to take another step onward. He just stood there, staring down the cavern as at a future stretching before him whose end he could not see. And he wondered at the past, at what wisdom or magic had led the ancients to create this place.

Finally he stepped back, pulled the door shut, and collapsed on the floor with his back against a wall.

Tamorabi pondered. *Is this why I am here? Have the Gods been waiting, looking down from the sky into the realm of men, until they found... me? Did they choose me, then drive me here to find this, to restore their glories? Are they that cruel? Or was it their last forlorn hope and I chose them? They did not drive me here with the whip of my grief, they merely abandoned their nest here and died, in the hope someone would one day find it and divine its secrets.*

He was a humble hunter. His tribe were not of the Concord but nor were they its enemies. Their lands overlapped the ill-defined edges of the Concord, and if that sometimes led to friction, theft and murder on both sides, more often it led to trade; sometimes even the exchange of sons or daughters in marriage.

So Tamorabi knew of the Sages, even if to him they were near mythic titans with minds dwelling in the sky. He knew what he needed to do.

Tamorabi left the Temple, for Temple it must have been, and stood outside in the city. The towers rose as grimly and as dead, and the cold wind whistled its way down the streets of ruin; but did he hear, in the whispering song of the wind, a subtle undertone of joy? Had the eons-long wailing dirge of the Ancients at last been answered?

He looked around him. It was unlikely anyone else would come here, but he carted rubble and brush over the entrance to the Temple and arranged it so it looked as ancient and dead as the rest. Then at last he retraced the steps of his search, and left the city.

~~~

Frenislan the Wise sat in his office, reading the theses his students had submitted for his examination, occasionally jotting a mark or a comment on them. Sometimes he guffawed at a childish fallacy or pompous expression; more rarely, he pursed his lips at an unexpected insight. His true love was his own reading and research, but he did not begrudge his role in teaching the next generation. He saw himself as part of a noble history: a branch on the growing tree of humanity's quest for knowledge. Perhaps not the most magnificent branch, but a branch nonetheless, connecting the roots of the past to an unknown but glorious future. And if he were not the strongest branch on the tree, who knew what delectable fruits might come from it in the future? Sometimes the smallest plant bore the sweetest berries.

His town was a small one, little regarded in the Concord, assuming anybody beyond its immediate neighbors and the scribes of the Archives even knew it existed. His title of The Wise had been given to him by the townsfolk, who had been impressed by his judgements in settling their disputes. He imagined that the great Sages in the magnificent cities deeper inside the Concord would laugh at his title as much as his clothes, should he ever be introduced to them. But he did not care. He was what he was and thought himself, if not the wisest of Sages, then wise enough. He would work for his allotted span on Earth and leave it a better place than when he had arrived.

He lifted his head at a gentle tapping on the entrance to his office.

A student stood there diffidently, head bowed.

"Speak."

"A stranger to see you, Master."

"What kind of stranger?"

"A dirty one, Master. A hunter, I would think, from far away."

"My regular court is tomorrow. Tell him to come then. If he has money there are plenty of inns. If not and he is a hunter as you say, he can camp among the woods in his usual manner."

The student nodded and withdrew.

Frenislan was engrossed in a particularly intriguing paragraph, knowing there must be a flaw in its reasoning but unable to pin it down, when the gentle tapping was repeated. The same student stood there and Frenislan frowned.

"You again? What is it, another visitor?"

"No Master, the same. He implores you to see him now. He says he has journeyed far and long with information of the greatest import. He says he must speak with you in private."

"Well? Evaluate. Does he seem to you mad? Dangerous? Deluded? Or might there be something to it?"

The girl shrugged. "He seems tired and agitated, but sane. He seems sad but not aggressive. But such men have close horizons, and can see import in the trivial, and imagine their personal problems that loom so large to them will seem equally large to others."

Frenislan smiled. "So you have known many such men, that you feel qualified to judge him so?"

The girl blushed, and stammered, "My... my apologies, Master. No... no, I have merely heard, and deduced."

He waved his hand in forgiveness. "You do not need to apologize. Merely know your limits. If you are to become a Sage you must recognize where knowledge ends and opinion begins. But your perception and logic do you credit in this case."

Now the girl smiled, but blushed even more. "Shall I tell him to return tomorrow?"

"No... no... It is probably nothing, as you say. But hear me. Another part of being a Sage is tending the threads of friendship that bind the Concord. The man thinks his quest is important enough to interrupt a Sage. If it proves unimportant, still he will be grateful that I listened to him, and when he returns home he will tell his people that we treat even poor strangers well and with respect. But if it is important and I delay him until tomorrow, he will be angry and I will have erred. So best to see him now. Have the guards make sure he is completely disarmed—check his boots!—then show him in."

Again the student nodded humbly and withdrew.

Frenislan sat up straighter in his chair, tidied his desk, folded his hands and waited, a picture of serene authority. In a few minutes the girl came back, escorting a large and muscular man. Frenislan examined him. As the girl had said, he looked like a hunter, with rough clothes, long dark hair and windburned skin. His eyes had the faraway look of men used to wilderness and space, but their blue depths reflected echoes of deep and complex passions, as if even now his mind was torn between sorrow, excitement and dread.

"Greetings, friend! What is your name, and what is your need?"

"Greetings, oh Great Sage. I am Tamorabi. I am a hunter, not of your Concord, though my people consider ourselves your friends. But I have made a great discovery and know no better place to turn."

Mightier Sages might have questioned his sobriquet 'the Wise', but Frenislan had a quick mind, which rapidly joined the dots between 'hunter', 'wilderness' and 'discovery', and he leaned forward. "You have found some artifact of the Ancients?!"

"I have found more than an artifact, Great Sage."

"Speak then, friend Tamorabi."

"I was drawn to one of the Graves of the Gods, the bones of a mighty city where few dare enter. Do not ask how or why. Know only I was drawn there, perhaps by the Gods themselves. Men say the ghosts of the Gods sing there, Sage; singing a dirge of the loss of their world. It is true. I heard it. But then I heard something else. Beneath the mourning was a song. A song of hope, it seemed to me. A song that called to me, as if it had waited for me across the ages."

The man stopped, as if exhausted by his speech after so long and hard a journey, and Frenislan felt a twinge of disappointment. *The girl was right. A superstitious hunter, hearing music in a dead city. The wind in the ruins. Perhaps of some interest to the study of sound. But probably not worth a journey to find out.*

"So you feel the Gods sang to you? What did they say?"

"Perhaps they did not sing to me at all. Perhaps they just sang, hoping someone would hear. I heard. So I followed the song. It led me to a ruin, where one of the ancient walls had recently crumbled. I was sore afraid, but my death means little to me now so I explored. There was a door, sealed against the world. I broke its seal. Air rushed in, through some magic of the Ancients. Then the door opened. And inside... inside were... wonders."

Frenislan leapt to his feet, thoughts of serene authority gone. "Wonders, you say! What wonders?"

The hunter reached into the pockets of his vest, and placed three small objects on the desk. "These are just a token that I speak the truth. There is more. Far more."

Frenislan eagerly examined the objects. One was a globe of some hard, lustrous metal that looked like a model of the world, which the Sages knew was a sphere; one was a tube with glass at both ends; another a sheet of metal with geometric patterns and symbols engraved upon it.

"Take the tube, and look out your window through it," Tamorabi suggested.

He did so and jumped. He took it away from his eye, put it back again. Though it, distant objects looked much closer.

"More, you say! What do you think this place is?"

"I am no Sage, my lord. But I have puzzled at the images on the walls, and puzzled at the artifacts. I moved nothing except these tokens. It seems to me to have been made by the Ancients themselves, made to survive all the uncounted eons since their deaths: made so that we may recover their secrets."

"How... how big is this place?"

"It is a curved room, oval like an egg, taller than a man but less than two; about double that in length. But..."

"But?"

"There is another door at its end. It opens onto a corridor, leading I know not where, for I dared not go further. But I saw enough. There are more such eggs. How many, I cannot say."

29. GODSNEST

Frenislan sent his best students, along with some guards, to accompany Tamorabi to the place they were already calling Godsnest, while he sent himself deeper into the Concord carrying Tamorabi's treasures. He could have sent couriers with a message, but thought secrecy was best at this stage; all others who knew about Godsnest were with Tamorabi and under strict instructions to tell nobody else. And there was one particular Sage he wanted to approach, and she was unlikely to answer a summons by a courier from the edge of the Concord.

A score of days after he left his home, he sat on his horse before the gates of the fabulous town of Riverbend. Along the way he had stayed in several towns, but to the polite enquiries of his host Sages he had spoken merely of confidential dealings he could not discuss. Sages were used to open sharing of knowledge, but they were also used to rivalry and secrecy; if they suspected the latter was the truth of it they remained friendly, restricting themselves to subtle probing in an attempt to discover clues to his secret. After all, they reasoned, if he was holding some great secret from them, their best route to sharing in it was to remain his friends.

Riverbend had been planted in the fertile soils deposited in a bend of the mighty Snowmelt River. Over the years it had grown in wealth from the increasing trade along the convenient thoroughfare the river provided. Its wealth had allowed the establishment of a great center of learning, and it was to its current head Sage that Frenislan had come.

~~~

Sage Cherigaline felt no need to expand her name with 'the' anything. Though several such epithets had been offered to her along the course of her distinguished career, none had stuck.

One that had never been offered was 'the Patient'. Yet here she found herself, seated at her desk, eyeing a visitor from some spot she had never heard of at the edge of the Concord, patiently waiting for him to speak.

Frenislan found himself finally standing before the great Sage Cherigaline, suddenly too nervous to speak. When he had entered her august presence and been introduced as Frenislan the Wise, he had inwardly flinched.

He saw a middle-aged woman, with brown hair cascading in waves that framed her still handsome face, whose main feature was its pair of large dark eyes, alive with an arresting intelligence. He knew that what she saw was a man of similar age but undistinguished appearance, partly balding, in clothes that could not match the fineness of hers even before he had ridden a horse for weeks in them.

But though her eyes had flickered at his name, and darted over his clothes, beyond a faint gleam of amusement in her eyes and an even fainter upward curve to the corners of her mouth, she had not laughed or given any other sign of dismissal of his person. But nor had she spoken, and he knew she was testing him. Suddenly he wished he had left 'the Wise' at home where it belonged. But he knew his words and name would be the least important things he was bringing her.

"Greetings, Sage Cherigaline. Thank you for seeing me so quickly."

She smiled, just a little. "Greetings, Frenislan the Wise. It would be impolite of me not to, since you have come so far. It must be a matter of some importance to bring you all this way to me."

"You know of my humble village?"

"I know how to find out what I need to know, if I do not," she replied ambiguously. At that moment a servant entered carrying a tray of refreshments, and placed it on the surface between them. "Sit, Sage Frenislan. Take food and drink. And tell me your important matter."

"Thank you, Sage Cherigaline," he said, sitting, but too nervous to reach for the delicacies. Then instead of speaking, he took three items from his pouch, and laid them before her.

Her eyes widened, and she examined each in turn. She looked down the tube, and seemed to jerk slightly. Then she held it up to her eye, turned around, and scanned the gardens of her domain.

She put it back down, her hand shaking slightly, and stared at the objects for a while. Then she stared at him, as if he were as mysterious as them.

"Where did you find these?"

"I did not. A hunter found them and brought them to me."

"When?"

"Two ten-days ago."

"You either have an extremely fast horse, or you must have left that very day."

"The next."

"You know what these are, I presume?"

"They are artifacts of the Ancients, astoundingly well preserved."

She regarded him speculatively. "Forgive me if I speak frankly. You are a minor Sage from nowhere. I don't know any Sage who would not give their eye teeth for a discovery like this. It could make your name! Give you entry to the highest reaches of society! Anyone else I know would keep this to themselves, study these objects to glean as much as they could from them, and only then amaze the world with a discovery already neatly wrapped in their own erudite analyses! Yet you do none of this. You rush straight off to a more famous Sage, like a student who has found a strange new bug! Do you not believe your own name, Frenislan the Wise?"

"Perhaps I am living up to it. Or maybe proving it false instead."

She regarded him silently with those dark eyes of hers, before replying, "What do you mean?"

He hesitated, his mouth suddenly dry. He reached over and took one of the drinks she had offered, gulping it down. Then he looked directly at her. "I do not know this for a fact, so I may be proving I am a fool. But I believe the hunter's tale. If he speaks the truth these are just a token. He has found, not three items of astonishing value, but a whole room of such objects. And not merely a whole room, but several rooms. And not merely a treasure trove filled with random jewels, but a trove with a design: the design to teach us, long after their deaths, the secrets of the Ancients themselves!"

"Is this some joke?" she asked, barely audible. But her eyes were drawn to the objects and stayed there.

"That is why I came," he continued. "To enlist your help. To enlist everyone's help. If I am right, what we have here is the key to everything!"

She said nothing for long moments, and Frenislan waited silently. Finally she lifted her eyes back to his.

"Yes," she said hoarsely, then grabbed a drink herself and tossed it down in one action. "Yes. You have done well, Frenislan the Wise. But first we must be sure it is true. Where is your hunter now?"

"I sent my best students, with guards, to return with him to the place he found. When they have seen it with their own eyes they will send their fastest courier to me here with the news. That will take some days, however."

She nodded. "You have done well."

Then she laughed. "If this is true, I have just uttered the greatest understatement in history."

She picked up the globe, examining it closely. "Remarkable. Truly remarkable. No doubt you have not been idle when you stopped to rest on your long journey. What do you think this is?"

"We know the Earth is a sphere. We know little of other lands but we know the shape of most of ours. See this place here: it is a similar shape. Not the same, as if the sea has drained from the edges of the land since this globe was made. I think this is a model of the entire world."

"How do you think these objects are so well preserved? Are the rest like this, or are these the only ones?"

"The hunter said that when he opened what he calls the egg, for inside he could see it is rounded like one, there was a great inrushing of air. Perhaps the Ancients sealed it and removed all the air, so the metals inside would not rust, and no life could feed upon its contents. It was not mere luck that these things were preserved. It was by design. The hunter is not an educated man, not by our standards, but nor is he completely ignorant. He says he could puzzle out things that show the history of the world, and other things that instruct in mathematics. He thinks the Ancients knew they were dying and built this place with the best of their arts, so that it might survive the eons until men were ready for their rebirth."

Cherigaline held the globe a moment longer, then extended it toward him, though she seemed to have trouble letting it go. "These are rightly yours, Frenislan the Wise. We shall await news from your people. Until then my house is your house, and my School is your School. Study these things, and learn what you can from them."

He nodded his head gravely. "Thank you, Sage Cherigaline. It is a great honor. An even greater honor would be if you would help me in this task."

Cherigaline smiled, and reached over to clasp his forearm. "Then let it be so. I think, in this case, that the honor is all mine."

~~~

Cherigaline and Frenislan were in conference. They had spent several days in productive labor and had had frequent meetings to discuss and argue their findings.

"Look at this," Cherigaline said. She opened a box, and Frenislan gasped when he saw it contained the viewing tube, nestled safely in the soft velvet cloth lining the box: safely, other than the fact that it now lay in pieces.

"What happened?" he cried.

She smiled. "Don't worry. I examined it closely and it seemed designed to be taken apart then put back together. You see these threads? The parts unscrew. It is quite an ingenious design. I admit I felt fearful about doing it, but your hunter's theory about the Ancients wanting us to learn from these things gave me courage. Would they leave it to us just to display their own cleverness? Or in a way that lets us divine its secrets? How better to learn from a complicated device like this than to take it apart and discover how it works? And so it seems."

"So what did you learn!?"

"Have you noticed how light shining through something clear but curved may be brighter in some places, dimmer in others? Like the shadows of light and dark you see under ripples in clean water?"

"Yes... yes, I know what you mean."

"Well, look at this. I call this clear part a 'lentile', because it is shaped rather like a lentil seed, don't you think?" She carefully picked up one of the clear end pieces by its edges, held it in the sunshine above her desk, and moved it over a piece of pale wood resting on its surface. The shadow of her fingers was normal, but that of the lentile was odd. It had a brighter area inside a darker ring, and as she moved the lentile closer to the wood the dark border became wider and darker, while the central circle became smaller and brighter: until it became a very bright, almost point of light. After a moment, smoke began to curl from where the point of light touched the wood, and she placed the lentile back in its box.

"If you look closely at the lentile, you can see it is very clear, symmetrical and finely ground. I've never heard anyone speak of it this way, but if we'd been paying attention to our own eyes we would have noticed: the direction of light can change when it passes through something curved. The lentiles take advantage of that to actually focus the light to a point. I haven't really worked out how or why yet, but evidently if you put two lentiles the right distance apart, they work together to magnify a distant view."

"Yes... remarkable. But why did the wood burn?"

"I'm not sure. But everyone knows sunlight is warm. Perhaps light is warm, or perhaps warmth and light are somehow the same thing and both are focused by the lentile. In any case, just as the point is very bright, so it is very hot. But that's as far as I've got. What have you discovered?"

He grimaced. "As far as you've got, eh? You make me feel I should change my name to 'Frenislan the Slow', for I have found nothing so dramatic as the nature of light and heat, and how to see into the mountains with it."

He softened his sigh with a smile, then steepled his fingers under his chin and began his own report. "First I decided to examine the metal sheet covered in markings. As we guessed, it is almost certainly some kind of mathematics, but I cannot understand it. I can make guesses about the meaning of several of the symbols, but not enough to work out the rest or even be certain of my guesses. So I put that aside, as from what Tamorabi said, the Egg has much more in it to guide us.

"So to the globe. Look here, at the top and bottom."

He handed it to her, and she examined the poles closely.

"I think the top one represents the northern ice fields, and I suppose that if the north is capped with ice so is the south. But they are too far to the north. I think that means that in the time of the Ancients there was much less ice. The Earth must have been warmer, and the ice correspondingly restricted to more distant regions. That also fits the strangeness of the map. If we assume the total amount of water on Earth is fixed, then if we have more ice on the land, surely there must be less water in the oceans. So our oceans are lower and therefore the land extends further out into them. That would also explain why there are no Ancient ruins near our coastline. And another thing. There are remains of primitive people in places now under the sea. This globe gives us a simple explanation: the Earth is again warming, the ice is melting, and the seas are rising again."

She nodded slowly, turning the globe over in her hand. "Yes. Yes, that makes sense. And we know there is land far to the south of us… that also fits this large landmass here. But there is so much land… over the ocean. A whole world…"

A chime sounded and was followed by the appearance of an assistant. "Eminences, a rider has arrived asking for Sage Frenislan. As you ordered, I have brought him straight here. He awaits just outside."

Frenislan and Cherigaline looked at each other. "Show him in."

A young man entered, and Frenislan recognized one of the guards, a youth from his town known for his skill at horsemanship. His eyes were wild, and he forgot the niceties of permissions and greetings, saying only, as his eyes met Frenislan's:

"It is true! It is all true!"

And he tumbled more artifacts onto the floor.

30. The Fall

News of the find spread rapidly through the Concord, but the Sages agreed that too many people at Godsnest would be not only hard to manage but even harder to keep fed and healthy.

So a plan was made. Some choices were obvious. Others were both less obvious and too many, so a ballot was held. The lucky Sages and their brightest students left as quickly as they could pack and say goodbye. The others had to live with the promise that once items were properly examined where they were and their removal deemed prudent, they would be sent to be studied by the most qualified Sages throughout the Concord.

One decision caused much grumbling, but was probably the best for peace among the Sages. Tamorabi held that the Gods had chosen him to find Godsnest and made him pay a terrible price for their choice. So his condition for revealing its location was that he would be granted overall leadership of its investigation. Frenislan had agreed and the Concord honored that. Part of the Concord's success was based on its reputation for the integrity of its agreements, even if they were made with unwashed, uneducated primitives. That was how so many formerly unwashed, uneducated primitives had become the forebears of today's washed, educated citizens.

Tamorabi would defer to the Sages only in matters of research. By priority and standing Cherigaline was virtually unchallenged to be leader of the research team. More challenged was her decision to appoint Frenislan the Wise as her chief deputy, but if any dared express such challenges they broke upon the rock of Cherigaline's indifference.

She had found she worked well with Frenislan and admired his mind, and there were plenty of other valuable uses for Sages of greater reputation but less certain synergy.

And so the great study began. The remaining eggs were unsealed, and as expected contained more wonders. An access well to a deeper tunnel was discovered but it contained no eggs. The tunnel was clearly man-made but its function was obscure. Rusty remains of iron strips and other decayed detritus of some former glory were found along its length, but it did not appear to be part of the nest, just another relic of the Ancients, like the city above.

Tamorabi sent gangs of workers along it, first to explore, then to clear. One end of the tunnel was completely collapsed but the other seemed to be intact, despite being blocked in places by cave-ins or the results of water seepage over the millennia. So Tamorabi sent his gangs to dig through these blockages to see how far they could go. Who knew what other wonders might lie beyond?

They managed to penetrate several miles from Godsnest. But they found no sign of more nests or eggs. What they did find were a few cave-ins that seemed to be close to the surface, and when they cleared them it proved to be so. They opened deep inside the city but led to no further treasures anyone could find. A few hundred yards beyond the last such access point the tunnel was collapsed again, and after a few weeks of futile labor deemed impassable.

The people of the Concord, having grown up under the influence of the Sages, were by and large open to new knowledge and keen on what it could bring them, so they watched the news from Godsnest with great interest. The leaders of the Concord promised them great things, and looked with sharp eyes at the globe of the world, which promised great things in the future. Even the news of a new and dangerous barbarian chiefdom could not dim the glow of the glorious future beckoning them from the Eggs of Godsnest.

~~~

Praximar the Mighty sat in his tent, considering the news. Twice he had darted in to attack the borders of the Concord with success, and the Concord was beginning to stir like a nest of hornets poked with a stick. They were beginning to take Praximar more seriously, and he had been planning how best to deal with the larger armies they would surely field against him. He knew their arrogance and that they would underestimate him; however he knew a good general had to guard against his own arrogance, and not underestimate them.

And now he had news of some great find they had made, a treasure trove of the Ancients themselves. He had little use for knowledge and little understanding of its value. He thought the Sages with their exaggerated desire to learn new things were fools, and soft. Even the bravest whined like children as he taught them the penalty of resisting him; while the others, while useful, were cowards, willing to see him pleasure their daughters and even their sons in order to save their own perfumed skins.

He knew this trove was highly esteemed by the Sages, and on some level was aware that the treasure they most valued was knowledge. But to him treasure was gold and gems, and that is what he saw in his mind's eye when he learned of this Godsnest they had found.

The place was some distance from here but not too far. It was well guarded, and if he delayed too long, and the Concord learned to fear him more, it might become too well guarded. He could defeat any army on open ground of his choosing; he could defeat this one, but not if it became much stronger. Not this year with this many men; therefore, perhaps never.

And so the next day his army melted back into the forest, and the Defenders who awaited his attack on the nearest towns wondered why he never appeared.

The first the defenders of Godsnest heard of the coming of Praximar was when a breathless scout barged unannounced into the quarters of Chief Defender Katamatos and announced that he had seen a column of the barbarians slinking through the forest, upon which he had fled to report the news before being seen himself.

Chief Defender Katamatos was not especially worried. He had a strong position and many men, more than enough to rout any barbarian attackers. He installed his sentries and pickets, set up his traps and waited. While he waited he sent out probes and feints to test the enemy's strength and resolve. He was pleased with the results. "The barbarians," he opined to Tamorabi, "are as predictable as they are undisciplined. They will fear us and turn aside, or if not we will crush them. We have no need to worry."

But Tamorabi did worry, and set his own plans into motion.

To Katamatos' displeasure the barbarians continued to probe his own positions, proving too willing to disengage but not willing enough to stay away. Finally he maneuvered them into battle, or thought he did. Within hours Katamatos lay dead on the field, the bulk of his army dead or scattered, and only a small core, too loyal or trapped to flee, remained as the last ring of defense around Godsnest.

Praximar did not press his attack. He withdrew a short distance, while still surrounding the defenders with an unbreakable ring of iron. He would give his scattered enemies time to worry but not enough to regroup or counter-attack. As the sky began to redden he approached the defenders with a flag of truce over his head, his elite fighters by his side and a wedge of the best of his other warriors behind.

"Men of the Concord!" he bellowed. "You have fought bravely! But you have lost! Surrender, and I will let you go free! If you do not surrender, every last man and woman among you will die!"

Tamorabi strode to within hailing distance. "Will you give us time to consider your offer?"

"You have until the sun sets. Then you surrender. Or then you die."

Tamorabi nodded curtly and withdrew. There was little time.

"There is no need for you to die," he told the young man now in command of the Defenders. "Go to fight another day. I will delay them long enough. I know how these barbarians think."

The man looked at him. "I am no coward. Nor are my men. We stand with you to the last."

"No. You would throw away your lives for nothing. Trust me and go. If Praximar does not agree to my terms then you may stand with me. Otherwise... the best you can do, for Godsnest and the Concord, is to escape with your lives. Do not throw them away to no purpose."

As the sun touched the horizon, Tamorabi walked back out to where Praximar stood at the head of a column illuminated by flaming torches. Tamorabi looked around him, at the skeleton of the city that had called him, at the brightest of the eternal stars beginning to dot the darkening heavens, and his heart called out to his woman and child: *And now I come to join you in the night where all must go.*

"Praximar! In the eyes of the Gods, yours and mine, I challenge you to personal combat! If I win, your army will withdraw! If you win, Godsnest lies open to you. If you agree, then my army will depart in peace! If not, perhaps we will die: but so will many of your own men!"

Praximar glared at him from beneath his fierce brows. *This man has both wisdom and courage. He knows that no Chief of my people would dare deny a call to personal combat. But he knows he dies tonight.* The man was large and muscular but could be no match for someone like Praximar. He looked at the remnants of the enemy army, considering. *Would they dare face me again after this day? They are too few to bother me even if they would. And if I let them go now, the treasures will be mine as soon as I dispose of this one man. Then I shall sweep through their precious Concord and all will be mine.*

"I accept your challenge! On my honor, your men may depart in safety!"

He nodded to his men, who withdrew from the left flank, opening a gap through which the remnant army began to depart; alert for a betrayal that never came.

Tamorabi stood erect and proud, casually holding a large battle axe as he watched the last of his men leave; watching the reflections of the flames flickering off the enemy's armor and eyes.

And so they glare, their glittering eyes, gathered in the gathering dark. And so they burn to destroy the good, their only reason their greed. My love, my son, who lit my life: the night is here and I am coming to you. I did what I could for you and it was not enough. Now I have done what I can for the world, and perhaps this time it will be enough.

As the last of the Defenders filtered into the streets of the city and were gone, Tamorabi stood tall, his eyes sweeping around the earth and the sky one last time. He heard a faint clang as a door shut inside the Temple and he raised his axe.

Praximar stepped forward, as his men began thrusting their weapons into the air and chanting their barbarian songs. Tamorabi watched the spectacle. *And the glittering eyes they whirl and howl and burn and hate, in night and fear and blood.* Then he let out his own howl that echoed through the city, rushing to join the other voices of the dead. Then he charged toward his enemy, whirling his axe.

~~~

Vermaxakon was afraid, cold, hungry and alone. His parents had hoped for great things from him. He had hoped for great things from himself. His family were from a powerful tribe, not the most powerful nor the wealthiest but well above the average. It had seemed so perfect. Highly intelligent, quick-witted and ambitious, Vermaxakon had looked forward to learning at the feet of one of the great Sages before eventually becoming one himself. The timing could not have been better, with the amazing discoveries at Godsnest bursting forth at the very start of his career.

Then it had all crumbled in a matter of days, when the barbarians had come and laid waste to so many lives and dreams.

So now, rather than living in safety and comfort among some of the greatest minds of his time, each morning awaking to discover new wonders, instead he was shivering in cold and fear. But at least he was alive. Tamorabi and many others had sacrificed their own lives for that.

None of them wanted the treasures of Godsnest to fall into the hands of the barbarians, who would take what they wanted and destroy the rest. The best that would come out of it was that the barbarians would learn ways to be even more effective. Instead of a new age of enlightenment, the treasure of Godsnest would be corrupted, spawning nothing but centuries of even deeper darkness.

So most of the Sages and students at Godsnest had taken whatever they could carry, run down the tunnel under the city, and escaped into the ruins far from the barbarian horde. From there they would disperse in all directions, some into the forest, some toward the mountains, others back into the lands of the Concord. They would flee far from the barbarians or else find a place to hide and wait until it was safe to return. Whatever they could not take was burned or broken, as far as was possible, and finally the access to their escape tunnel was collapsed and hidden as well as their arts could accomplish.

Vermaxakon had the misfortune of taking refuge in part of the forest near where the barbarians had chosen first to pour into and then to camp. His barren hilltop eyrie was reasonably safe: not the highest, so of little strategic value even if the barbarians ever thought of strategy; far enough from the barbarians that they could ignore it if they wished; clearly of no supply value, being rough and rocky; and with a small but well-hidden cave system in which a man could hide.

Unfortunately it was still too close to the horde to risk a fire, visible activity or foraging in the nearby forest. Hence his current state of fear, cold and hunger. However he knew the barbarians would not stay long, so he waited. And perhaps he could prove of some value, for he had taken one of the two-tubed long-viewers. With it he could study the enemy and maybe learn something of use to the Defenders, should he live long enough to report to them.

He drew from his pack what he suspected was the greatest treasure he had absconded with. The Ancients had tried their best to use materials that would survive the millennia of their long sleep. But even for them gold must have been rare and expensive, for there was little of it to be found in Godsnest. But now Vermaxakon held a thin gold plate in his hand, rectangular and about a handspan wide and a little taller. He turned it in his hand, admiring its sparkle, careful that no flash of its yellow fire would betray him to the enemy. It was covered in inscriptions in the old language, its characters small but legible.

They had not yet deciphered the writing of the Ancients. There had been too much to do in too little time, and now their time was gone. They had learned enough to realize that the Ancients had had several languages, and that they had left keys that would eventually allow translating all of them. What treasures lay buried in those words could only be imagined. They did not know how many languages were represented, only that there were a number of different styles of character and therefore at least that many languages— unless the Ancients had used some more arcane system of multiple alphabets.

It had also been apparent from the placement of objects that Godsnest had been constructed over a period of many years. There had been many debates over that. Had Godsnest been built with some other function, perhaps a museum, and then been adapted to outlive its creators by uncounted generations? Yet the structure of the Eggs seemed to indicate a plan for long range storage from its inception. But why? If its builders had known it was needed, why had they allowed the disaster to overtake them when they'd had so many years to choose another path?

The golden tablet's position had indicated it was one of the last objects to be placed inside before the sealing of the Eggs. That and its composition made Vermaxakon and many others suspect that it was some last message from the Ancients, made of gold to highlight its importance. It was clear from the objects in Godsnest that there were other materials equally immune from the decay of deep time. But none were as recognizable as gold, the queen of the metals; perhaps none whose value could be more reliably signaled across the millennia.

Nobody knew who might succeed and who might fail, who would live or die. So from among the healthy young men the guardian of the tablet had been chosen by lot. Now Vermaxakon took a last look at his treasure, as if hoping to divine its meaning from the foreign markings covering it. Then he carefully wrapped it and hid it away. He hoped he would live long enough to see its secrets revealed.

He hoped he would live long enough to see another morning.

As the sun drew nearer the horizon he scanned the barbarian host. It looked like they were preparing for some action tomorrow. As it became darker he saw campfires and imagined he could smell the roasting meat. He sighed, put away his long-viewer and settled down for his own uncomfortable night, cursing the barbarians to whatever hell they believed in.

In the morning he woke, and realized that what they had been preparing for was battle. An army of Defenders was arrayed nearby, and the barbarians were streaming into the trees. He had a good view of a wide valley and settled down to watch.

Before long he spied the barbarian general himself, Praximar, striding arrogantly down the valley flanked by his guard. Then he saw Praximar whirl to the side, then stagger backwards as something flashed through the air and hit him.

~~~

Praximar fell backwards as a sharp blow struck him in the chest. He looked down at the gouge in his armor, where the metal missile now quivering in the dirt had been deflected. Judging from the arrow's hard metal and how violently it had struck him, he thought his new armor had probably saved his life. He laughed at the irony.

He had been disappointed by Godsnest. It had been conspicuously lacking in gold and gems, and indeed contained little of value, and he had wondered how the Concord scum had betrayed him and stolen his rightful due. So furious was he when his men had found few treasures and no clue to how the thieves had escaped, that he had struck a metal panel on the wall violently with his axe. But the panel had barely been dented, and he looked at it with renewed interest. He had it and its partner ripped from the wall and, with much labor, beaten into armor for himself, the strange pictures inscribed on the metal witness that Praximar was favored by the Gods themselves.

Steal from me, will you? Well it may be that I gained a greater treasure, and the Concord will suffer a greater loss.

Then he shouted at his men to hunt down the assassin, and continued on his way.

The battle was close fought, but Praximar's battle plan proved worthy, and a wedge of his men tipped by his elite soldiers pierced a critical line of the Defenders. It was enough. By the day's end, the army of the Concord was routed.

High on a hill a man of the Concord saw it, and wept.

~~~

With the spine of the Concord's resistance broken, Praximar and his horde pressed their advantage. The lands of the Concord were taken; its chief cities razed, conquered or surrendered. Even Praximar's horde had limits to its reach, and some cities more distant from the action were allowed to sue for peace. This they did lest they be crushed in their turn over the next few years.

But whatever remnants may have endured, the Concord ceased to exist as a unified political entity. The refugees from Godsnest who survived their trek settled down in the wilderness, or among the unaligned hunters, or in secret in the cities and towns of the former Concord. There they tried to keep the knowledge of the Ancients alive as they had sworn to do.

Praximar cared much for power and little for knowledge. If he'd ever had any doubts about that, the fate of the effete Concord had proved the wisdom of his course. His empire, which he named Praxia, now ruled most of both the barbarian lands and the Concord, and he was happy. If there had been too few jewels for the taking in Godsnest, the accumulated wealth of the Concord more than compensated for its deficit. Where that wealth had come from and what human qualities were needed to produce it were of no concern to Praximar. It was there, and he could take it, and that is all he cared to know. To ensure he kept taking it he imposed governors on the cities and towns, whose secondary role was to keep order and whose primary role was to cream wealth from the subjugated lands. These burdens succeeded in generating a satisfying stream of gold flowing into Praximar's treasury. He was unaware of the invisible price for this: the greatly reduced creation of wealth available for creaming.

As had often been the case in human history, though the invaders had devoured the civilization of the Concord, over time elements of that much larger civilization began to absorb the soul of the invaders. This began with the Governors in the more remote areas; it continued with Praximar's own son. Then that son's son rose to power, and fell in love with a daughter of the Concord. She was the granddaughter of one of the Sages who had preserved his life and part of his station by pledging allegiance to Praximar. From her the grandson learned the value of knowledge and wisdom; for her, he lightened the load that his dynasty had placed on the Concord.

As time went by, the iron fist of Praximar and his sons evolved into a group of Lords under a supreme leader, now known as the Parax. Due to the precedent of some unfortunate events, the Parax was no longer the first son of a first son, but could come from any of the Lords. All of these were also descended from Praximar, sometimes by circuitous and possibly imaginary routes. And so the fist became a hand of many fingers, still ruling Praxia but somewhat weakened by rivalry.

Slowly the shackles on minds and production were loosened. Much of the knowledge of the Ancients had been lost again in the ashes of Praximar's victory, yet much had been saved. As the people became wealthier and wisdom became more highly prized, the knowledge that had been preserved began to grow, merge and spread. Praxia remained an empire with a strong, and to many overbearing, central government. But if science had been held back, and even now could not flower as luxuriantly as it might have, still it began to advance.

As it approached and then began to exceed what the Ancients themselves had done, their technology allowed them to uncover more remnants of the glory of past ages.

They even found another nest, but this one had ripened prematurely. Its outer layer had been penetrated by some wandering group of starving savages. They had not understood the treasures of knowledge within, only the glitter of gold and gems. Whatever they had taken was long scattered and lost over the untold decades or centuries since. What remained, most broken, some intact, was buried in the mud and debris of those centuries. Whoever they were and whatever their fate and their reasons, they had not gone past the first egg. So the inner eggs had remained intact.

But by then, whatever extra knowledge could be gleaned from them was modest. Humanity had not gained as much time as the creators of Godsnest had hoped. But it had gained some, and perhaps it would be enough.

31. THE DYING OF THE LIGHT

The three of them stood on the beach, looking toward the sky. They were not alone, for hundreds of others had gathered also, but it seemed to Accimbali that they were alone. Just he, his wife and their seven year old daughter, alone on the sands of time.

The ocular implants in their eyes, automatically adjusting to the light, let them watch the sun in perfect safety as the black circle of the moon crept across its face, a small bite that grew into a blackness with an edge of fire. Then the world went dark, and it seemed as if a black circle had been punched through the sky, surrounded by an ethereal pearly light. *If only we could punch a hole through the sky, I would not have to make this decision,* he thought.

He did not know why, when he had heard about this eclipse, that he had announced that they should take the time and go to see it. But when he looked at his daughter's rapt face, he knew. *It is good for her to see such wonders. I who am about to betray you, my dearest child; at least I can give you this. It is of such moments of wonder that the joy of life is made. I cannot pay for what I will do, but I can at least give you this.*

~~~

Two weeks later, back in their own home Accimbali sat at breakfast with his family. His wife examined him curiously. For months now he had seemed withdrawn, and too frequently she would glance at him and see him looking at her or their daughter with a look she could not name. It was if some terrible burden was torturing him; something he could neither reveal nor change. But it was not as if he were withdrawing from them. If anything, his embraces were more passionate, his need to hold them greater; as if his love were the only thing standing between him and some abyss that only he could see.

She had asked him about it, not knowing what it was she should be asking. But he could not or would not speak of it. All he would do was reach out to her, and hold her hand; and smile at her. But his smile made her afraid. It was a smile of tenderness; but also a smile of loss.

Their daughter reached for a glass of juice and saw him looking at her. "What is it, Daddy? Why are you looking at me funny?"

"Come here."

She giggled, and ran to sit on his lap, throwing her arms around his neck. He hugged her, tickling her neck with the stubble on his chin, and she squealed with delight. He held out his other arm to his wife, beckoning her to him. She looked puzzled, but there was something about his gesture: as if it were a command not to be questioned, just obeyed.

He held them both, and whispered, "You know I love you, sweet ones. I will love you without end. You know that. Know it always."

His daughter reached up, touching the dampness around his eyes. "What's wrong, Daddy? Are you going away?"

But he would not answer, only tickled her until she squealed.

His wife said nothing, but she rested her hand on his shoulder and he saw a sheen of tears in her own eyes. Then she whispered "Is it today?", and he knew that at some level, she who knew him so well knew the burden he bore. He did not answer, which was answer enough.

Then he drew them both to him and held them tight.

Finally he rose and stood looking at them for a while, like a man drinking in a sight that must last him a lifetime.

"I will love you both to the end of time."

They both went to the door as he walked to the transport tube. He hopped in but did not take a seat. He turned to look out of the open door, and lifted his hand in farewell. Then he was gone.

I cannot do it, he thought, the image of his wife and daughter burning in his mind. *If I do it you will cease to exist. Even death is not so final an end. In the eternity of spacetime you will never have been, never even been imagined. If I succeed, billions will be saved. But who are the billions to me, when it is you who must lie on the other side of the scale?*

But he knew he would do it. *If it were the billions against you, perhaps I would leave the billions to seek their own salvation. But it isn't, is it? Your fate is sealed as much as theirs. Perhaps for the few months I could grant you, still I would trade those billions, even for such a little time. But I cannot. Not even that.*

He knew what he would do. He remembered a poem from ancient Earth, one that had been discovered in the troves of ancient knowledge that had survived the holocaust:

> Do not go gentle into that good night,
> Old age should burn and rave at close of day;
> Rage, rage against the dying of the light.

He knew too well how he would rage. The billions of years of life on Earth had honed life into precisely that rage. As the end came, they would fight. Even knowing the futility. Even knowing that the more they succeeded, the more they grasped an extension to life out of the horrors to come, the worse would be their final end. That end could be fought. But it would come and claim them all.

He could not save himself. He could not save them. He could only save the world. It would have to be enough.

As the transport carried him to his destination, he saw nothing except the image of his family watching him go, and the memory of what had brought him to this.

It is my decision. It was always my decision. I have damned you, and I will be forever damned for it.

32. HAVEN

The nearby orbiting white dwarf stars were discovered by the scientists of Praxia three quarters of a century before they were found by Pachmeny in a timeline that never existed. The implications were realized five years after that and ever since then, the scientific resources of Praxia were bent toward finding a solution.

Some scientists were confident of finding an answer: after all, knowledge was growing at a breakneck pace and had already gone beyond that of the Ancients. Unfortunately they could not say what the solution might be.

Large shelters far underground might provide a haven for some; might even provide a nucleus for resettlement of the surface decades or centuries later. Construction of many such shelters and research into the best ways to ensure their long term survival were begun. Beyond an elite chosen for their essential skills, equality of access was to be guaranteed by a lottery. But many wondered who the true winners would be: those given places in the shelters, perhaps gaining nothing beyond a long lingering death, or those left behind to perish more suddenly.

Fleeing to other stars was another option, but nobody knew how. The best extrapolations of known methods of propulsion could achieve fabulous speeds, but even they were a mere fraction of the speed of light, and the inhabitants of such ships would not long outlast the death of their home world before being overtaken by the same holocaust. But here too research proceeded apace, in the hope that some breakthrough would allow acceleration close enough to the speed of light, soon enough for it to matter.

For a while the equations of spacetime excited great interest. The scientists who studied such arcane knowledge had found that those equations allowed piercing the geometry of spacetime with a kind of tunnel, which potentially could jump great distances without needing to accelerate at all. Maybe great ships could be built, able to generate their own tunnels to travel faster than light. Or what if a fixed tunnel could be made on Earth, spanning many light years of space? If such a tunnel could be created, perhaps it would allow an exodus to another world, far away from the fury to come. And unlike solutions involving shelters or ships, both needing to fit people inside and keep them alive, potentially far more people could be saved if all they had to do was to leave their homes and walk onto a far planet.

But by the time Accimbali began his own studies disillusionment had set in. The equations might allow tunnels through spacetime, but only under conditions that nobody understood or had any idea how to achieve. Research continued, but more out of grim wishful thinking than any real optimism that success was achievable in principle, let alone before the end of the world.

But advances had been made, and if nobody knew how to create a stable tunnel or one larger than microscopic, at least the general conditions under which one could be initiated had been elucidated. Nobody had yet succeeded in the task but at least it seemed theoretically possible.

Accimbali succeeded.

~~~

Accimbali sat at a starkly utilitarian table, feeling the eyes of the Lords and other luminaries arrayed before him, boring into him. He gazed back calmly. Over the years he had learned calm. No matter what emotions roiled beneath the surface it was better to present an untouched mask to those above him. Passions were regarded with suspicion, as passions implied personal goals and therefore less than perfect devotion to the needs of the Group. Civilizations might have risen, fallen and risen again, but one thing had stayed constant: the remarkable coincidence between the needs of the Group, the ambitions of its leaders, and obedience to their desires.

Today was a day when passions were raging beneath the calm face of the scientist. *Today I am playing for the fate of the world.*

"We have poured a lot of time and resources into your project,

Accimbali," pointed out Barramor, currently Headman of the Committee for World Defense. "Are you telling me you have failed? You promised us travel to the stars. And now, when travel to the stars has become necessary, you tell us it can't be done?"

"I never promised travel to the stars, Great One. What I said was that my own research, coupled with our better understanding of some of the obscure equations preserved from antiquity, seemed to hold hints of means to tunnel through spacetime. The Ancients called these tunnels 'wormholes', though even they had no more than theoretical hints of them. The hints held out promise of rapid travel over immense distances, a way to bypass the lightspeed limit. Hints, not promises. Good enough hints to be worth investigating. But yes, I have failed: while such tunnels do appear to be possible, they cannot be used for travel between the stars. They are too unstable. Perhaps with greater understanding we might find a way. But I do not think it is possible, not within our lifetimes. It would need an understanding of a layer of reality beneath or beyond our most advanced theories, one for which we lack even hints, let alone guideposts."

"Then we are doomed," declaimed the Parax himself. "All we can do is hide, and hope it is enough despite all our calculations to the contrary. Or hope that others can find a way to send ships to the stars, while yet others find ways to shield them from the supernova. In either case our resources are better spent elsewhere."

Accimbali looked slowly from face to face, then quietly dropped his bombshell. "Yet there may be a way."

"You just said it was impossible. Explain."

"The equations are those of spacetime. We cannot tunnel through space. We can, however, tunnel through time."

He waited for the gasps and mutterings to die down, saying nothing more.

Finally the Parax turned his gaze on him. "Explain."

Accimbali drew a deep breath, and allowed his gaze to wander over those present. He knew his greatest danger lay in Sharalay. They had been students together, briefly torrid lovers, both members of a secret society which had no name only a shared philosophy. It had no leaders, but had existed in the great Universities for centuries. It had survived by being invisible.

There had long been tension between the remnants of the Sages of the Concord and the barbarian Lords of Praxia. Even when the larger culture around them had absorbed the invaders, the rulers retained a pride in their barbarian roots, and might and power were valued more highly than wisdom. Wisdom, knowledge, and the Sages who embodied it were handmaidens of the Group and servants of its leaders.

Had not history itself proved that this was the natural order?

The sages and their intellectual heirs thought differently. Such thoughts arose most naturally and vigorously among the young. But whether the millennia of evolution of brains or minds had brought men more patience, or greater timidity, or simply more wisdom, their resistance remained in the shadows. Theirs was a resistance not meant to overthrow a regime but to keep an idea alive. A resistance that knew the invaders had already been largely tamed by the remnant, superior soul of the vanquished, and now waited to complete that job: to finally see the rule of force subjugated to the gentle rule of wisdom.

So they had no name, no leaders, and no aim but the pursuit of wisdom, and the dissemination throughout society of men and women armed with that wisdom. For a goal that would not be reached within their lifetimes, but their lives would have helped achieve. Their one rule was that there would be no active protests, and certainly no action against the Lords. Those of a more fiery temperament were eased into their own path.

There they either learned wisdom in time, or died.

Like many cultures throughout history where strength was key to success, women had played a subservient role in Praxia. As it became more civilized such prejudices had begun to recede. This had been accelerated by the discovery of the impending catastrophe, just as in past societies the pressures of war had achieved likewise. By Accimbali's time all positions and careers were theoretically open to women; however old prejudices die hard, and if paths were open to them still they were strewn with obstacles. A woman could succeed but she had to be exceptional.

Accimbali knew that the others present were all intelligent, else they would have not reached their current positions or, having reached them, long survived the plots of others who sought the same thing. For the same reason they were driven and ruthless. But their intelligence was of a more practical kind. An intelligence focused on goals and the machinations of men; not the intelligence of an artist or scientist. He knew he should not underestimate them, but was comfortable in his greater knowledge: he was confident he could answer any questions they were likely to ask.

Sharalay was another matter, he knew when his gaze was briefly stopped by her perceptive dark blue eyes. She was personal scientific adviser to the man she sat next to, Thegrado, most powerful of the Lords and both presumptive heir to the Parax and his chief rival. The ascension of heir to ruler was neither guaranteed nor always due to the voluntary retirement of the previous incumbent.

For Sharalay, a woman, to be his personal advisor was testament to both her brilliance of intellect and the focus of her drive. Accimbali knew it was probably also a testament to her willingness to be one of Thegrado's many mistresses. Everyone knew the man jikked around like a rabbit in heat. Society hadn't evolved that much, and unless Thegrado was particularly liberal in his thinking, brilliance would not be enough for a woman to rise so high by his side unless she also lay at his side. Looking into the dark pits of Thegrado's eyes, Accimbali doubted his thinking was very liberal.

Like many intellectuals, Accimbali was supremely confident in his own intellect. But back when they were students even he had sometimes wondered whether Sharalay's incisive mind bettered his. Now he wondered whether that brilliance had survived, and if it had whether it would be fast enough to deduce what he would not be saying today. And if it was, where her true loyalties now lay.

Looking into her eyes, he could see the first but could not read the second, and his mouth dried briefly with fear. *It is too late to change course now. Now I cast my dice in the lap of the gods. Perhaps she will see nothing. But if she does see, she is my greatest danger—or greatest opportunity.*

"A wormhole through space is unstable," Accimbali began. "In theory it can be held open by forms of matter and energy that we can put into the equations as mathematical terms, but bringing those into reality is currently beyond even our imagination.

"But extending a wormhole back through time creates tensions that are mathematically similar, in a sense creating virtual negative energy. Even so it requires a great amount of power and is not especially stable. But it is stable enough for a large body, a human body, to move into the past. It will last only half an hour or so, but that is long enough for many purposes."

The room was silent for long moments, and Accimbali could almost see the thoughts running through their minds as they first tried to see, then grasp, the implications.

Finally Barramor asked, "How sure are you of this?"

Accimbali shrugged. "I am as certain as I can be of the mathematics. To confirm it in practice will need experiments using a lot of precisely directed energy. That is why I am here."

Then Sharalay said, "But back in time to what place? We are moving through space all the time."

"Spacetime is bent by matter, so fortunately for our purposes the wormholes are anchored to the gravitational well of the Earth. So we would end up here, not falling into the empty space between the stars."

"You say about half an hour," said Barramor. "That is not very long. What happens then?"

"Then it closes. Without experiments we can't be sure of the details. However my investigations indicate that sending large masses into the past cause spacetime distortions which will probably prevent repetition in times too near. So we could achieve a number of small scale journeys but they would be to different times."

"How different?"

He spread his hands. "I don't know. We are at the edge of my understanding at this point. I think at the scale of a single human body it will only be a few days. But then it increases exponentially. If we send a hundred people through then I guess… decades. Decades between migrations. And if we tried sending only one or two people at a time, the distortions accumulate into much the same delays."

They are now thinking that this is of little use for saving the world, but it might save their own skins. They are wondering how much they care.

He saw men exchanging glances, as if assessing how much others expected them to care. Then Sharalay spoke. "But travelling into the past… then doing things in that past. What about the Ancestor Paradox, the contradictions you get if you change the past in a way that prevents your being born, in which case where did you come from?"

"I imagine it is impossible. Perhaps that is part of the reason why the limits to transfer are there: nature's way to prevent paradoxes."

She nodded, then sat silently. He could see the thinking in the depths behind her eyes; saw a look of puzzlement, then a slight widening of her eyes as the puzzlement began to morph into horror.

He blinked slowly, then idly scratched his left ear. *Our old signal for danger, the need to keep silent. She will remember it. But will she notice it? And if she does… will she obey it or betray me? Is she still loyal to our past and the ideals of our youth, or is she now one of those we despised? Now I will learn and perhaps I will die for nothing. Now the fate of the world is as much on her head as mine.*

He watched her stare at him, saw her lips open; then she nodded again as if satisfied and leant back in her chair.

"I see. Yes. Obviously we need more study, but clearly nature will not allow us to achieve the impossible."

The Parax had watched the exchanges silently but now spoke. "You have done well, Accimbali, but as amazing as your achievement is—if it is real—it is not the answer we were hoping for. Still, surely it is better to save some than none. And as you say, this is the edge of your understanding. Perhaps further investigation will expand our options. I am favorably inclined to give you all the resources you need, within reason. Does anyone else have any comments or suggestions?"

Those in the room looked around at each other, except for Sharalay, who remained frozen in her chair staring at Accimbali, and there was a general murmur of assent to the Parax's words.

"Accimbali?"

"Thank you, Noble One. I shall present a more detailed plan to you all as soon as I can. But may I make one other request?"

The Parax nodded in assent to continue.

"I would ask Thegrado's permission for Sharalay to work with me on this task. I am aware of her brilliant mind and think she will be of great value to this enterprise." *And Thegrado will be happy, as his woman will be inserted as a spy at the highest levels; and the Parax will be happy, as it will strengthen Thegrado's obligations to him.*

"I have no objection, Noble One," said Thegrado graciously.

A faint smile played over the Parax's lips. "We shall make it so, then. Sharalay, you will make yourself available to assist Accimbali in any way he wants. Accimbali, develop your plan and present it for approval, but I don't foresee any problems. Since you have asked for Sharalay's help, I will expect an independent appraisal from her as well, once she has had time to examine your findings in detail. You are both dismissed."

Accimbali and Sharalay rose, bowed in assent and farewell, then left the group to their other deliberations.

~~~

As they walked out then sat in the transport taking them to Accimbali's offices, they continued an animated discussion of Accimbali's discoveries, though still avoiding the questions he could see raging behind her eyes.

Finally they sat in his private office, and he offered her a drink which she now held in her hand. She took a sip, but then something broke inside her. She stood abruptly and banged her glass down on his desk, the amber liquid sloshing over its sides, and glowered down at him, leaning her weight on her fists.

"By the fact that you didn't want me to ask some obvious questions, I can only assume that you don't have good answers to them," she accused in a voice now hoarse with barely suppressed emotion. "Worse, I can only assume that it isn't that you don't have answers, but that you don't want to give them. Given the way you warned me to shut up, I assume that our noble Lords won't like it either. So spill it, Accimbali! What's your game? Or to be more precise, have you gone utterly mad?"

Accimbali calmly sipped his drink, watching her.

"You are still beautiful, Sharalay. Especially when you are angry."

"Jikk you, Accimbali! Maybe I'll go straight to Thegrado with my suspicions. Answer my jikking question."

"And still the same old Sharalay," he said with a smile as she fumed. "Just as fiery and, considering your questions, just as brilliant. So I am glad you are here and you obeyed my request. I didn't know what side you were on."

"Maybe I'm on nobody's side. Except mine, the truth's, and by implication, our great Lords'. Don't think just because I'm here that I'm on your side. My suspicions can strike me suddenly at any time. So answer the *jikking* question!"

He nodded and put down his drink, rather more gently than she had. "All right. No, I have not gone mad. At least," he added with a bitter laugh, "I don't think so. I wish I had. But if you had any deeper questions perhaps you should ask them now."

She glared at him. "Fine. I can see how you want to play this. Admit nothing, see how much I know. And I suppose if I were in your position I'd do the same. So as you wish. Your answer to my question about time travel paradoxes was a steaming pile of horse manure and you know it. 'Oh, if we're careful we can get away with it?' Seriously? This isn't going to work unless we go back a long way. Nobody is going to want to go back to our own dark ages. We're going to want to pick some era long ago, when life can be easy and small numbers of refugees can be safe from rampaging natives. Aren't we?"

"Yes. So?"

"So you know as well as I do how contingent the future is. The tiniest change can rewrite history. If we do this our present will be obliterated. We will save at most a few hundred people, at the cost of everyone else's lives. Worse, whatever world replaces this one is still dead. So what are you really trying to do?"

"Surely saving some people is worth it? Don't you think?"

"What I think is that this is going to be a very expensive exercise. What I think is that you are building your own escape tunnel to save your own skin, which you will get away with because our dear leaders want to escape with theirs too, the rest of the world be damned!"

"Sharalay, the rest of the world is doomed regardless. We have twenty years left. I think it will take ten of those years to develop the technology to turn the theory into practical reality. Another few years to refine things. This is our only chance, and our Lords will not agree to it if there is no hope. And while they will fiercely proclaim their desire to save the whole world, they will agree to it even if the only hope is for them and their friends. But they must have that hope, or we are all dead."

"So that's it, then. It *is* your private escape route. But you know our Lords are not yet ready to accept it, so it is too risky for them to know the truth. So we don't ask too many questions, and we rely on any suspicions they may have to collide with their personal wish to survive, so they remain silent too?"

He stared at her in silence for a while, then picked up his glass, swirled the ice, and sipped. "Sit down, won't you? Finish your drink."

She looked at him for another few moments, then gave a sigh which could have been bitter, resigned or damning, and sat back down. She picked up her drink, downed half of it in one gulp and glared at him.

"Jikk you, Accimbali. I think I'll just spill it and watch you burn, you bitchspawn."

"You could tell them, but do you think they would thank you? They might praise your devotion and loyalty and service to the people: for a couple of months. They must, because their public faces are all for the people; and to be fair, with the best of them even in reality. But they didn't get where they are without being fundamentally all about themselves and their own advancement. I have looked into Thegrado's eyes, and I think you know as well as I do how he would reward you. They will know you have cost them their lives. Whatever it costs me it will cost you more."

"Jikk you. But I repeat myself."

"You know it is true. You feel it even in your own soul. When faced with your own death, if this way out were offered to you, you know you would take it. Don't blame me. Don't blame them. And not one person in the world you feel sorry for would do otherwise."

She lowered her eyes and replied softly, "I... I don't know."

They were silent for a while. Then Accimbali sighed.

"You are a brilliant woman, Sharalay," he said. "So I must lay all my cards on the table. You will find out anyway."

She looked up at him, puzzled.

"I wish I did not have to tell you this. I wish it because you might betray me, and then the game is lost and with it the world. I wish it because it is something hard for anyone to bear, and I do not wish it on anyone else, least of all you. But your genius dooms you to know, because I need you."

He looked into his empty glass, looked into hers, and poured them each more, as she continued staring at him in silence.

"I can only trust you with the truth and hope that—for the sake of what we had, what we were, or what you still are—that you will not betray me. The Lords must believe there is a way out, at least for them, or they will bury us. They are all survivors, but their vision is narrow. If they can see a way to survive they will do what they have to do. If they cannot, if instead they see only their doom, then they will hang on to hope for another solution: even if it gives them just an hour more of life, even if it means dragging down the whole human race into destruction for the sake of that hour."

"What... what are you trying to say?"

"There is no way out. Not for them, not for us, not for anyone alive today."

"So... what? Are you saying this is all a lie? For what purpose?"

"Oh, it is not a lie. But you are right. We cannot travel into the distant past without losing the present. But it is worse than that. It is not that we can escape and leave the rest of the world to its fate. The present can intrude into the past for only a short while. It can do things, things that persist: but just like the future, it will cease to be. If a man goes back into the past and changes the past, he too will cease to exist."

"But then... but then what is the point?!" she cried.

He stared into the depths of his drink for long seconds, then lifted his eyes again to bore into hers.

"You have read the tales of the discovery of the legacy of the Ancients. But have you considered how and why that legacy was left?"

"Why... to preserve their knowledge, knowing their end was near."

"But have you considered the nature of their legacy? Built to last millennia, but also to be hidden for most of those millennia. They must have taken a long time to build. As if they knew their end was coming long before it arrived. They accepted their end, or could not prevent it, yet left their knowledge for others."

She stared at him, then whispered, "As if they knew... knew their own future. Their own far future."

He nodded. "Perhaps it means nothing. There is much we don't know about the Ancients. Perhaps those caches were to them no more effort and time than building a warehouse is for us. But I don't think so. Not when we compare them to the other remnants the Ancients left behind."

"What... what are you getting at?"

"I think you see it yourself now."

She nodded, dismayed. "I think I do. But tell me. It is time to tell me all."

"Maybe you were right the first time, and I am mad," he sighed. "But I think we are not the first to live in this time. There was another timeline, which had suffered the same disaster we have. For whatever reason, perhaps they simply ran out of time, they could not save themselves. So they changed the past: at the price of their own existence. They warned someone, someone able to preserve enough of the Ancient wisdom to give their heirs on a second timeline—us—a head start. As it turns out, it does not seem to be much of a head start. But maybe it will be enough this time."

"Enough... for what?"

"To change history again. Not to preserve knowledge through the disaster that overtook our ancestors. To stop the disaster from ever happening."

She tossed back the rest of her drink, and silently extended her glass for more. "But if we could do that... then we would grant the world millennia of progress. Not to start again, but to build on what they already had. We could... we could..."

"We could save the world."

"At the price of our own lives. At the price of everyone's lives. At the price of our entire history."

"Yes."

"It is insane."

"Yes. But it is our only hope. You know as well as anybody on Earth what we have tried and what we have failed. Do you think we have a chance at an alternative? Some way to make our tunnels cross light years of interstellar space, or make starships able to carry thousands of people? Starships fast enough to outrun the storm, or tough enough to weather it?"

"No," she whispered.

"No. We are all dead already. But we can give the world another chance. We will die, the billions of people in our history will never have been: but there will be new billions, people who never were but who now will live. Then perhaps our race will find a way to escape its doom."

"Do we have the right? To do this? Maybe we have no right, and we should pass the decision on to others."

"If we are right we have no choice. We must bear the burden ourselves. To do otherwise is to cast the existence of our species to chance. We cannot risk it.

"But we do not need to decide now, just leave our options open. We have years. Perhaps the technology will not work. Or we will be surprised and better solutions will be discovered: in which case we will take the lifeline given us and leave the past as it is. To change the past is risky, as how can we know we won't make it even worse? So when the time comes and the end approaches, if there are no better solutions then must we do what we can. But if there *are* better solutions, then I will destroy our technology myself rather than see it used."

~~~

The years since that day had been busy.

He had not intended to marry. But life has its own logic, and if he was fighting a war to save all life, he could not deny his own life; nor refuse whatever happiness he might win in the time he was granted.

He had not intended to have a child. But love has its own logic, and after billions of years of the survival of the living, life did not easily let go of its legacy. And still he hoped that there would be a solution. That he was not bringing a child into the world only to erase her life by his own hand. That somehow there would be a better answer, that they all might live.

Over all those years he told himself that there would be an answer. Perhaps even one he found himself, and he would be the savior of those he loved as well as of the billions; not their killer.

But now he knew there would be no answer.

He and Sharalay had brought nobody else into their secret. It was too risky, and not needed. Their reports were written truthfully where possible, if incompletely. Their experiments were in the open, though their true intent might be disguised. Sharalay's brilliance extended into the realm of computer programming, and she constructed a layer between the output of the instruments and the inputs to the recording and analytical engines. It would take a person of exceptional intellect to penetrate her deceptions. Such people were rare; any who came were not allowed near the secret code, their talents diverted elsewhere.

In public their relationship was one of cool, slightly hostile professionalism. It helped preserve the illusion that they were a check on each other; each respecting the other, but each maneuvering for their own advantage. It was a story easy to sell to men whose own lives turned on the same axis.

In private their relationship had an air of desperation and triumph, depending on their progress. Too often the triumph was itself the cause of their desperation, knowing its end if they failed in their greater aim of finding a less fatal solution.

For a while, in secret, they became lovers again, their lust driven by their desperation and triumph to its most logical climax. But it could not last. Each saw death in the other's eyes, and their passion could not survive it.

Each found their own solution. Sharalay, powerful enough now in her own right to be immune from any displeasure of Thegrado, even if he himself had not moved on to other conquests, sought release in a string of short term relationships. They were not casual affairs. But they too could not survive the look of death, this time the one she saw gazing back from her own eyes. For a while each one brought her hope, the pulse of life damming the darkness in her soul. The light of lust in their eyes was the light of life, the legacy of a billion years. But when the light began to turn to love, she could not bear her own betrayal, and then she cried in incurable desolation, and moved on.

Accimbali found another: a woman whose intellect challenged him and who was working on space drive technology. When he met her she was young and filled with as much optimism as fire. She believed there would be a solution. She was delighted to bring a child into the world as a right and proper expression of their love, sure that the child would live long. As the years drew on, the fire began to fade with the optimism; Accimbali would sometimes see her gazing at their daughter with a look of equal love and despair. But it did not last. She would never give up until the heavens destroyed her; she would never believe she had failed until failure claimed her and no breath remained in her to struggle. It was one of the reasons he loved her; it was the fuel that let him survive what he saw in the mirror.

If their triumphs and despair were linked opposites, so were their hopes and fears. He retained the hope that he would never hold the fate of the world in his hands. Part of what let him was the good possibility that the war could not be stopped: but that was also his greatest fear. As the years went by and that fate drew closer, he would often recall one of their conversations. Soon after they had begun working together and their passions had reignited, Accimbali had woken one morning to see Sharalay lying on her side, eyes wide open, staring not at him but through him into space.

He squeezed her shoulder.

"Sharalay? What are you thinking of?" he asked.

She slowly gazed at him for a few seconds with her eyes still empty, then she focused on him. "You said... to change history. To stop the war. But what if the war can't be stopped? There are some theories of history that insist it is the outcome of vast impersonal forces. How do you fight... that?"

It was a good question. Little was known about the war that had ended the Ancients, beyond the evidence from their ruined cities that it had been terrible. There was one fragment inscribed on a gold plate in a language of the ancients. No doubt had it been found by Praximar the gold would have been melted down and the knowledge lost, its meaning scattered among the atoms of a crown on Praximar's noble head. But some long forgotten brave Sage, recognizing that it must hold a special value to be made of gold, had spirited it away in the Great Preservation that had saved much of the knowledge of Godsnest.

Without it Accimbali's task might have been impossible. But it told the story of the start of the war. The world of the Ancients was fractured along many political and ethnic fault lines, but its two greatest powers had been the 'USA' and the 'USSR'. Two nations separated by two letters but a vast enmity. At one end of the world you could almost walk from one to the other. At the other end their territories were separated by an ocean, with numerous smaller states huddled between them. The gulf between their philosophies was even greater, though perhaps less so in how their leaders applied them to their own policies and lives.

The War had started when the Soviets had launched a large scale nuclear attack on the United States, who had retaliated in kind. Other nations, allies or opportunists, had been drawn in. The tablet was unclear on why the Soviets had attacked, though it related a claim made by one of their diplomats, before he was executed, that their early warning system at a place called 'Oko' had reported an attack coming from the United States.

It was not much to go on, but it was a place to start looking.

So to Sharalay's question he had simply replied, "Praximar."

"Praximar? What do you mean?"

"Consider how the world might have been different, had he never been born. Or died of the fever while a child."

"If history is made of forces not men, then it would not matter. Praximar did not conquer the Concord on his own. He was merely the sharp point of a barbarian horde. Maybe it would not have made a difference. Or maybe whatever difference it made would not have changed anything."

"Yes, that is what they say. But Praximar was one of the greatest generals who ever lived. There had been many barbarian invasions before and all had been squashed. Without him the same would probably have happened. And the Concord had just uncovered Godsnest. Before long, they would have been unconquerable.

"And think on how small a thing it might have turned. Everyone knows the legend of the assassin's arrow deflected by armor of Ancient metal. Praximar used it as proof that the spirits of the Ancients had chosen him. Assume it is true. We might as well, as the armor is still on display for all to marvel at. Two metal plates. Left behind by the Sages fleeing Godsnest because it seemed of too little value among all the other treasures. Two pieces of scorned metal that led to the ruin of the Concord."

"If you are right... should we choose an easier task? Go back a shorter way, and kill Praximar. Save the Concord."

"I don't think we dare. Saving the Concord might buy us a century, but would even that be enough? I suspect the builders of Godsnest hoped their trove would be found much earlier, but they miscalculated. I don't think we can blame them. Who can calculate the tides and misfortunes of future millennia? Perhaps if we killed Praximar all we would achieve is two other people lying here now, no closer to saving the world than we are."

"I am afraid. Afraid of failing. Afraid of succeeding."

He grasped a fistful of her hair, kissed it, and buried his face in it.

"Afraid? We should be afraid. But we must be bold. We cannot save the world by making small steps. Those others. The ones I think have already done this. They tried something small. Perhaps it was all they could try. They gave us breathing space, and my admiration and gratitude can't be overestimated. But that's all they gave us. They have passed a baton through time to us. We have to finish the job, and for that we need all the courage and boldness we can muster."

"But the war. Two mighty nations and their client states! Whole armies! Thousands of nuclear warheads! A sheet of metal won't be enough."

He sighed. "I know. But we have to look. What was it that ancient Sage said? 'Give me a place to stand and I shall move the world?' Perhaps we will find no place to stand, or too many. In that case... well, there is always Praximar."

~~~

So surreptitiously, in the midst of the other research, they had sent probing tunnels to the time vicinity of the start of the war, and began zeroing in on its immediate causes.

Their world was already familiar with the structure and writing of the long dead Russian language. With their probes and computers it was not too great a task to reconstruct how it was spoken. With their neural linkage technology, nor was it a great task for induced learning systems to train a human brain into fluency in both directions.

When finally they knew the truth, Accimbali and Sharalay stared at each other without speaking, each knowing the other's thoughts. It could be done.

They still could fail. Perhaps the man they had found would not believe. Perhaps he would not believe enough, and would falter when tested and fail to act. Or perhaps he would act, but history was ruled by impersonal forces after all: and a day, a week, or a month later, the disaster would come regardless, unstoppable as an avalanche begun by a snowflake but not caring which of a million snowflakes was the cause.

But they did not act. Or maybe it is why they did not act. Instead they waited, in a mixture of fear and hope in which the fear continued to grow to absorb the hope.

Their positions gave them access to the latest scientific information. The science in their world was the best humanity had ever achieved, but even it had its limitations when faced with the gulf between the stars. They knew when the supernova would blaze its deadly glory over the Earth, but not exactly. They knew when was too soon and when it must be past. Between those two points was uncertainty, a range of probabilities peaking in the middle of a range spanning nearly a year.

The public were unaware of this. They thought that the event was still some years beyond that point, and were encouraged by frequent news of great, if still secret, progress. Those who knew the truth were enjoined to secrecy under the most dire penalties. Accimbali and Sharalay knew, and watched the fall of days with growing dread.

They knew that if they acted too soon they could be the worst murderers in history, destroying a world that might have been saved had they only waited long enough for the means to be discovered. But if they waited too long they might be unable to act at all. The equipment was buried deep and well protected; but in the face of the fury to come, even that was no guarantee it or they would survive. So as the date approached on which 'no chance' would tick over into 'a tiny chance', their fear began to gain an edge of terror.

Finally they agreed. It had to be the last day of certainty. They were already gambling the survival of humanity on their actions. They could not add to the gamble. They could not hold possible victory in their grasp and risk its loss to chance.

So now Accimbali found himself in a transport capsule, having hugged his wife and daughter goodbye, knowing he would never see them again. That he, they and his world would have never been.

Experiments with animals had been done. They had been sent back to deserted places, not too many centuries in the past, to minimize the risk of damage to the timeline. The Lords knew that risk was there so were prudent. But when it came to their own journeys, the risk did not matter for they would no longer be here. The animals had been monitored and appeared healthy. Then a burst of energy had been sent through the observing tunnel and vaporized them: they did not want the risk of inserting a creature from the future to run wild in the past, scattering unknown consequences into the winds of causality.

Or so Accimbali had told them, with the connivance of Sharalay's data interception routines. In fact the animals had been sent to wilderness areas only a few years in the past, with a judicious selection of locales and seasons to hide the fact. They dared not risk anything more. And the animals had to be vaporized, as the last thing Accimbali wanted was for the Lords to see them vanish of their own accord.

Accimbali had told them that today would be the final experiment. He would take the risk on himself and go back to one of the times they had chosen. There was still risk, he said. The tunnels were at heart a quantum process. There were theories, held by many, that quantum events were indeterminate until set into reality by the observation of a conscious mind. This, Sharalay had argued, presented a risk that the animal experiments had not fully resolved. If there was a link between consciousness and the quantum realm, she pointed out, who knew what might happen to a human-level consciousness that traveled through such a tunnel? Perhaps the traveler would go mad, or lose their mind completely: an empty shell, present in body with their consciousness forever lost among the quantum pathways.

In public, Accimbali and Sharalay argued vigorously over this point, he dismissing it as a foolish interpretation of the equations. But reluctantly he agreed that, whatever his opinion, it could not be entirely dismissed as a possibility. So in public, the two came to an agreement that it must be tested.

Accimbali volunteered. Despite his enforced compromise with Sharalay, he said, he was completely confident that no harm would befall him, and he was proud to be a pioneer, the first of those who would follow him to this particular era. Many among the Lords secretly admired his cunning. They knew that whatever promises were made nobody, not even them, could be sure they would be among those who escaped. In one swoop, Accimbali both made himself a hero and guaranteed his place in the past.

Or he might die. But, Accimbali argued, that did not matter. If he died then he had failed. There was nothing more he could do, no way to save anybody: and if he'd stayed, his own death might have ended up more prolonged and painful than it would be this way. But if he were still alive after a day in the past then the main exodus could begin.

The leadership agreed. Having an official experiment scheduled made Accimbali's plan much simpler. If the Lords had demurred they would have still found a way, but it would have been harder and far riskier.

And now Accimbali stood in front of the chamber. He surveyed the assembled luminaries, and then turned to Sharalay, standing beside him at the controls of the machine. He knew they expected some words on an occasion like this, so he stood at attention, saluted the Parax, and spoke.

"This is the end of a journey of many years, but it is also the start of a new journey. One where no man has gone before. I salute you. I salute you all.

"Many of you, I will see on the other side."

With that, he turned to include all those present in his salute. Then he extended his hand to Sharalay and gravely clasped her arm. He knew the others could see the tears in her eyes, but only he knew their full meaning.

He stepped into the chamber where a faintly glowing black dot awaited him. Then it rose to engulf him, and he was elsewhere.

The crowd watching the visual feed gasped. They saw the trees of a forest, the glow of a sunset painting shades of pink and yellow over high clouds.

Then Sharalay pressed a hidden button, there was a spark and a bang from the machinery, and the image went black.

As the room erupted in cries of consternation and questions, Sharalay turned gravely to the audience and just stood there, saying nothing, answering nothing.

Now nobody can see where you really are, Accimbali. Nobody can follow you or stop you across the gulf that separates us. Farewell, my co-conspirator, my fellow traveler, my friend, my lover. Are you a hero or a devil? Am I? Well, hero or devil, do your job well. You cannot save me, you cannot save us, but perhaps you can save the past and the future.

33. The Meeting

The man sat at his desk, watching the displays on the electronic panels arrayed before him. He sipped his coffee, bitter and black, its black bitterness alleviated only by the two spoons of somewhat gritty sugar dissolved in its depths.

Had he been asked to name the defining aspect of his personality, and had he cared to answer, he would have said 'phlegmatic'. On any other day. But not today. Today he wondered if he was going mad.

Could it be true? Impossible! It must be some trick!

He had been telling himself that ever since the previous evening. Now he thought back to that time as he continued to watch his displays and sip his bitter coffee; for once, less bitter than his soul.

~~~

It was his habit after work to stop at a bar near his home. He would sit at a table near the back, indulge in a shot of vodka and a piece of pickled cucumber. It was his time. A break between work and home, so the pressures of the former could fall away and leave space for the cozier existence of the latter.

The owner of the bar knew of his habit and always kept the table free for 'my Colonel Stanislav' at this time.

So Stanislav was surprised, and somewhat irritated, to see a stranger occupying his table this evening, with the owner of the bar nowhere to be seen. But the stranger had seen him come in and was looking at him, as if he had been awaiting his arrival.

"Good evening, Lieutenant Colonel," the man said as he

approached. "Please. Take a seat."

The hairs on his neck stood on end. These were dangerous times, and his country was dangerous enough at the best of times. Who was this man, who acted as if he knew him? He could be Secret Police, suspecting him of some imaginary crime against the State, in a State where even some thoughts could be a crime. Or he could be an agent of another country, here to tempt him into such a crime, whether by bribery, threats or blackmail. Or perhaps he was just a drunk who recognized his uniform.

"Thank you for inviting me to my own table," he replied somewhat acerbically. "Did Alexei not tell you I like to be alone?"

"Alexei found my gold persuasive, not only to let me sit, but to give us both privacy and his best vodka. It would even pay for that urn," he added cryptically. "Here," he said, pouring a shot of the chilled fire, "Enjoy."

He left it untouched. "Who are you? If you are the Secret Police you do not need to throw money around to speak to me in private. If you are some drunk you would not. That only leaves a criminal or a spy. Perhaps I should shoot you myself and gain another medal."

"Colonel, I am none of those things. I shall tell you my story, then you may shoot me or report me if you wish. Is that fair?"

He looked at the man coolly. If this was entrapment he could always claim, with justification, that he had continued the conversation only to trap the man himself.

"As you wish. Now what do you want?"

The man looked at him speculatively. "If I tell you, you will probably shoot me anyway. So I will show you. Will you humor me, and put this on your head?" he asked, extending a thin metal band made of a lustrous metal that shimmered in the light, like some kind of industrial era diadem.

Stanislav took it and turned it over in his hands, learning nothing more. "What is this? A joke?"

"Put it on your head. To play, tap your right finger. To rewind, tap your left. To pause, tap both at once."

"Play! Pause! Rewind! Are you mad? What are you talking about?"

"Put it on, and you will see."

Giving the man a searching glance, Stanislav slowly put the ring over his head. He twitched in surprise when it contracted to fit firmly but comfortably around his head.

"What in...!?"

"Tap."

He tapped, then jerked backwards. It was as if he were suspended in space, watching the history of the world unfold around him. The destruction of his world in nuclear war. A voice spoke, and it seemed to him that it spoke not into his ears but directly into is mind, as it explained the three-dimensional imagery also filling his head with its horror.

"Oh my God," he muttered once, then was silent.

Near the end, the scene changed. He saw himself, at his post. He saw a warning, the warnings he had trained for. He saw himself make the decision he would have made. He saw the world end.

"Oh my God," he whispered again.

And then he was shown the truth. It was a false alarm. There was no attack. The death unleashed upon the world was unleashed... by him.

Then the scene faded, and again he was looking through his own eyes, and all he could see was the stranger across his table.

"What... what the hell was that, *blya*?"

"That is the future of the world."

Stanislav just stared at him, too appalled to question or doubt.

"But I... but I... No. No. It cannot be!"

"Yes. One decision destroys the world. Your decision."

"How do you know all this?!"

"That is the future I am from."

"Why are you here? To punish me? To kill me?"

"To save you."

"To save me? Why? How?"

"Not you in particular. I do not know your fate after today. But to save the world. Prevent the war. You have seen the truth. Tomorrow the thing you saw will happen. Your system will detect an attack. It will be a false alarm. You must report it as such."

"Tomorrow!?"

"Tomorrow."

"This is some trick!"

"Do you think your time has the technology you just witnessed with your own eyes? With your own mind?"

"No... no... but... maybe! Some advanced experimental system, perhaps... some trick... to trick me... into ignoring a real attack..."

"Then I have something else to show you."

With that, he took out another small object and showed Stanislav, not letting him touch it. Just a small ovoid, of a size to fit in the palm of his hand, with what looked like a large lens at one end. He pointed it at the large urn in the center of the room and pressed a button, upon which the urn vanished in a crackling flash of light, leaving nothing but a pile of dust settling onto the floor.

"Do you think if the Americans could do that they would bother risking their own necks in a nuclear war, and spend their time in bars fooling Russian officers?"

Stanislav just gaped at him.

"Colonel, it is true. Accept the evidence of your own eyes and your own reason. Tomorrow you will destroy the world. You will kill yourself, your wife, your family, everybody you ever loved and ever will love. Your home, your country, your race.

"Or tomorrow you will know what you have seen and report a false alarm. You will be the man who saved the world.

"So, Colonel," he said, reaching for his own shot. "Drink with me. Drink to the future of the human race."

Stanislav reached out and picked up his glass, examined it critically as if it held all the bitterness of the years, and tossed it back.

"And what of you?"

"You can choose to escape your fate. The rules of travel through time are inescapable. I will cease to be."

"So you have come back to save us at the price of your own life?"

"You are a military man, Colonel. You know I am not the first nor the only man to do that. But in my case I have less courage than you think. I am not here only to save you. I would be dead anyway, soon enough. Your war will cost humanity millennia of progress, and in losing those millennia we lose everything. It is the extinction of the entire human race that I seek to prevent. It is what I was born for, and what I will die for."

Stanislav sat back with a sigh, staring at the man, unable to believe, unable to doubt.

Then the man… vanished. He was there, then where he had been was a black void, then he was simply gone.

Unseen, unheard in his hiding place, Alexei gasped. The man had given him not worthless rubles, but actual gold. More than enough to buy vodka and privacy. But a man couldn't be too careful, he'd told himself. These days a man had to be cautious, and he owed it to himself to keep an eye on strangers bearing gold, though he had been able to make out little of their conversation. He patted the gold in his pocket... but it was gone. He felt cheated. But he knew there was no person on Earth he could complain to. It did not occur to him to think that the man who had cheated him had paid him something far more valuable than mere gold.

Over at his table, Stanislav looked around. Everything the man had left on the table was also gone. There was no magic crown, no sign the man had ever been here.

Am I going mad? Did I imagine all this?

Then he looked at the expensive bottle of vodka, with beads of water condensing on its chilled sides. He looked at the two shot glasses. He looked at the pile of dust on the floor.

I never liked that urn anyway.

Then he reached for the bottle, and poured himself another shot.

~~~

His mind jerked back to the present and his eyes widened. The early warning system was reporting the launch of a single intercontinental ballistic missile from the USA. Then the system reported a second launch. And more.

The system is new and not yet fully tested, he wrote. *Nor would the Americans launch only a few missiles. My assessment is it is a false alarm.*

He sent his report to his superiors.

Then he sat back, to sip his coffee and watch his displays.

There were no more alarms, false or otherwise.

34. A Most Exclusive Club

Ron looked out the window of his temporary country mansion, lost in thought. He had done well over the years, the lies and deceptions not weighing too heavily on his soul.

And now it was 1983, and Ron was afraid. *I do not know whether to fear that I have done it all for naught, or that I have not done enough.*

Yet his fear felt particularly sharp and in focus today. *Perhaps his visit entangled me with the timelines, and I can sense the coming apocalypse.*

He frowned. *Or my mind is going. The ramblings of an old man.*

He rang a bell, and one of the servants came to him, bearing the drink the servant knew he would request at this time of day. "Stay," ordered Ron, tapping the ash from his cigar into the silver ashtray on the low marble table beside him.

Ron looked to the far horizon, the blue Californian sky temporary home to a flock of clouds. *Today, it is today, I am sure of it,* he felt.

But nothing happened. The sky remained blue. The world continued turning. Ron looked at the peace of the sky, frowning. *Yes, that's all it is. The ramblings of an old man.*

~~~

The next day Ron looked out his window at a sky still peacefully and almost smugly blue.

But today Ron didn't feel disturbed. He felt more lighthearted than he had in years, as if some great weight, so long felt it became forgotten, had been lifted from him. *It is as if a cusp has been reached, and passed. And the future is free. Or am I rambling again?*

Then Autumn became Winter, then 1983 became 1984, and the world did not end.

Ron felt happy. Sometimes the happiness burst out into slightly hysterical laughter, as he wondered again whether he were the greatest fool in the history of the world.

~~~

Ron sat in his study, the smoke from his cigar curling around his head like a fragrant mist. The dark wood of the desk felt sensual under his fingers, its polished grain both rough and smooth under his fingers.

He looked with distaste at the sheaf of reports resting provocatively on that wood. The distaste came because of what the reports reminded him of.

He used to think of them as his Legacy, a term now even he found rather pompous. Now he just called them Ron's Follies. They were a few small gold tablets hidden safely around the continent. Each told a story, the background to the great war of 1983: the War that Never Was. There they waited. Waited for the details of the war to come, details he wished to bequeath to the ages to come. But the war never came and the tablets remained unfinished, shining in mockery at his hubris. The reports on his desk were the latest distillation of the network of spies he had set up to help gather the information to complete them, and which still mindlessly churned out its data long after it had ceased to matter.

If there was a God looking down on the world he figured it must be Loki, ever ready to torment men with his pranks and the irony of their own arrogance.

Why do I still bother? he wondered, eyeing the reports balefully.

Ah well, I guess old habits die hard. Screw you, Loki, a man needs his hobbies.

So he reached for the reports and began to read.

He had read through the two paragraphs without really paying attention, but when his brain finally noticed, his eyes stopped with a jerk and darted back to read them again.

Holy Frigga, you must be joking!

For all that he had lost over the decades, his great imagination was still intact, and churned away while he stared at the page in blank surprise. Then he burst out laughing.

When at last he looked up from his desk, tears still streaming down his cheeks, he saw that Jensen had appeared in his doorway. *He is like a personal sprite, materializing when I need him then vanishing again from the world.*

He burst out laughing again. He seemed to be finding everything funny today.

If this hilarity at his appearance offended Jensen it did not show. His only reaction was a discreet, "Is there anything I can do for you, sir?"

Ron wiped his eyes. "Oh Jensen. Dear, dear Jensen. How would I survive without you? There most certainly is. Bring me a glass of that two thousand dollar Scotch, will you?"

"Sir."

"On second thoughts, bring the whole goddamn bottle.

"Then come join me."

Then he laughed again, and it echoed through the house for a long time.

~~~

Stanislav stopped. It was nearly two years since he had held the future of the world in his palm, and he had settled comfortably back into his routine.

After all, if he was anything, he was phlegmatic.

The stranger sitting at his table noted the way he stopped, marked the stunned look that briefly blanked his features, and waved him over with a cryptic smile.

Stanislav walked slowly over to the man but then just stood there, uncertain.

"Sit down, sit down," the interloper said. "I won't bite."

This man was old and spoke passable Russian with an American accent. *Maybe this time it is a spy.*

Stanislav appeared to relax. "Ah. An American." He sat and added, "Who the hell are you?"

The man studied him. "Here I sit at your personal table, a stranger acting like I own it. Yet I saw no annoyance or irritation. Instead you looked like a guy who suddenly wonders whether he's really awake or is having a bad dream. I almost heard you thinking, 'Oh no, not again.' Now I wonder why that is?"

"You are an American. What are you doing here? How did you get here?"

"Guilty. Let's just say that I have an organization with tentacles in all kinds of strange places. Let's say that I've had a personal interest in you Russkies for a long time, so I made sure that some of my tentacles reached even here and that I could speak the language. Let's also say that something happened, or more accurately didn't happen, when it should have."

"Surely it is dangerous for you to come here, American."

"Eh. What's a bit of danger? My days are numbered anyway. I wouldn't miss this for the world."

"Miss what?"

"Have a drink, Colonel."

"You came all the way from America to have a drink with me?"

"Sure did."

"Why?"

"Because I believe, sir, that you and I are members of what must be the most exclusive club in the world."

"Club? I have never seen you before today."

"I hear you did something very good in 1983. Strangely enough, on exactly the day when I was expecting something very bad."

Stanislav paused. "How could you know that?"

"As I said, I have ears. Low level ears, but they pick some things up. Like a bit of chatter that you reported something as a false alarm, something most military folks would have gone the other way on. Or like finding out you had a peculiar visitor right here on the night before."

"I don't know what you're talking about."

"That's fine, I can do the talking. Do you know why I care?"

"Too much vodka?"

"Oh, I don't think there can be too much vodka for this. Tell me, Colonel. Do you believe in time travel?"

Stanislav sat very still, shocked, trying not to show it. "Surely impossible," he managed.

"Let me tell you a story, Colonel. Many years ago I was sitting in a bar. Some stranger came up to me, spinning me a tale. Total crap, obviously. Then he showed me stuff. And do you know what he showed me?"

The old man looked at Stanislav, who offered no guesses.

"He showed me that in 1983 the world would be destroyed in a nuclear war! That nobody could stop that war! That the only hope for the human race was that I would spend the rest of my goddamned life hiding away knowledge to survive the war, to give the future a hand, so they would be ready for an even bigger disaster coming from the heavens!

"That's what he showed me!

"And do you know what happened?!"

Stanislav just stared at him.

"NOTHING!"

The man tossed back a shot of vodka and chased it with some pickled tomato. "You Russians know how to drink, you know," he muttered.

"And then what do I discover?" the man continued more calmly, almost silkily. "I discover that some Lieutenant Colonel in Russia was manning a nuclear early warning system, his system detects *multiple* missile launches, and what does he do? Calm as the coolest cucumber, he declares it a false alarm and goes on picking his nose."

He glared at Stanislav. "The very year it was supposed to happen. The very *day* I *felt* it was going to happen. Now what do you think of that, Colonel?"

Stanislav just stared, and shook his head slowly.

"Well, let me tell you what I think. My guy, my guy from the future, said they didn't have the technology to prevent the war. So all they could do was help the future along. My job. Maybe it wasn't enough, but maybe it helped. Maybe the next version of the future still couldn't save themselves, but they were more advanced. *They* were able to penetrate the quantum mess surrounding the war.

"They found the guy who pushed the button or whatever it is you guys do here to end the world.

"They found you."

Stanislav's face had gone white.

"So they got the same idea my guy had. Someone came back to show you your future, and stop you making one godawful decision. And you went from being the guy who ended the world, to the guy who saved it."

His eyes bored into Stanislav's.

"Didn't you?"

Slowly, Stanislav reached for his own shot glass and downed it.

"You don't expect me to answer this nonsense, do you?"

"No."

"You realize that you are mad, and I don't believe a word of it?"

"Yes."

"Then," said Stanislav, filling first the stranger's glass and then his own, then raising his, "Za Vstrechu!"

They downed their shots and Stanislav added, "And to the most exclusive club in the world."

EPILOGUE

Hireld Banekaro stood on the beach, holding his daughter's hand. The dark ocean gently lapped against the sand, the force of its waves blunted by the reef far off shore.

The glow of the sun was beginning to appear on the horizon, its advance rays dipping the edges of the clouds in gold and crimson.

Behind them the coastal trees grew lush and green, though in the predawn light the green was more black than verdant. Still, a few birds had noticed the lightening sky and had begun their tentative greetings to the new day.

It feels like the Earth in its dawn. The rhythms of nature, as they have been for millions of years.

And so it was, though he knew that deep beneath his feet and extending under the ocean before him and the forest behind him was a mighty city, home to millions of souls.

The rest of the Earth was much the same. Men no longer needed to despoil the Earth to live. Much of it was left to return to its natural state, where people were free to wander, enjoy and commune with a world as it had been when their species was young. However far mankind had travelled, at some level of their souls they still needed that. Perhaps they always would.

Yet in many places the cities burst forth from the earth and towered above the landscape in all their glowing glory. For the works of man were honored too, their achievements a source of pride. If raw nature was something to admire for its beauty and even its savagery, humanity saw itself as nature's crowning glory.

Over the long existence of the race it had been a crown they sometimes wore precariously. But today, they knew, they would earn it.

Hireld and his daughter looked toward the sky. At a thought, their modified eyes, part biology, part machine, magnified and identified; when it was needed they would protect their sight from the brightest radiation, yet let them see the subtlest play of colors. Both of them were looking at two bright points of light, dancing impossibly close to each other impossibly far away.

"Daddy, who was Pachmeny?"

"She was a very wise woman. The first person to discover the stars that even we call by her name. She lived in a different timeline from ours. But the wormhole engineers found the traces of that timeline, and others. We honor her, for without her and her people, our race would have ended and we would never have reached the stars."

They had not needed to come here. The same eyes that extended their natural sight could have shown them this scene no matter where they were. But even now, humans felt the need to be there. For their physical presence to mark their witness. Perhaps if they advanced even further they would no longer need it. Or perhaps, like the forest behind them, they always would.

Then the heavens turned white, as the front of the supernova's rage finally reached Earth. When they looked away, they saw the violent colors of the aurora streaming past the birthplace of mankind, as the electromagnetic and quantum shields diverted the deadly radiation safely into space. So it would be for a long time, until the death throes of the stars finally abated.

Hireld held his daughter close, as they watched the end of the world pass them by.

Afterword

On September 26, 1983, Lieutenant Colonel Stanislav Petrov was monitoring the nuclear early warning system at Oko in the Soviet Union when it reported multiple nuclear missile launches from the USA. He judged that it was a false alarm, and his decision is widely credited with saving the world from nuclear war.

In a talk on time travel, I used this 'Petrov Effect'—that history can turn on small decisions—as an example of why time travel would be extremely dangerous. You have no way to know what effects it might have and you could easily make things worse.

Unless you were faced with a disaster so immense that you couldn't make it worse.

Which led to an intriguing, opposite idea. If you were a time traveler wanting to stop the Great Nuclear Cataclysm of 1983—who might you visit to whisper things into his ear, on the night of September 25?

And it wasn't even the first time. On October 27, 1962, the US navy blockading Cuba detected a Russian submarine trying to run the blockade, and the Americans started dropping depth charges to force it up. The submarine was out of contact with the surface and both the captain and the political officer decided war might have broken out: and it was armed with a nuclear torpedo. On any other submarine that would have been enough to launch that torpedo. But on this vessel a third officer's agreement was needed: Vasili Arkhipov, overall commander of the flotilla, was also present. After much argument, Arkhipov's opinion prevailed and the submarine surfaced, to be sent on its way by the Americans.

War, needless to say, had not broken out, so another Russian military officer had also saved the world from nuclear war, two decades before Petrov.

Ian Fleming once said, "Once is happenstance. Twice is coincidence. Three times is enemy action." Perhaps these two coincidences don't mean anything except we were extraordinarily lucky twice. But they are enough for a novel.

Robin Craig
February 20, 2018

ABOUT THE AUTHOR

Dr Robin Craig has a PhD in molecular biology and a keen interest in science and philosophy. He believes that novels, like all art, should be one in thought, theme and style: to nourish the mind as much as the soul. His books specialize in blending fact and speculation in dramatic and engaging stories, driven by strong characters and intriguing, topical philosophical themes.

In addition to near future science fiction exploring contemporary issues such as artificial intelligence (*Frankensteel*), genetic engineering (*The Geneh War*) and cyborg technology (*Time Enough for Killing*), his books include time travel (*The Time Surgeons*), alternative history (*The Passion of Judas*) and a collection of short stories (*Past, Present, Future*).

He also writes non-fiction. In addition to 14 scientific papers and a long-running philosophical series in *TableAus* (the journal of Australian Mensa), he has published numerous philosophical essays on Amazon.com and was a contributor to *The Australian Book of Atheism* with his chapter *Good Without God*, an essay on the importance and validity of secular ethics.

Dr Craig is an independent author. If you like this book please spread the word with reviews and recommendations to your friends or library... and enjoy more of his books!

To keep up to date on new and upcoming works and events, like his Facebook page: fb.me/authorcraig